KNEEL

CANDACE BUFORD

Recycling programs
for this product may
not exist in your area.

ISBN-13: 978-1-335-40251-6

Kneel

This edition published by arrangement with Harlequin Books S.A.

For questions and comments about the quality of this book, please contact us
at CustomerService@Harlequin.com.

Inkyard Press
22 Adelaide St. West, 40th Floor
Toronto, Ontario M5H 4E3, Canada
www.InkyardPress.com

Printed in U.S.A.

To Jonathan, who always believed in the dream,
even when I'd lost sight of it.

1

Our soles crunched the gravel of the near-empty parking lot as we walked to my car. I tightened my hold on my duffel bag, looking past my best friend, beyond the patchy lawn of the schoolyard and the gangly water tower beyond that—in the direction of the interstate. With glassy, hooded eyes, Marion's gaze drifted in the same direction, which didn't surprise me one bit. Sooner or later, everyone had their eyes on the way out of Monroe.

At the car, I gripped the back of my leg and massaged a knot in my hamstring, which ached with every move I made. Football practice had run long *again*, and as much as I wanted to win our first game of the season on Friday, all I wanted now was to go home, eat my mama's meat loaf, and melt into the couch. I opened my trunk and piled my backpack and duffel bag onto one side. I waited for Marion to toss in his gear, but he was too busy howling with laughter at my car.

"Oh, snap!" He brought a fist to his mouth. "My boy rockin' cardboard windows now."

"Don't start." I slouched against the door, groaning as he bent to inspect the new repair—a slab of cardboard I'd taped to my window this morning. It wouldn't roll up, and since the weather called for rain, I'd gone for the fastest fix I could find. Marion looked up with a smirk.

"The red duct tape is a nice touch. Dog, I can't…" He covered his face with his hands.

"At least I got a ride." I cackled and moonwalked backward, wincing slightly through my hamstring pain, but it was worth it. Marion gave me the finger, his smug grin growing wider. Then I clapped my hands, urging him to hurry up. Storm clouds from the gulf crawled across the sky, and I wanted to get on the road before it started pouring. "Let's roll."

"I feel like this thing is going to fall apart." Raising an eyebrow, he paced the length of my car—which was his ride home several times a week. "This can't be safe to drive anymore."

He had a point. Older than I was, my hand-me-down Honda Civic had seen better days. With a broken window, leaky AC, and an engine that sounded like a freight train, it wasn't in the best shape. But it got me where I needed to go—and right now, that was home.

The road skirted the edge of the parish line between Monroe and Westmond, the white town on the other side of the freeway. A passerby might mistake our two towns for one. They were *so* close to each other, separated only by the interstate. But locals understood the century-old fault lines between the Black and white sides.

With my car looking as janky as it did, it would draw unwanted attention—especially from Westmond folks. And when white people got nervous, they called the cops. That's what had happened a few weeks ago to Dante Maynard, a Black kid from Shreveport. In the middle of August during the last week of summer break, he was shot and killed in a gas station parking lot for no reason other than *looking* suspicious.

The way I saw it, their fear was misplaced. Black kids were being killed by *white people*. And they were scared of *us*?

But what I thought didn't matter.

With darkness approaching, it didn't matter that I was a regionally ranked tight end or that Marion was arguably the best quarterback the state had ever seen. It didn't matter that we had never been in trouble. All that mattered was that we'd be driving while Black in a car with a cardboard window.

"You got three seconds to get in. Then I'm taking off," I said, brushing past him.

I crammed my body behind the wheel as Marion tilted his face toward the stormy sky. Shaking his head, he picked his bags off the pavement and disappeared behind the car.

The Civic shuddered as Marion slammed the trunk shut, then dipped to the right as he slid into the passenger seat. He pushed his chair all the way back, making it easier for the seat belt to stretch around him. "Coach says Mississippi State might be there Friday. Just heads-up."

I nodded as I pulled onto the road, mildly interested in Marion's rundown of his conversation with Coach Fontenot. But I knew better than to get my hopes up. Coach always sent tapes of our games to recruiters and invited them to watch us play live. He was encouraged by their noncommittal responses, but I knew how to read between the lines.

Looks like you have yourself a good team.
We'll have to make it over to Monroe sometime soon.
We'll let you know if we can swing it.

"He don't know who coming or going," I mumbled under my breath as I got onto the freeway.

The truth was, college recruiters were hard to come by, and offers were even harder. Every baller this side of the Mississippi had their eyes on a way out of dying towns just like mine—and the golden ticket was a Division 1 scholarship. There weren't enough to go around, and that uncertainty made me uncomfortable. I tried not to think about it. All I could do was focus on my game and hope that was enough.

"Your dad coming to the game?"

"You think I could stop him?" I raised my eyebrows. Pops didn't make every game—sometimes he had a plumbing job. But he certainly wouldn't miss the season opener.

"Hope he doesn't try to coach from the sidelines. You know how Coach hates that."

I cringed, picturing my dad's chubby cheeks barking orders from the bleachers. As much as I loved his enthusiasm and support, I hated the spectacle he made at our games.

Marion rifled through his sweatshirt pocket and pulled out a bag of chips. Squeezing it open, he set it on the center console. "Want some?"

I was pawing for the bag when a loud rattle filled the car. I tore my eyes from the freeway, debating whether or not to pull onto the shoulder.

"What was that?" Marion grabbed the strap of his seat belt, his eyes growing wider as another gurgle rippled through the air.

"No idea." My chest tightened as we reached our exit ramp for Calumet Street, the steepest part of an otherwise flat Louisiana landscape. It was the line that separated Monroe and

Westmond—exactly the worst place to break down. I prayed that we'd be able to make it up the hill and turn right at the stop sign, which would put us squarely in our neighborhood. The car chugged up the hill. "We good. It's nothing."

Come on, baby, you can make it.

But the strain was too much for the car. With a hiccup, the old clunker shuddered and sighed as the Honda died. Before it had a chance to slide back onto the freeway, I braked and put the car in Park. Just in case, I pulled up the emergency brake.

"I knew something like this would happen." Marion ran his fingers through his short dreads. "What are we going to do now?"

"Dog, just let me think." The ramp was deserted, except for an SUV that whizzed by. The driver rolled up her windows before turning left toward Westmond. Given the state of my car and the color of our skin, we'd be hard-pressed to find someone to help us unless they were from our side of town. I shook my head, sighing as I ran through ideas. "What about at your stepdad's shop? There must be a mechanic there."

"You know damn well Ed's not going to lift a finger to help me." He scowled.

"Right," I said, mentally kicking myself for even mentioning his stepdad. He was terrible to Marion, always spewing hateful things—things meant to tear him down and eat away at his confidence. He rattled Marion so much that Coach had barred him from coming to our games. But as bad as Ed was to Marion, he was even *worse* to Marion's mother. That's why she took off sometimes. In a lower voice I asked, "Have you heard anything from your mom?"

"No." Marion gritted his teeth, turning to look out the window instead of at me.

Mrs. LaSalle usually came home after a few days, maybe a week—after things cooled down. But she'd been gone for almost two weeks. That weighed heavily on Marion. I could see it every day in the tightness of his eyes.

"She'll come back." I elbowed him across the center console. "She always does."

"I know." He looked at me over his shoulder, a lightness returning to his expression. He smirked. "I can't *wait* for her to come home and light Ed's ass up for all the shit he's put me through lately."

"That's the spirit." I grabbed my door handle, smiling at the image of Mrs. LaSalle whipping her house in order. I hoped that day would come soon. But now we needed to help ourselves by popping the hood of the Civic to see what was wrong. "Let's see if we can fix it ourselves."

"Like we know how to fix a car!" He threw his arms up. "Let's call a tow truck."

I didn't have money for a towing service. I barely had enough money for gas.

Cussing under my breath, I shoved the door open and rounded the front, grumbling as I felt for the lever beneath the hood. "How many times I tell Mama this car was on its last leg?"

"I'm not trying to be out here in the white neighborhood at night." Marion stood beside me, bouncing on the balls of his feet. He looked nervously at the neighboring fields, at the stalks of corn casting shadows in the creeping darkness. The sun had just dipped below the horizon, taking the safety of daylight with it.

"Chill. We're around the corner from our side of town. We'll be okay," I said, but I didn't believe it. I reached for the battery but yanked my hand back when I felt the hot metal. "Ouch!"

"Are you serious?" Marion hissed at my reddened fingertips. "You can't catch a ball with a banged-up hand."

The momentary sting disappeared almost as quickly as it came. The pain was nothing compared to my elbow, which was currently wrapped in kinesiology tape underneath my sweatshirt, begging to be iced and rewrapped. My body was my greatest asset, and I couldn't risk another injury before Friday's game.

All the surrounding car parts were hot to the touch, so we fanned with our hands, hoping to speed up the cool down.

A shiny black BMW with tinted windows made its way up the ramp. I didn't expect it to stop—just blaze by like there weren't two kids stranded on the side of the road. It idled at the stop sign but, to my surprise, didn't turn left. Instead, the white reverse lights flickered on. My fingers twitched nervously as the sports car backed up. Would they jump the battery, or us?

The dark window rolled down and my breath hitched as I recognized the driver—Bradley Simmons, one of Westmond's varsity football players. I grumbled under my breath. By the malicious gleam in his eyes, I could tell he had no intention of helping us.

"Yo, homie." He leaned over the caramel-colored leather seat, and even in the waning light, I could see that his cheeks were red from a summer tan—probably from an expensive vacation on a beach in the Caribbean or Cabo or wherever rich white people wasted time. He pointed to the on-ramp ahead. "The impound lot is one more exit down."

"You're hilarious, Brad." I really didn't have time for trash talk from a Westmond football player. Not in the darkness, away from the watchful lights of the field.

"What? I just want to catch up. Haven't seen y'all since we whipped you in the playoffs." He cocked his head, a pout pursing his lips. The echo of that disastrous game—the one that had knocked us out of the state championships and haunted me for the better part of a year—filled the silence between us.

Jackson and Westmond High had been evenly matched, tied for first in the regional rankings. But they'd had home field advantage and played with the knowledge that the refs wouldn't scrutinize their fouls as closely as they did ours. We were up by two touchdowns by the last quarter, but that changed when two of their players sacked Marion. And I mean *sacked*—brutally pinning him to the ground and dislocating his shoulder. I'll never forget the sound of Marion screaming in pain, the image of him writhing on the ground as tears filled his eyes.

Westmond played dirty—on and off the field.

"Keep driving." Marion stepped forward, instinctively reaching up to his left shoulder. "Unless you tryna help."

"With this garbage?" He pointed at my boarded-up window. "I wouldn't know where to start. Better off leaving it."

My heart rate ticked up, hammering loudly in my ears. Wasn't it enough that he had everything? The better-funded school, the fancy car, the state championship ring all belonged to him. And still, he felt entitled to my time, my smile. It wasn't fair. But I had to keep my cool.

Brad leaned closer, waving his finger in a circle around us. "*Y'all* are garbage. Y'all know that, right?"

I started to take a deep breath, but Marion snapped before I had time to steel my nerves. Rage flashed across his eyes as he shoved off the car.

Oh, shit!

"That's it!" He stalked toward the BMW with his hands curled into fists.

I lunged and gripped his shoulder, but he tried to wriggle out of my hold.

"Get off me!"

"Take a sec, bro!" My voice shook as I struggled to keep him in check. Marion wasn't a fighter, but it looked like he was about to make an exception. I couldn't let him do it, no matter how much I wanted to see that sneer wiped off Brad's sunburned face. I put a hand on Marion's chest to keep him at bay. "Don't let this fool win."

"How's your shoulder, homeboy?" Brad sneered. "Ready for round two next week?"

The threat ignited Marion's anger even more, and I pushed harder against his chest. I couldn't blame him—he had every right to be upset. Last year's injury was the kind that could have ended his football career before it even started.

"Why don't you get out your car and say that to my f—"

He was drowned out when Brad leaned into the center of his steering wheel and blared his horn. I released my hold on Marion to cover my ears.

"Sorry." Brad cupped his hand over his ear, pulsing the car horn between bouts of laughter. "I can't hear you."

Then his tires lurched forward, kicking up loose bits of gravel as he sped through the stop sign and disappeared into his town beyond the tree line. He hadn't done us any favors. In fact, he'd made the situation worse. Because honking his horn and screeching his tires was like shooting a flare in the sky, alerting every cop in the vicinity to our presence.

That was his privilege. He didn't need to worry about getting hassled by police. But that was our reality.

"I'll be damned if I let him call me trash." Marion stood huffing in the road, his fists still clenched as he looked toward Westmond.

"Man, forget him." I was angry, too, and I wished there was something I could do. But guys like Brad could get away with starting fights. Guys like us couldn't. I slapped Marion's shoulder. "What does Coach always say? We get 'em back—"

"—on the field," Marion finished the well-worn phrase, his chest still puffing as he turned away from the intersection.

We retreated to the car and fanned the engine. In the hushed darkness, I could feel Marion calming, which allowed me to release my tensed muscles. We fell into an uneasy silence, letting the hum of the cicadas overtake us. No one passed. Nothing moved. Still, we stood there—two boys on a backwoods road, headed nowhere fast.

2

Our ears perked up at the sound of tires churning up the exit ramp behind us. Headlights flooded the ground around my feet, and my jaw instinctively clenched. I hoped it wasn't a cop, *especially* not one of the officers involved in Dante Maynard's shooting.

I waved for the car to go around, but they flashed their lights—thankfully the yellow headlights of a truck, not the blue and red of a police cruiser. Straightening, I squinted toward the driver and exhaled when a familiar face leaned out of the window.

"You need help?" Henry Dupre asked.

"Thank you, sir." I hadn't realized my hands were shaking until relief stilled my nerves. "You couldn't have come at a better time." I jogged to his side of his truck, the Dupre Produce Delivery paint along the side barely visible in the waning light. He sank back to his seat, revealing his daughter on the passenger side. My pulse sputtered, but I recovered quickly with a shaky wave. "What up, Gabby."

"Hey, Rus." She nodded curtly, brushing her natural hair

to the side before turning on the overhead light. A blush crept up her light brown cheeks, covering the trail of freckles beneath her glasses. She turned away, suddenly more interested in the book in her lap than me.

Mr. Dupre cleared his throat, snapping my attention back to the matter at hand.

"I think it's the battery," I said with confidence, though I was sure something else was wrong with the car. Batteries don't gurgle. But we needed to patch up what we could and get home. "If you could give me a jump, I'd be grateful."

"All right, son. But let's get you off this hill. You know the gas station around the corner and down a ways." He pointed to the right, across Gabby's lap, and I nodded. "Put your car in Neutral, and I'll push you from behind. Don't worry, this old thing is stronger than she looks."

Marion and I stuffed ourselves back into my car and waited for Mr. Dupre to tap the bumper. My hand hovered over the gearshift, ready to change into Neutral. I could feel Marion's eyes boring into me. Preemptively, I shot my hand up.

"I know what you're thinking. But there's nothing there, so just let it go."

"Okay, so we're still playing *that* game." Marion cradled his head in his hands, groaning. "The one where we pretend you don't like Gabby."

"Of course I *like* her. Just not like that." When I felt the bump from behind us, I released the brake. "She looks good, though, right?"

"Sure. Sure. I mean, she's no Aysha." He bit down on his lip, his nostrils quivering. I knew he was holding in a laugh, so I pushed him against the window. I didn't want to be reminded of my ex-girlfriend and how we'd fizzled out at the beginning of summer. Marion's body rumbled as he let out a snicker. "What? I'm agreeing with you."

Slowly, Mr. Dupre eased us up the hill, his engine wheezing through the added strain before tipping the Civic onto level ground. A few blocks later, we pulled into Emmett's Quick Stop, the local Black-owned convenience store and gas station. He swung around the pumps to face us bumper-to-bumper then hopped from his truck.

"Let's have a look at what we're dealing with." Henry sidled next to me, his calloused hands finding the lever to pop the hood quicker than you could say Sunday. He yelled over his shoulder. "Gabby, hand me those jumper cables, would ya?"

"Quit playin' and get in there." Marion shoved me out of my door, mumbling something about how I needed to slay the baller way.

But I didn't feel like a big-shot baller—not after being heckled on the side of the road.

Itching to be useful, I rushed to grab the bundle of cables from Gabby's arms. "I can help with those."

"They're not that heavy. I can handle it." She shook her head as she pivoted away from my outstretched hands. "Rus, I've got it."

My lips smacked as I struggled to rebound. I wasn't used to flat-out rejection, not as the captain of the football team. Shoot, even my teachers gave me a wide berth. But Gabby wasn't going to cut me a break. That wasn't her style.

Henry Dupre cleared his throat.

"I'll need to run current to the battery for a bit before giving it a go. Pass me your keys." Mr. Dupre tucked the jumper cables under his arm and held his hand out, flicking his fingers back and forth. I gladly handed him the keys— he looked like he knew what he was doing, which was more than I could say for Marion and me. He stuffed them in his back pocket then turned his attention to the tangled clump of cables. He grumbled under his breath. "Let's see if I can separate this dang knot."

A light rain started trickling down, and Gabby dashed to stand beneath the awning of the store entrance. She wiped raindrops off her face, eyeing Marion and me as we left Mr. Dupre between the headlights and walked over to huddle next to her. An unlikely trio, silence stretched before us.

Gabby and I used to be friends—we'd known each other since elementary school. We'd been tight, but that all changed freshman year when I invited her to my first high school football party.

I'm not going to lie. I was feeling myself back then, and all the high fives and hollers from Aysha and her clique of high school royalty drew me deeper into the party—farther away from Gabby, who stood in a corner, looking out of place. After an hour of snapping selfies and chugging beers, I realized Gabby had bounced. At the time, I didn't own up to what I had done to drive her away. I was too busy feeling hurt. I ended up going home with Aysha that night, and we'd dated ever since. Until, that is, this summer. Gabby and I hadn't said more than a dozen words to each other since that party, even though we sat near each other in English class this year. But if I was being totally honest, she'd always had my eye.

The last time I checked, Gabby despised the town's "hysteria" over organized sports, especially football, so finding something to talk about as we stood there in our football sweats was no easy feat. The Civic roared to life, breaking my train of thought as I looked to Mr. Dupre.

"We'll let the cars run for about twenty minutes. Make sure the charge takes." He wiped his blackened hands on a dirty rag. "If you come by my warehouse, I can set you up with some new connector cables."

"How much would that be?" I hung my head, thinking of the ten dollars in my wallet.

"I keep spare parts around. Have to maintain the fleet." He slapped his thigh with the rag in his hands. "It's on the house. Happy to help both of the captains of the Jackson Jackals. Isn't that right, sweet pea?"

Gabby shrugged, like she didn't care about my baller status. I bit the inside of my cheek and scuffed the ground. How was I going to chat her up if she was immune to the strongest card I had to play?

"Anyone want some grub?" Mr. Dupre opened the door to the convenience store, the bell over the threshold chiming.

Marion followed closely behind him. "You know I can't turn down a chance for some beef jerky." He smirked as he looked over his shoulder. "You good?"

"I'm straight." I turned to Gabby. "You a jerky fan?"

"Gross." She scrunched her nose and shook her head. "I don't eat meat. Thanks, though."

So she was a vegetarian now. Meeting one of those in the Deep South was like finding a unicorn. She was lucky her dad owned the local produce distribution center. If not for him, the only lettuce you'd see for miles would be on a Big Mac.

Marion disappeared inside, leaving the two of us on our

own. Gabby shrank to the cinder block wall with a sigh. Her gaze occasionally darted to me, her glasses catching the lamplights as she scanned my tracksuit and muddy shoes. She had a sharpness to her stare, like she was looking beyond the trappings of football. I squirmed in place, feeling a little vulnerable as she appraised me, hoping she didn't find me lacking.

Our eyes locked, and I wondered if she might see my interest in my upturned brows, but she looked away quickly, her nostrils flaring as she studied the asphalt.

"I liked your presentation the other day in Ms. Jabbar's class." I stepped nearer, naming the one class we had together—the one thing we shared. Ms. J had already jumped into assignments, and Gabby had made an incredible first impression on our teacher. "Your report about sectional feminism."

"*Intersectional* feminism." She blinked up at me, the ghost of a smirk tugging at her lips. She eyed me with that same sharp, piercing gaze—one that would make any football player on the field feel exposed. I gulped.

"Right." I nodded like I knew the difference. "That was real chill. I'm one hundred percent on board with that."

God, I sound like a chump.

"Whatever." Gabby rolled her eyes. She thought I was a chump, too, and maybe I deserved that, especially after I ditched her freshman year. She pushed her glasses up her nose. "No one else got it either."

Feeling my cheeks heat, I ducked out from under the awning, deciding to take my chance with the rain. I paced around the building and released my breath in a whistle at the sight of a wall of rain-soaked flyers. There must have been fifty of them. Fifty pairs of Dante Maynard's sad eyes staring back at me, the hood of his Shreveport High School basketball sweatshirt casting his face in shadow. The bold letters scrawled on the bottom of the pages read Justice 4 Dante.

"Did you know him?" Gabby asked from behind me.

I whipped my head around, startled by her lightness of foot. Like a shadow, she stood behind me, gazing up at the wall.

"Nah." I shook my head, backing up to view the wall better. By now, everyone in Louisiana knew about the high school basketball player who got shot outside the Shreveport Kwiki Mart. Cops saw a hooded figure with black hands and assumed he must have been up to no good. What the officer thought was a concealed weapon in his pocket was just a bag of M&M's. "But it hits too close to home."

Dante had been the captain of his team, just like me.

"I know what you mean. It could have been anyone. Still could." Gabby picked at the corner of a poster that was coming undone. "I heard the cop transferred to Westmond—Officer Reynaud."

I nodded, and a shiver rolled up my spine.

"Oh, hell nah," Marion said as he rejoined us, biting off a mouthful of beef jerky. "We don't need to be anywhere near this mess. Just watch—a cop car gonna pull up and take all our asses to jail. Because whoever's slapping up these posters and vandalizing buildings, he gonna get caught."

"He's right. We better head home." I needed to eat dinner, finish my homework, and get some decent shut-eye if I wanted to be prepared, even though I wasn't too worried about Friday's game.

Our season opener against Deerlake would be a walk in

the park. They were near the bottom of the district rankings after all. The real prize was the win against Westmond, and that game was scheduled for the week after. I had a score to settle with them—now more than ever—and I was counting down the days until I could face them on the field. Maybe then I'd get a chance to wipe that slick sneer off Brad's face.

"Come by anytime, and I'll change out those cables," Mr. Dupre said as I opened my car door.

"Thank you, sir." I looked to Gabby, itching to invite her to the party on Friday, but I chickened out. "See you around, Gabby."

"Drive safely." She tucked her hair behind her ears and quickly turned, as if she couldn't get away from me fast enough. But the redness of her cheeks told a different story, and that made me smile.

As I turned off Calumet Street and into our driveway, Mama stepped onto the porch and waved, the screen door clapping shut behind her. Our house wasn't much to look at from the front curb, with its flat, chipped-white exterior and faded blue shutters. People like Brad might have called it *garbage*, but if they came closer, they'd see Mama's window boxes of bluebonnets, smell her cooking wafting from the kitchen.

It was home, and I'd never been happier to see it.

Marion and I grabbed our bags from the car and made our way up the warped steps.

"I was starting to worry. Hey, baby." She stood on the tips of her toes to rub the top of my head, then looked over my shoulder at Marion. "You staying for dinner?"

"Yes, ma'am." He nodded, sticking the roll of beef jerky into his sweatshirt pocket. "If you don't mind."

"Mind? Boy, give Mama a hug."

Marion melted into my mama's arms, sticking his tongue out at me. He liked to joke that he was Mama's second son, that she loved him just as much as she loved me. And he was right—he got all the affection and none of the scolding. But I didn't mind. He got enough scolding at his house.

"Coach keeps y'all later and later every day." She glared at the sky, at the trees bending under the weight of the wind. "Got you out here in this howling wind and rain."

"Coach knows what he's doing. Working them boys hard," Pops said from down the hall. The laces of his work boots dragged against the linoleum floor as he walked up to the screen. "Besides, Cheryl, a little wind never hurt nobody."

"Eli, it's hurricane season." Her eyes narrowed at him.

September was the height of hurricane season in Louisiana, when all the storms seemed to find their way to our corner of the Gulf of Mexico. It also corresponded with the start of football season, when my days started to heat with the building pressure of getting scholarship offers.

"It's gator season too." I chuckled. "Maybe he'll throw us in the swamp to make us hustle more."

"Lord, help us." Mama slapped her side and joined me in a hearty laugh. She swung the door open, shooing Pops aside to make room for Marion and me. "I know y'all hungry. Come on in."

The faded green couch was a welcome sight for my weary body. I collapsed on it, feeling the springs creak as they surrendered to my hefty weight. I'd put on fifteen pounds since last year. It was that high protein diet Coach had us on. Marion, too, had bulked up. He could barely fit in the rocking chair on the other side of the living room where the AC unit rattled the windowpanes.

"Back in my day, we stayed on the field till midnight. And look what it got me." Pops pointed to the middle shelf on the wall. He wiped a smudge of dust off his 1998 State Champions trophy, which sat next to his MVP trophy. "Nobody can take this away."

I sighed. I'd heard his football stories many times before.

Mama's brows furrowed as she scooted past Marion on her way to the kitchen. "I could wring Fontenot's neck for keeping you until eight o'clock again. He better not do this every night."

"We actually got out an hour ago," Marion said. Knowing it didn't take an hour to drive home from school, Mama raised her eyebrow. He was quick to add, "The Honda broke down."

"Right on the exit ramp." I threw my arms up, then slammed them back to the couch. A plume of dust escaped the cushions. "I actually was afraid to turn it off. I hope it starts in the morning."

"How did you get it going again?" Pops asked as he shuffled to the fridge.

"Mr. Dupre gave us a jump," I said, conveniently leaving out the part about Brad's harassment. It was in the past and would only worry my parents. I shot Marion a look, praying that he wouldn't bring it up, but by the twinkle in his eyes, he had another topic in mind.

"And don't forget Gabby," Marion said, his eyes flickering with amusement.

I grabbed a *TV Guide* from the coffee table and tossed it across the room, hoping to wipe that mischievous smile off his face. It missed him by a few inches, but with the way he clamped his mouth shut, he'd gotten the message. I was still kinda flustered about my interaction with Gabby, and I had no interest in involving my parents.

"Now, there's a name I haven't heard in a minute. You two used to be so close." Mama leaned against the kitchen counter, which overlooked the small living room. "Poor girl hasn't been the same since her parents got divorced. I see her driving her daddy's truck all over town. He must be keeping her busy."

Pops took a measured sip from his beer—too measured. He didn't want girls to steal my focus. Before my dad could give me a lecture about unnecessary distractions, I steered the conversation back to the car.

"Anyway, Mr. Dupre offered to change out the battery plugs." Mama rubbed her chest at the base of her throat—a nervous tick. I rushed to put her mind at ease. "Don't worry. It won't cost anything."

"Isn't that charitable of him." Pops grunted into his bottle of Bud. He was a proud man, who'd built his business from the ground up. He didn't like anything that felt like charity, but I wasn't as prideful. As hard as I worked at football, I figured I deserved the little perks that came my way. It's not like we were Brad's family. We needed all the help we could get.

"You do whatever you can to save that car," Mama said. "Otherwise, we'll be down to your dad's truck. Between the three of us, that's not enough."

"We'll make it work, *mon cher*. Don't fill his head with

worry. He just needs to keep his focus. Eye on the prize." His gaze drifted to the trophy shelf mounted beside the couch.

Using her hips as a rudder, Mama pushed Pops aside, balancing a plate of golden corn bread and smothered meat loaf above her head.

Finally. What I'd been waiting for all night. I unzipped my hoodie and tossed it on the arm of the couch.

"What's this?" Pops crossed the room in wide strides. Crouching in front of me, he appraised the tape wrapped around my elbow. He cradled it like a newborn baby, like all of his hopes and dreams were distilled in the crook of my arm.

He wasn't the only one who prodded at me like a prized stallion. Coach did the same thing, and sometimes random people felt entitled to my space and body. And I just had to smile and nod, because mouthing off never got me anywhere. I loved playing the game, but not this part—the layers of fretting and worry that piled on top of my passion were exhausting.

"Pops, quit it." I tried to pull my elbow away, but he gripped it harder. I gritted my teeth as he applied pressure right where Coach had told me to take it easy. "It's nothing. I mentioned this clicking sound to the trainer. She said to ice it and see if it brought some of the swelling down. It worked. Enough said."

"You gonna be good for Friday's game?" He looked at me over the rim of his glasses, scanning the rest of me.

"Yes, sir." I wiggled under his gaze, hoping he wouldn't ask if anything else was wrong—I didn't want to tell him about my aching hamstring.

"He'll be good, Mr. Boudreaux." The rocking chair

creaked as Marion slid to the edge of it. "I'll go easy on him, lay off those power throws."

"They need a good meal before they finish their homework and get some rest." Mama gently squeezed Pops's shoulder. He braced himself on the edge of the coffee table and heaved himself into a standing position.

"You listen to your mama," Pops said as he brought her fingers to his lips. She snatched her hand away and cupped her cheek, trying to hide the blush pooling beneath the surface. Pops winked at me. "Go on, get after it. But don't forget to say grace."

Marion and I bowed our heads, mumbling a prayer while peeking between our clenched eyelids. The moment Pops sank to a barstool at the kitchen island, Marion and I dove for the heaping pile of food. Our forks dueled with each other for the best slice of meat loaf.

"You'd think we don't feed y'all," Mama said as she watched us scarf down food. She shuffled over to our duffel bags by the door. "Don't forget to throw your uniforms in the laundry. You'll need clean shirts tomorrow."

"Oh, that reminds me..." Pops pushed back from the counter and disappeared down the hall. After a moment, he returned with a shirt in his hands. He unfurled it, revealing a custom-made fan T-shirt with my name and number. "What do you think?"

"Pops..."

Cleats and uniforms weren't cheap, especially on a substitute teacher and plumber's salary. Our school wasn't like Westmond. We didn't have corporate sponsors to provide gear or boosters to subsidize our expenses, which meant the cost fell on my parents. I felt guilty every time they shelled out money for my sake.

"We talked about this." Mama stared at Pops, her jaw growing slack. "I thought we agreed to use the shirts from last year."

"I know, but then Noah gave me a good price on the box of shirts." Pops rounded the counter, putting distance between Mama and the anger brewing behind her eyes. He grabbed a piece of corn bread and popped it in his mouth. "And I just did a job over at Jean's restaurant. Where'd you think I got all this corn bread?"

"It's gonna take more than corn bread and T-shirts to pay the bills this month." Mama reached across the counter, grabbing Pops's sleeve. His smile faltered, and he chewed slowly like his mouthful of food had turned to cement. Mama's eyes narrowed to slits. "Can I talk to you in the other room? Now."

Pops tucked the T-shirt under his arm and took off in the direction of their bedroom at the end of the short hall. Hot on his heels, Mama slung her dish towel on the kitchen floor as she stormed out of the kitchen.

"There they go," Marion said.

"I wish he would stop." I stuffed another forkful of meat loaf in my mouth before shoving off the couch. The sound of muffled yells traveled through our tiny house. I slid the accordion door separating the hallway and the front of the house shut.

"At least you got someone in your corner. At least he cares," Marion said. "Is it still cool to crash here, or should I bounce?"

"Yeah, you can sleep in the tree house," I said with a smirk, nodding toward the back door. Tucked away in the woods behind the backyard, our old fort towered above the bayou in one of the oak trees. A crumbling relic of our childhood, it was no place to spend the night—especially with a storm dumping buckets of rain on the poorly patched roof. It probably wouldn't hold his weight anyway.

It was obviously a joke. There was no way I'd let Marion sleep out there on a night like this. But as I bent down to grab Mama's dishrag off the kitchen floor, I noticed him gripping his bag next to his chair. His legs bobbed up and down like he was ready to be on the move. Marion had plenty of practice disappearing. Between my parents' fussing and my badly timed joke, his lip jutted out just enough for me to feel bad.

"I'm playing, man." I tried to laugh it off, tried to make the air lighter.

"Oh, yeah." Marion breathed a sigh of relief. "Good one."

The curtain rod above the kitchen sink bowed as I gathered the fabric to the side. The trees swayed in the wind as they were battered by the storm. It was only a mile and a half walk to Marion's house, but it was on the edge of the parish, near the bayou where the line between wet and dry was murky on a good day—the farthest from the luster of Westmond you could get.

"You heard Mama. We should finish our homework and get some rest." By now, the dirt road leading to the Bayou Glen trailer park would be waterlogged. Mama wouldn't want Marion to walk home, and neither did I. "Let's set up the couch. You know where to find the sheets."

"You sure?" He tilted his head in the direction of the hallway, where the sounds of bickering still thundered.

"Don't worry about them. They'll get over it."

They always did. I just hoped it was sooner rather than later. Mama was the glue that held the family together. When she wasn't right, nothing was. And I'd need my house in order to be able to focus on my game, especially the one against Westmond.

3

Gabby strolled through the lunchroom the next day in a lumpy sweater and board shorts, slicing through the crowded room with a tray of food. Her gaze was glued to her phone as she pushed past a sea of acrylics and weaves, of skinny jeans and hoop earrings, obviously uninterested in talking to anyone in her path. This was why people thought she was antisocial, cold even. But she was talking to *someone*.

She smiled, biting her lip as the fingers of one hand rapidly flew across her phone screen. Someone was making her smile like that, occupying her thoughts. I wondered who it was.

"Do you think she's seeing someone?" I asked as I watched her take her lunch tray out of the cafeteria. Marion followed my gaze, catching a glimpse of Gabby just before she disappeared down the hallway. He stared at me, his mouth open wide, but I pressed him. "For real."

"You're kidding, right?" He shook his head, then slid his tray down the lunch line, bumping mine.

"I mean, she's always off in that truck, going somewhere."
After I'd seen Gabby last night, she kept drifting into my

thoughts. She was always on the move, and that intrigued me. "Maybe that's why we never see her out."

"Get real." He waved his hand dismissively. "Bet her last kiss was with you."

"Don't trip." I bumped his tray, a little harder than he'd bumped mine. "That was like ten years ago."

It had been nearly a decade, but I could still remember standing barefoot underneath the jungle gym during first grade recess, my toes wiggling in the pea gravel as we leaned into each other. I'd had many kisses since the one I'd shared with Gabby—some better than others. Still, a part of me wondered whose lips Gabby's had touched since then.

I fished out a few crumpled bills from my pocket and waited for Marion to do the same. The cafeteria was packed, the tables teeming with students, but when we headed to our table, everyone instinctively moved out of the way, parting like the Red Sea to make room for us.

It was a tight squeeze between the mismatched tables that peppered the cafeteria—the old white ones mixed with the new gray ones brought in from district surplus. Underfunding limited our facilities. Then rezoning had filled our school over capacity, and the lunchroom was chock-full of students, all trying to squeeze into the round tables. Of course, Westmond could have absorbed some of the students—we were in the same school district. I'd heard that their cafeteria was twice the size, with different food stations and endless selections. But the parents complained, threatening to pull PTA funding if the district increased their class sizes.

It wasn't about class sizes. It was about the type of students that would blemish their pristine halls—poor Blacks

and whites from the edge of the district, who could have
really benefited from more room and resources. But that
wasn't compelling enough for Westmond, so Jackson packed
its buildings to the gills. But Marion and I didn't need to
worry about finding a spot.

We headed to the back wall of windows, over which hung
a faded school banner: Home of the Jackson High Jackals.
Underneath it was a pair of empty tables.

The football tables. My spot.

I spread my afternoon notebook and readings onto the
chipped gray surface, taking advantage of the quiet to catch
up on work. I raised my eyebrow at Marion as he swiped
through pictures on his phone, resisting the urge to tell him
to look over homework rather than the Gram.

I was just finishing up my English homework when Terrance sank onto the chair next to me, followed quickly by
Darrell—the biggest dudes on the team. He leaned across the
table, reaching for my notebook.

"Yoink!" Darrell plucked the edge of my worksheet right
from underneath my pencil, leaving a trail of lead across the
page.

"How many times I tell you? Wait till I'm finished." I
snatched my paper back, shaking my head. "I'm not trying to
fail just because you need to cram for next period."

"Man, forget you. Yo, Terrance." He nudged the quiet
giant to his side with his elbow. "You do English last night?"

Terrance rifled through his bag, producing a crumpled set
of papers. His face reddened beneath his many freckles, as if
he were aware that he had a pitiful excuse for homework.
Terrance was *really* smart—like rewire-your-car-GPS-to-

play-movies smart. I groaned under my breath as I read Terrance's worksheet over Darrell's shoulder. Terrance had clearly scribbled the summary from Wikipedia onto the page, and I doubted he had actually done the reading. He'd probably been too busy tinkering with his dumpster-found electronics to actually focus on homework. But that kind of extracurricular work didn't show up on his report card. I shook my head.

"Coach is going to bench you both if you dip below a two-point-five again," I said.

"No he ain't." Darrell wagged a finger, pushing up his dark-rimmed glasses. "I'm the best lineman he got."

"Hey!" Terrance slapped the table.

"I guess Terrance too." He shrugged, popping a Cheeto into his mouth. "He can't afford to lose us. And he sure as shit can't lose you and Marion."

"Even if Coach Fontenot and all the other teachers go easy on us, college recruiters won't. Your ass going to wind up in JUCO."

"Yeah, dog." Marion nodded in agreement. Playing junior college ball in the community college circuit was the kiss of death for most ballers. Their level of talent and scouting visibility was nothing compared to a powerful D1 school. He leaned forward, whispering like he had inside information. "Mississippi gonna to be there on Friday. Maybe even Auburn."

"Oh, I got the field covered for sure. You let me worry about my shit. Gonna light it up!" Darrell held his hand up, and Terrance slapped it. They both withdrew with a wiggle of their fingers, their signature high five they'd done since middle school. "Relax. It's only the season opener. Deerlake is gonna be a walk in the park."

"They're nothing compared to Westmond." I shook my head, flashing back to last year's playoffs once more. I couldn't let that happen again. I scooted over to Darrell. "I've been meaning to talk to you about the D line. When y'all snap up, you gotta—"

"Blah, blah, blah," Darrell said, cutting me off. "Somebody tell this negro to worry 'bout his own game."

"Speaking of spitting game…" Terrance said, his eyes gleaming. He tapped Darrell's phone and licked his lips as Darrell unlocked the screen. He set it on top of my homework, showcasing a picture of a very done-up girl with thick arched eyebrows and plump shiny lips puckered like she was ready to kiss you through the screen. Yeah, she was fine—and she knew it.

"Boom! She cute, right? And she gots *friends.*" He clasped his hands together, wiggling his fingers. His toothy grin widened. "She bringin' all them to the party Friday."

"Dress code—fly." Terrance held his hand up for another high five. Then he pounded his chest. "Slay the baller way."

"That means if you invite Gabby, tell your girl she can't show up in a T-shirt. Or that Mr. Rogers sweater she walkin' around in today." Darrell doubled over, slapping the table. I swung around to scowl at Marion.

"What'd you tell them?" My cheeks heated. Marion was a shameless gossip sometimes, and he'd obviously told the guys I was trying to chat up Gabby.

Marion covered his mouth and looked away, confirming my suspicion.

Great.

I was saved by the bell ending lunch. I shoved my notes in

my backpack and slung it over my shoulder before pushing away from the table. I had English class with Gabby next period, and I didn't want to be ruffled before I saw her. I made a beeline for the hallway, making a cluster of students scatter out of my way. Footsteps squeaked behind me.

"Relax. We're just playing." Marion slapped my shoulder. "You have our full support. Right, guys?"

They nodded vigorously.

"It's been a minute since you smashed. Aysha was, like, two, no—*three* months ago. Hold up. Do we need to have a little birds and bees discussion? Let me learn you something right quick." Darrell turned around, walking backward down the hallway. He batted his eyelashes and gripped my shoulder. "When a man and a woman love each other very much—"

"Man, shut up." I swatted his hand away. "It's not like that."

"But for real, though. Nerdy chicks are the *best*. They're just happy to be with a baller." His shoulder clipped the corner of the hall, and he lost his balance for a second, which served him right. "I bet Gabby got some real freaky—"

Just then, we turned the corner—right where Gabby was taking a pile of books out of her locker… Her eyes narrowed to slits as she scowled at us. She'd obviously overheard.

Gripping her backpack strap across her shoulder, she shut her locker and strode down the hall in long steps, her arms pumping at her sides, taking her far away from our banter. But the distance would be short-lived because, unfortunately, I had the same class.

"Darrell!" I banged my forehead against a neighboring locker, rattling the cold steel.

"Maybe she didn't hear?" Darrell shrugged, scrunching up his mouth.

"She def did." Marion stopped between us. Slapping Darrell on the backside of his head, he said, "Time and place, dog."

"Run." I straightened, flaring my nostrils. "Now."

I rushed into the classroom, almost tripping over Ms. Jabbar, who was leaning against her desk at the front. She followed me with her gaze as I scrambled to the other side of the room—probably wondering why I was in such a rush, since the second bell hadn't rung yet.

My desk wobbled as I skidded into my assigned seat, panting. Scooting across the aisle, I grabbed the edge of Gabby's desk.

"Don't listen to them." I took a deep breath, leaning toward her. "They trippin'."

"Um, yeah. Obviously." She sighed as she searched my face. For a moment her frown softened, and I thought I'd be forgiven. But then she shoved her bag to the corner of her desk, knocking off my fingers. "I just thought you were different. Guess I was wrong."

I balked, preparing to defend myself, but the teacher interrupted.

"All right, settle down, y'all." Ms. J shoved off her desk and clapped her hands at the trickle of students filtering through the door. Her eyes scanned the room, zeroing in on my chair in the middle of the aisle. Folding her arms, she said, "Whatever y'all are talking about, it's going to have to wait until after class."

The chatter faded as everyone turned toward her. Darrell

slid through the door just after the bell rang, and she tapped her watch, an indulgent smile sliding across her face. I glared at him as he took his seat a couple rows over. He mouthed an apology, his eyebrows upturned, but I shook my head.

"While you get settled I'm going to hand out your graded assignments from last week." From her desk she grabbed a stack of papers so tall it almost reached her chin. She combed the aisles, placing our short-form papers on each of our desks. My stapled pages landed on my desk with a flutter. She jabbed the paper, right on the B+.

"Very nice, Russell," she said with a proud flare of her nostrils. My chest warmed. I'd worked hard on this homework assignment, though not as long as I maybe should have. Football had taken its pound of flesh, and that was a full letter grade down from that elusive A+.

When she got to Gabby's desk, she also paused for a moment. "Excellent. Really insightful."

Comparing Gabby's compliment to mine, I knew she'd gotten a better grade than I had. I squinted toward her paper, trying to see what she'd written. How did that brilliant mind of hers work? I was determined to find out.

"Please, get out your packets of E. E. Cummings's poems. Let me see your highlights, your markings in the margins." Ms. J flicked her wrists in the air with a flourish as she continued to stroll between the desks. She stopped in front of Gabby's color-coded highlights to give her a thumbs-up. When she turned to look at mine, I flipped it over to show her my notes jotted hastily on the back page. That earned me an encouraging nod before she moved to the other side of the classroom.

I leaned forward, admiring the scribbles in the margins of Gabby's packet, the multicolored highlights that splashed across her page. As if she felt my gaze, she turned around, her cheeks reddening before she slid her notes out of view.

"So, what did we think of the readings?" Ms. J asked the class when she returned to the front of the room.

"I liked the 'Olaf' one," Karim mumbled from the front row. At least someone from the defensive line had done their homework. I'd read that poem over and over again last night. It was my favorite one in the packet too.

"I'm going to choose to believe you like it because of the challenging message. Not because you went online and looked up the explicit original version of the poem." She bent over so that she was eye level with Karim, nodding slowly until he nodded back.

"Good, because I don't need more angry parents picking apart my curriculum." She rose from her crouch. "That being said, it's one of my favorites too. Turn to 'i sing of Olaf' on page six. Who wants to tell me what it's about?"

Darrell slouched in his seat, trying to make himself smaller. He likely hadn't finished his reading, and by the looks of the shifting students around the room, he was not alone.

This was not lost on Ms. J. Lifting her copy, she began reading the poem aloud, her long nails strumming against the edge of her desk, keeping meter with the rhythm of the poem.

"i sing of Olaf glad and big
whose warmest heart recoiled at war:
a conscientious object-or"

She read it with such gusto we couldn't help but be riveted, especially when she reached the end and her voice cracked. She looked up and asked, "What's happening here?"

"It's about a guy getting beat up," someone from the back of the class muttered.

"Okay, that's a good start." She wagged her head from side to side, not completely satisfied with the answer. "Who else wants to dig in here? Yes, Gabrielle."

Gabby lowered her hand to her desk. "It's about a conscientious objector being tortured."

"Can anyone tell me what a conscientious objector is?" Her gaze skipped over Gabby's raised hand and fell to me. "How about someone else? I'll go with Russell this time."

"It's someone who's against a war. In this case, World War I." I jutted my chin out as Gabby cast me a sidelong glance. "Like Muhammad Ali during the Vietnam War."

"Well done. For moral reasons, this man has chosen not to engage in violence. And as LaShon noted, he's being beaten up. By whom?" She raised her eyebrow, a challenge.

Gabby and I both raised our hands. The rest of the class looked on with mild disinterest, except for some of the other football players who scrunched up their faces at my eagerness to participate in class. But I didn't care what they thought right now. I wanted to redeem myself in Gabby's eyes, to show her I *wasn't* like the others. Ms. J sighed and called on Gabby again.

"By his own colonel." She scanned through her notes. "But he refuses to change his views."

"Ah, so there's the heart of the story." She beamed with

pride, giving Gabby a fist bump before returning to the front of the room. She hopped up to sit on her desk. "So, what does it mean to you?"

"It means you better do what you're told," my teammate Karim said from the front row. He squared his broad linebacker shoulders. "It's like the pledge of allegiance. We have to do it."

"Is that what you got out of it? Perhaps it shows an instance where following orders goes against everything you hold dear. Maybe it means speaking truth to power is sometimes hard. Maybe it's a call to arms against apathy. Think about that." She paused with a shrug, giving us space to explore our own thoughts. "Write me a five-page paper on what 'Olaf' means to you. What does patriotism look like in your eyes? You have a whole month for this assignment. So today is Thursday the fifth, so you have until October 4. Got it?"

A collective groan rippled through the classroom, but my mind was swimming. When we'd studied the Revolutionary War, Mama had told me our ancestors—the ones we could trace—hadn't fought in it. *That was a white man's fight*, she'd told me. Because even though the colonies were fighting for justice and the rights of men, it wasn't for *all* men. Not men with dark brown skin like me.

But "Olaf" said something more, something that really stuck with me. In a society that glorified war, Olaf stood for peace. He kinda reminded me of Dr. King, with his nonviolent civil rights tactics.

I couldn't help but think about Colin Kaepernick. He took a knee to highlight police brutality against Black people, for kids like Dante Maynard. Dante lost his life because cops like Officer Reynaud were so filled with prejudice, they couldn't think straight. And what did Kaepernick get in return for his peaceful, nonviolent protest?

He was villainized, and he lost his job—his ability to live his passion. Ain't no poems about him.

Foolish. That's what Pops had called his protest, and maybe he had a point. Karim's comments rang in my ears: *It means to do what you're told.* Black and brown people had to fall in line, or get punished.

Ms. J was right about a lot of things, but I found it hard to believe that "Olaf" applied to everybody. Because the people in power decided what tyranny was. And the people in charge…well, they were overwhelmingly white, and they couldn't see their own prejudice. They didn't want to. They didn't have to. *That* was the real American way.

The rest of the period passed in a blur with me stealing glances at Gabby, wondering what was going on beneath her curly mane, in that sharp mind of hers. She turned her head to the side a few times, almost as if she was watching me too, but I couldn't be sure. Unlike last night, she was more cautious with her interest. I wondered if she was still hurt from Darrell's trash talk in the hallway, because any warmth we'd rekindled last night felt like it had dissipated. I felt the chill of her cold shoulder as she continued to ignore me.

Finally, after wrapping up the day's discussion, Ms. J knelt beneath her desk and lugged a box of papers to her chair.

"Our next assignment is one of my favorites, *If Beale Street Could Talk* by James Baldwin. Now, the powers-that-be consider some sections of this book to be a little too mature, so we'll be reading excerpts. That means your tirelessly devoted teacher stood in the library for hours copying and binding these new handouts."

She held up a thick packet of papers. There must have been forty pages stapled together. I hissed under my breath. I liked Ms. J—she really cared about her class and her students. But she was the hardest teacher I had. *By far.* We'd only been in school for three weeks, and we were already on our third assignment.

"And since we all love the environment—nod along with me." She nodded, pointing to her head, signaling for us to do the same. "Yes, since we want to save the planet and my copy machine privileges, I only made half as many copies as there are people in class. That means we're partnering up for the next project."

"How are we supposed to read a book side by side?" Darrell piped up from the back of the room.

"I'm sure you'll work out a schedule with your partner."

Gabby raised her hand, and Ms. J pointed to her.

"If we can get our own copy, can we do the assignment alone?"

Our teacher chewed on the side of her mouth, considering the possibility. Then she shook her head.

"No, let's collaborate. Come on, find a partner. If you don't, I'll choose for you." The class shifted at her instructions, eager to choose their own partners.

"Psst!" Darrell whispered, but there was no way I was partnering up with him. He'd stick me with all the work. Ignoring him, I scooted across the aisle toward Gabby and flashed the most charming smile I could muster.

"What do you say?"

Gabby looked around her desk at the pods of two huddled together, at her girl across the room who had already paired off with someone else. Even Darrell, who'd muscled his way to the front of the room, had nabbed Karim for a partner. It was down to the two of us.

"Fine." She gave a weak smile at Ms. J, who turned her back on our corner as she made her way back to the front of the room. Once she was out of earshot, Gabby whipped around. "What's your number?"

I smiled and sent a silent thank-you to Ms. J for throwing this assignment at us—for throwing us together.

"You can keep the packet," Gabby said.

"But how are we—" I was cut off by Ms. J, who was clapping her hands again.

"Make a poster board of the themes of the story. You have until October 21 to complete this assignment. This is part of your midterm grade, so take this seriously and don't leave your work until the last minute. I'm giving you plenty of time to really make this special. If you need supplies, they're up here. Grab whatever you need when you come get your handout."

"Look." Gabby shoved her phone in the front pocket of her backpack and zipped it shut. "I'll get my own copy of the book online. So, like I said, you can keep the packet."

I crossed my arms, frustrated that she was drawing such a hard line with me.

"Fine. Will you do your own project too, or am I included in that?"

"Oh, you'll work on this project if you want a grade." She stood and slung her backpack over her shoulder. "But we won't be meeting at your house. Don't want to give your *boys* anything else to talk about."

I dropped my forehead to my desk and moaned into it.

"We can start on it at my dad's warehouse when you come pick up the battery plugs. Friday night work?"

"We have a game. And there's a party afterward. After we beat Deerlake."

"A victory party before you've even played?" She raised her eyebrows. "Isn't that a bit premature?"

"Not at all," I said. "We're gonna crush it."

She rolled her eyes.

"You should come through." It was out of my mouth before I had time to think about it.

She blinked, her breath catching. Maybe I'd made a mistake by inviting her. I mean, three days was hardly enough time to finish the reading. But I was a fast reader. And if I was fast, Gabby was faster. She could handle it. Plus, I wanted her at the party. I wanted to show her that I wasn't the same punk who'd left her side freshman year. I wanted a second chance.

"Rus…"

"Come on," I said. "We can talk about the project there— maybe divvy up the readings between the two of us."

She laughed. "Nice try. You know we won't get any home-work done at a party. How about Saturday instead?"

"I have to ice in the morning but could come by after?"

"Fine. Let's say three o'clock." She pulled out her phone, typing into her calendar as the bell rang. "You better come prepared. And FYI, watching the movie doesn't count."

Her wild locks quivered as she shoved past our row of classmates on her way to the door. As I watched her leave, I realized that she hadn't said yes to the party. But she also hadn't said no.

4

The wind whipped through the window as Marion and I drove through the back roads on our way to his house. It had been a while since I'd been on his side of the parish, and as we moved closer to the Bayou Glen trailer park, I grew more grateful for that.

"I can't believe I left my lucky gloves at home." Marion cussed under his breath with a shake of his head.

Superstition had no place in my routine. To me, a pair of gloves was a pair of gloves. But Marion swore by his gear, and if he was willing to drive all the way out to his stepdad's house to retrieve them before tonight's game against Deerlake, they were clearly important to him. And he was important to me.

Winning was important to me too. So we missed the team bus to Deerlake's stadium *just* for Marion and his magic gloves. We wouldn't be too late—their school was nearby in the next parish to the east—but I was the captain of our team, and I didn't want to be late for warm-up on game day.

"Still can't believe Pops let you use his truck."

"Yeah, the Civic wouldn't start this morning, so my folks

are gonna catch a ride to the game with Karim's mama. Hopefully Mr. Dupre can bring it back to life—we *need* two cars.
For real."

I tried not to think about Mr. Dupre or Gabby, instead focusing on turning onto the narrow drive that led into Bayou
Glen. The truck's tires crunched on the gravel road as I pulled
in front of a pale green double-wide with brown shutters. A
silver sedan sat in the driveway.

Marion bent forward and grumbled into the dashboard.
"Ed's here. You better wait outside. And turn the truck around
so that it's facing the exit."

"Okay." I nodded slowly. When it came to his stepdad,
Marion was always dead serious. I searched for Mrs. LaSalle's
car along the street but didn't see it. She still hadn't returned
home. Marion would be facing his stepdad alone.

"I'll be as fast as I can." He pushed his door open and
hopped down from the truck, skirting a stained mattress that
had been left on the road to rot. He looked over his shoulder,
twirling his finger while he mouthed, *Turn around*. Then he
disappeared around the side of the house, where I knew he'd
slide inside through his bedroom window.

I repositioned the truck, backing into a neighboring driveway before pulling out to face the other way. The noise dis-
turbed a dog chained to the trailer across the street from
Marion's. It ran full tilt at the truck, barking and snarling as
it strained on its chain.

The door to Marion's house swung open. He stumbled out,
falling to his hands. Ed followed, yelling something I couldn't
hear, but I didn't have to. His face looked like that angry pit
bull—nasty and vicious.

I flinched as Ed threw Marion's gloves in his face. Marion reached to the grass to pick them up, and when Ed stepped toward him, my hand reached for the door handle. If he shoved Marion again, he'd have to deal with both of us. But Ed tripped over his slippers, giving Marion a chance to skirt around him. I put the truck in Drive while Marion stormed across the lawn and climbed into the truck, his nostrils flaring.

Ed pumped his arms as he followed him, stopping to bang on the driver's side window. He wanted me to roll the window down, but Marion yanked my shoulder back.

"Just drive. We're done here."

"Y'all boys is soft!" Ed spewed from the other side of the glass. "You think you something but you ain't, understand? You ain't shit."

"Rus, drive!" Marion yelled.

I pressed the gas and the truck lurched forward, kicking up gravel as we sped away. Ed held his fist up, cussing and calling us cowards, but after a few yards, we couldn't hear him anymore. Marion fanned his hand, hissing through the pain.

"Are you going to be all right?"

"I've played through worse. You know that." He slipped on his right glove and flexed his fingers.

"He needs to go back to jail." I skidded onto the main road, afraid to slow down or look back. "Seriously, next time we call the cops."

"What? So I can end up in the system?" He sighed. He'd be eighteen in February, but if he got tangled up in foster care for the months until then, it could be just enough to derail his chances of getting into college on a football scholarship. He shifted to face me, his jaw set, eyes unblinking. "We've got one last season to play for recruiters, and I don't feel like stirring up shit with the finish line so close. You understand?"

"Man, you might not make it to next spring," I said.

I glanced at the limp hand he was nursing in his lap. If Coach Fontenot caught a whiff of a blown joint, he'd surely dig deeper into the reasons behind the injury. Shoot, he was still checking on my elbow, even though the trainer said I was all healed up. And it was only a matter of time before Ed did more damage.

"Promise me you won't call the cops, okay? Nothing good happens when they get involved."

It didn't feel right, but I nodded in agreement. It wasn't my secret to tell, and Marion was practically grown—it was his decision to make. I clenched my jaw and pressed the gas pedal harder, sending the truck flying down the country road. I didn't slow down until we reached the stadium parking lot.

The opposing lineman grabbed me by the sides and swung me around before I could gain any yardage. I struggled to keep the ball tucked to my chest as he pinned me to the ground. My head thudded against the grass.

I was vaguely aware of the whistle blaring, signaling the end of the play. But I was too busy trying to catch my breath. That big Deerlake player had *literally* knocked the wind out of me. My chest rose and fell in short spurts as I gasped for air.

"Move. Give him room." Marion elbowed his way past Karim and Bobby, and looked at me from above. "You okay?"

When I nodded, he extended his hand to help me get up. A muffled whimper escaped my lips when I felt my ribs creak, but I gave Marion the same look he'd given me as we sped away from Ed—the look that warned him not to blow up my spot.

Don't say a word. I'm fine.

The Deerlake lineman checked to see if I was okay and gave me a pat on the shoulder, which I appreciated. The last official game I'd played had been against Westmond, where no one was a good sport. Marion deposited me on the bench, his eyes still worried as he turned toward the field to set the next play. Beads of sweat trailed down my face, pooling at the tip of my nose before raining down on the turf. My shoulders burned, and I hung my head low, panting—still trying to catch a breath in this godforsaken heat.

I snatched a water bottle from the folding table next to me, avoiding the pleading eyes of my lineman, the dude who was supposed to have my back as I ran the ball.

"Rus, dog, I'm sorry," Karim said.

"Don't be sorry," I said, my voice cracking as I struggled to breathe. I spit on the ground, tasting blood on my lip. "Just do your job."

The season opener we'd thought would be a walk in the park was turning out to be brutal. Deerlake was relentless, making us work for every yard, every pass. They were ranked well below the Jackson Jackals, so they had something to prove. That meant they were going to make us work for the W.

And I was a target. Every time Marion sent the ball my way, two of their biggest defense players were on me. I'd been tackled at least ten times tonight. I couldn't take another hit like that last one. And the team trainer knew it too.

"That looked like a bad one." Ms. Duval knelt in front of

me, pulling her curly red hair in a tight bun. She always did that when she geared up for a long evaluation.

"I'm fine."

"I'll be the judge of that." She fished in her back pocket and brought out a skinny flashlight. Pointing it into my eyes, she said, "Look left. Blink. Look right. Are you seeing any spots? Any blurred vision?"

I was about to respond when Pops's voice ripped through our conversation.

"Coach!" His voice gurgled as he strained his voice. "COACH!"

I turned in my seat to find him gripping the railing above the track. Mama sat beside him on the bleachers, her hand gripping her chest. She caught my gaze and stood, leaning over my dad to mouth, *You okay?*

I nodded and did my best to give her a reassuring smile.

"Get him back on the field!" Pops yelled toward Coach Fontenot, who was pacing the sidelines. His arms were crossed, his gaze glued to the field, but I could tell by the way his jaw tightened that he heard every word.

One of the game security guards, likely an off-duty cop working the league for extra money, looked up at my dad suspiciously, his hand on his walkie-talkie.

"Pops, please." I swiped my arm at him, urging him to get back to the stands. But he didn't budge.

"Rus, you're fine, boy. Tell him." He bounced on the balls of his feet, turning his attention back to Fontenot. "He's fine, Coach. Put him back on the field. Let the boy play!"

"Hey." Ms. Duval gripped my shoulders and turned me

back in the direction of the field. She pointed to my swollen lip. "May I?"

When I nodded, she pinched the tender flesh and flipped
it downward. She released it with a sigh, then pushed off the
ground.

"Well, it doesn't need stitches." She removed her latex glove
and tossed it into the trash can beneath the water station.
"How's your neck? Roll it for me."

Closing my eyes, I dropped my chin to my chest and rolled
my neck, fighting through the stiffness. I tried not to wince.

"Okay, you're cleared for play. But…" She folded her arms.
"If you need to sit the rest of this one out—"

"I'm okay." There was no way I could sit on the sidelines
while my team was taking a beating.

I looked up just in time to see the opposition gain twelve
yards on us. I sprang to my feet, spurred on by a surge of
adrenaline.

"Come on, y'all!" I shouted, swaying a little from the rapid
motion.

We were supposed to crush this team.

"Horseshit! You see him grabbing my player!" Coach yelled
at the referee, spit flying out of his mouth. The ref gave him
a warning look. "Alls I'm asking is for you to call the holding when there's clearly holding!"

"Coach, take a breather." Our assistant coach gripped his
shoulder. But Fontenot shoved past him, rumbling down the
sideline to where I was sitting.

"Russell? Where you at? How you feeling?"

I paused for half a second, then nodded. "Good to go."

"Are you sure? 'Cause I don't need you burning out on the

first game of the season. Course, it would be a whole lot easier if your teammates played like they wanted some redemption for losing the playoffs." He turned to the players standing on the sidelines and raised his voice. "Or have y'all forgotten?"

"Put me in, Coach. Let me turn this around." I stepped up to the line. "I'm okay, I promise."

With the blare of the whistle, he stopped the next play. Waving to my relief player, he waited for him to jog to the sidelines before clasping my shoulder. "Turn this around, son."

I jogged onto the field, my loosened pads rattling atop my shoulders as I joined my teammates.

"I thought you was out for the rest of the game for sure," Marion said, unbuckling his helmet.

"And watch from the sidelines?" I slapped his shoulder. "You trippin'."

He leaned forward to give me a rundown, but a player from the other team shouted, catching his attention.

"Yo, say that again!" Marion stepped forward, a challenge. I tugged on the sleeve of his uniform, stopping him from going any further down that road. He turned to me. "Man, Rus. They trash-talking like crazy."

I left our huddle and caught Coach Fontenot's attention on the sidelines. I waved my arms above my head, asking Coach to use another time-out. We needed to regroup. The battered offensive team gathered around me.

"Don't let them get in your head. Keep your focus. Darrell, Terrance, y'all gotta hold their linemen back. They're killing us."

"You see the size of them?" Terrance croaked.

I nodded. Number eighty-eight was a beast. And sixty-seven was almost as big.

"Do whatever you gotta do to hold the pocket for Marion. And, dude," I said, turning to Marion. "You gotta stop running the ball. If you can't make a clean pass, throw it away on the sidelines and regroup. We can't afford another turnover."

I looked at the seconds ticking away on the scoreboard. Coach waved his arms from the sidelines, shouting as he signaled the next play with sign language only we understood.

"Hammerhead, delta, leftie. Y'all clear on that? Bobby, stay close as I set that edge."

Once we broke the huddle, I waited until the rest of my teammates were out of earshot before tugging Marion back. "How's the hand?"

"Better." He rotated it in front of me.

"Let's light it up, then." I rubbed the top of his helmet before getting in formation.

We lined up opposite Deerlake, a renewed fire simmering in our bellies. I stood to the right of Marion, a floater. A wild card tight end.

I chewed anxiously on my mouth guard. At the last second, I switched to the left side, just as Marion clapped his hands. The punter snapped the football and the wall of linemen collided. But I was on the move, a black uniform dodging and weaving through the fray. I hit the forty-yard marker, my long legs chomping at the turf as I ran down the edge of the field.

When I reached the thirty-five-yard mark, I looked over my shoulder, hoping that Marion would stick to the plan. The ball was in the air, slicing through the humid Louisiana night sky. Adjusting, I repositioned, almost colliding with

Bobby, but he fell back, giving me just enough room to extend my arms.

My gloved fingers grazed the edge of the football, making it wobble. It spun off-kilter, nearly toppling out of bounds, and I scrambled. Both my arms outreached, I jumped in the air and drew it into my chest, tucking it under my arm.

Then I ran full tilt—as if my life depended on it. Because it did. This was my last season of high school ball.

Twenty yards.

Ten.

Touchdown.

"Yes!" I slammed the ball onto the field with a primal growl.

The scoreboard flipped in our favor. I ran to the sidelines, my muscle aches easing with the fresh surge of adrenaline. I clasped Marion's outstretched hand. With a throaty croak I said, "Let's shut this shit down."

"Slay the baller way," he howled before falling back to the bench.

I exhaled sharply, relieved to see our score back on top. Gabby was right—planning a victory party before actually winning the game was premature. Thankfully, it looked like we'd eke out our first win of the season. I bobbed my legs up and down, eager to get to that party.

Eager to see her.

5

"Who needs a ride?" I looked around, spotting a few raised hands.

Even showered and changed, my teammates still looked a little banged up. We'd gotten that W, but just barely. And Deerlake had *nothing* on Westmond. We needed to step up our game if we had any hope of beating them next week.

But I'd save that for tomorrow. Right now, we had a party to catch.

We headed toward the parking lot behind our stadium. For a split second, I was looking for my Civic before remembering that Pops had loaned me his truck. I peered through the darkness. And that's when I saw it.

A mash of toilet paper clung to Pops's truck; the painted letters Boudreaux Baths and Plumbing on the side were barely visible. I picked at a strip, trying to tug it off, but beneath it was a goopy sealant, mortaring the toilet paper to the truck. It oozed a yellow gel.

"Eggs," I said, rounding the back to see the extent of the damage. And then I saw the writing on the back window.

Garbage.

The word was scrawled across the window in large, deliberate letters. Whoever wrote it wanted the whole town to see. Snail trails of white liquid slid from beneath the letters, the biggest one coming from the G. They oozed to the tailgate, making puddles against the lining.

I turned to Marion, words failing me, and by the way his lips silently smacked, he was speechless too. I turned the painted mess over in my head as if I could arrange it into something better, but I couldn't.

This was nasty, a personal attack that could only come from one team—and it wasn't Deerlake. They had too much sportsmanship.

"Westmond." I looked to Marion, my chest tightening with barely contained anger.

He nodded slowly. "It's gotta be Brad."

"Pops is going to kill me." I circled the truck. How would I explain this to my dad? I couldn't take it home like this.

"How are we going to get to the party?" Darrell paced near the hood, his phone screen glowing against his face.

"Man, shut up," Marion barked at him. "We obviously have a situation here."

"What? People are already showing up. You know I got a girl coming."

"There go a police officer right there. Maybe they can help." Terrance cupped his hands around his lips and shouted, "Yo, we need some help over here."

"What are you doing?" Marion ripped Terrance's hand away from his mouth. "Don't call them fools over here."

But it was too late. We watched in silence as two officers

sauntered over from their huddle near the south entrance of Deerlake's stadium, one with her hands in her pockets, the other adjusting his pants before crossing to our row. He held up a hand to stop an oncoming car so that he could take his sweet time.

My heart rate quickened. I didn't have anything I wasn't supposed to have, hadn't done anything I wasn't supposed to do, yet I was still on edge, feeling guilty.

"What do we have here?" The cop grabbed his belt loops as he looked at us over his glasses.

"Evening, Officer." I stepped in front of the group before someone said something foolish. His shiny silver name tag read *Reynaud*.

He was one of the cops who'd put a bullet in Dante Maynard.

Officer Reynaud strolled to my side of the truck, inspecting the scene. He looked up with a wry grin, releasing his breath in a whistle. "Looks like you have quite a mess on your hands."

"Yes, sir." My hand trembled as I gestured to the goopy mess, moving deliberately slowly so that he knew I wasn't getting any ideas, though I couldn't help but notice that his hands hovered near his belt, close to his holster. I wasn't going to let him catch anything less than calm.

"We take this kinda thing seriously." He put his hands on his hips and tilted his head. Something about his tone made me doubt that. He gripped his belt loops again, pulling his pants over his belly. "You wanna go on record with this? I can call it in."

"You think I should file a report?" I asked.

"You could." He shrugged. "Might be a lot of paperwork for nothing. This is such a hard thing to catch."

I glanced at the group of security guards gathered near the entrance gate and couldn't help but wonder if one of them had seen or heard anything. My car wasn't tucked away—it was in plain view. And if the guards had somehow missed my truck getting trashed, surely there was a security camera that overlooked the lot, maybe on one of the lampposts or on the side of the building. I peered across the lot, trying to spot one, but I couldn't find any.

"Thank you, Officer, but I think we'll just clean the car and call it a day." Marion stepped forward.

"Probably for the best, son." He lifted his chin then cocked his head, his eyes curious as they scanned Marion. "I was a quarterback in my day, at Jackson."

"Yes, sir. You held the record for the most touchdown passes until this year." Marion smiled, reaching to shake his hand.

"Until you." Officer Reynaud noticeably did not reach his hand to grasp Marion's. "'Course, that was a different time, back when the school was—well, it was different."

Marion's attempted handshake withered in midair, and he withdrew it with a quick cough. Reynaud's meaning wasn't lost on us. He was nostalgic for the days when Jackson was mostly a white school, before redistricting tried to correct the imbalance between the schools across the bayou and failed.

Why would you want to dwell on a past like that?

"Anyway, like I said, vandalism will not be tolerated." He kept his hands on his hips. "Speaking of vandalism. Y'all know anything about these flyers?"

He fished in his back pocket and pulled out a crumpled piece of paper, grumbling as he unfolded it and shoved it in my direction. It was one of the Dante Maynard flyers—just like the ones I'd seen with Gabby and Marion. Except this time the bold letters scrawled on the bottom of the page read: No Justice, No Peace.

"Well? You know who's doing this, son?"

"No, sir." I shook my head vigorously. I handed the sheet back to him, a hot potato I didn't want to be left holding.

"Been finding them plastered all over tarnation." He pointed behind me, in the direction of Westmond, then he rounded the car, his belly jiggling. "What about y'all?" He held the flyer at eye level, making sure each one of us got a good look. Suddenly we'd gone from being wronged to being the subject of a police inquiry. "Well?"

We shook our heads.

"Vandalism will not be tolerated, ya hear? Not on my watch. You be sure and let your friends know." He clasped his hands together. "It's time we put this whole issue behind us."

"Yes, sir." I nodded in agreement, although the irony was not lost on me. Vandalism had literally *just* happened on his watch. If he cared as much about my dad's car as he did about these damn posters, he wouldn't have told us it was for the best not to pursue it.

Still, I remembered my mama's instructions to always use *yes, sirs* and *please* and *thank yous*, especially with people like Reynaud.

"Thank you, sir." My hands flexed behind my back.

"All right, then. We better get back to it, but listen here, boy. You let me know if you see anything." He pointed two fingers at me and brushed the air between us, then backed away toward the other cop. "Y'all get on home. Don't cause no trouble, ya hear?"

The sound of fiddles and accordions from Bobby's zydeco music wafted through the open windows of Terrance's house, an old shotgun-style home just off the edge of the town square. By all respects, it was the nicest house of the group, with stained glass windows and a wraparound porch. His mother, Dr. Edmonds, was out of town at a conference. And she'd left the keys to the liquor cabinet behind.

The song abruptly ended, and the sound of arguing floated down to the driveway, where I stood with a wet sponge in my hand. I could hear Darrell yelling, "Bobby's lost his DJ privileges with his backwoods country shit."

Trap music took over, thrumming the windows with deep bass. I plunged the sponge back into the bucket, getting it nice and wet before turning my attention back to washing the truck. It sucked that I had to spend half the party washing my dad's car, but at least the paint on the back window was water-based and coming off easily.

"They need to turn the music down." I stood up in the tailgate, towering above Marion, who knelt by the front tires. "We don't want Reynaud thinking we're causing trouble."

"Man, don't worry about that fool." Marion waved dismissively. "He don't have anything on us. He can't touch us."

A silver car rolled up behind us, and a bunch of girls got out, including Aysha and her best friend, Donna. They giggled as they passed us, looking back to check out me and

Marion as they walked to the front door. Aysha made damn sure I saw her, swaying her hips as she walked up the steps.

After they rang the doorbell, Terrance popped his head out. He smiled when he surveyed the group, stopping momentarily to tell them this was a strict no-picture party before letting them inside.

"Man, how he gonna tell a bunch of Instagram babes they can't take any pictures?" Marion laughed from the other side of the car.

He had a point. Telling those girls not to snap pics at a football party was like giving them a glass of water on a hot day and asking them not to drink it. But those were the rules. If we wanted to let loose and dip into contraband, there couldn't be any evidence.

Marion dropped his rag in the soapy water. "I think that's as good as it's going to get."

"I just need to get this out," I said, taking another pass on the driver's side door. "Was this dent here before?"

"Dude, your dad is not going to notice no damn dent." He walked over to my side, while I brushed my fingers over the door. It was squeaky clean, and the dent was so small, you had to touch it to know it was there. I didn't know if it was new or not, but I guessed Pops wouldn't notice it.

Marion snatched the sponge out of my hand. "We should be in there."

"You right." I wiped my hands on my sweatpants, then pulled out my phone. "Hold on a sec."

"Dude, she's not coming." Marion slapped my shoulder. He knew I was waiting for word from Gabby, but he obviously wasn't as hopeful as I was.

"She might."

I knew it was foolish, but she technically hadn't said whether she'd show or not. So I'd held out hope. But the more I checked my phone, the more far-fetched it seemed. We didn't exactly have a history of having a good time together at parties.

"Nope." He shook his head, pursing his lips. "But you know who did come? Aysha. And she's obviously still into you, so *chop chop*."

I didn't feel a tinge of excitement when I saw her, didn't feel the gravity that used to draw me to her. When Aysha and I broke up at the beginning of the summer, it felt like we'd been broken up for a while. I was ashamed of myself for dragging it on so long. Maybe I thought I *should* date a girl like Aysha. I was the football team captain, and she was one of the most popular girls at school.

It worked on paper, but...to be honest, I didn't think we really *liked* each other.

But Marion was right: standing out here pining for Gabby wasn't the best way to spend my Friday night.

I took the steps two at a time and burst into the party. A wall of humidity hit me, a mixture of sweat and beer. I weaved through the room, stopping at the kitchen island for a Solo cup. Sitting on the barstools was Donna with a couple of the girls who'd just arrived. They squished together while Donna held her phone out for a selfie.

"Yo, no pictures." I ducked my head under the overhead cabinets, out of the frame so they couldn't see my face.

"For real?" One of them blinked at me.

"Seriously, take that outside. Please?"

"Can't take no pictures in no contraband party. But you can talk to me," Marion said as he sauntered over to their pouting faces. He turned on his full charm, as he led them to the couch.

I glanced around the room and caught Aysha standing by the keg in the corner. I decided to give her space. I didn't want everyone gossiping on Monday that they'd seen us talking at the party. Especially if Gabby might hear. I wasn't going to blow my chance twice.

I darted into the dining room where a cooler of beers sat on the ground. Darrell was holding court at the head of the long table, his legs propped on top of the mahogany surface as he chatted with his new girl. The fireplace behind him crack-led, which had me bursting into laughter. It was ridiculous to build a fire in this September heat—no wonder this party was so dang hot. But Darrell always had to put on a show.

His cousin Gary Tounior—or Homegrown Gary, as ev-erybody called him—hopped up when he saw me, a Swisher blunt hanging from his lips.

"There's the little munchkin." He grabbed my hand and pulled me in for a hug, patting me on the back. The smell of weed and charcoal clung tightly to him, even though he wasn't wearing a shirt. He *never* wore a shirt. Gary waved his arms, stretching the length of the room. "I heard them cops tried to rough y'all up tonight."

"Nah, it was nothing. They just asked a few questions," I said, pointing to the truck parked in the driveway. "I'm more worried about my dad's car."

"Yeah that's some rough ish. You say the word, and I'll take care of them, nah mean? Westmond wannabes, cops—you name it. I got your back." He tugged at his waistline, where he concealed his signature pistol.

"Aight, but it's cool." I gulped. I'd heard stories from Darrell and knew Gary wasn't one to dish out empty threats. "I'll handle it."

"You will?" He raised his eyebrow with a sneer. "Mr. Big Man Baller, you want some of this ish?"

He drew the blunt to his lips and sucked in a long drag, the butt lighting up as bright as the fireplace. He covered his mouth through a cough while he offered it to me. I shook my head.

"Nah, man. You know I can't." I fanned the smoke wafting through the thick humid air, making sure none of it made it to my nostrils. I could ignore the beer and Henny. But not the stuff that would show up on a random drug test for the next few weeks. "And that goes for all y'all."

My teammates within earshot concealed their blunts under the table, turning away from me so I wouldn't see their bloodshot eyes.

"I remember those days." Gary tilted his head, his gaze growing distant, and I imagined him mentally strolling down memory lane, back to the time before he dropped out and threw away any chance of playing college ball. He shook his head, coming back to the present.

Darrell joined us and snaked a bulky arm over my shoulder.

"Come on, Rus. It's a party. So take this," he said, popping the top of a can of beer before handing it to me. "And *party*."

I leaned against the wall, the can of beer sweating in my hand as I surveyed the scene. Marion sat in Dr. Edmonds's antique armchair, chatting with one of Darrell's Instagram

friends. I was amazed at how he was able to compartmental-
ize what happened earlier today. He was all laughs, all charm.
No one would ever think that hours ago he'd fought off his
own stepdad to get his gear.

I wished I could be like that, but the events of the day still
nipped at my mind.

Where is Gabby?

She had my number. I'd invited her to this party twice.
And even against Marion's advice, I'd texted her an hour ago.
Still, no response. I pulled out my phone, feeling like a total
chump for checking again, and a black screen stared back at
me. My phone was dead.

"Anybody got a charger?" I asked the room.

"It's a no-phone party." Donna chuckled. "Take it outside."

Hissing under my breath, I pushed through the packed
crowd, making a beeline toward the truck's glove box where
I knew Pops kept his car charger.

The cool night washed over me, and I leaned against the
truck door while my phone charged.

A flash of black across the street caught my eye, and my
spine instinctively straightened.

For a second, I thought my eyes were playing tricks on
me, but the shadow stirred again. A hooded figure darted
along the side of town hall, a bulky messenger bag thumping against his knees.

I dropped my phone to the seat, locked the truck, and
crossed the street, curious. In the dim glow of the streetlamps,
I could see that the entire side wall of town hall was papered
with more Dante Maynard flyers—just like the side wall of

Emmett's Quick Stop. This time the writing at the bottom read: Silence is Violence.

Suddenly a police siren rang out, and the hooded figure froze at the edge of the alley. I shifted to the side, hoping the shadow of the building would shade me from the streetlamps. The cops were probably looking for him. *This* was the guy who'd been plastering posters all over town condemning their latest shame—the killing of Dante. I clenched my jaw, inwardly chastising myself for being in the wrong place at the wrong time. I couldn't be caught with him. I'd be arrested for sure.

I yanked the sleeve of his hoodie and pulled him into the shadows. He made himself flush with the wall, gripping his chest like he was trying to slow his breathing as a cop car cruised slowly by.

When the danger passed, he pushed off the wall, dropping the stack of flyers. He held his hands up—in surrender or in preparation to defend himself, I don't know. He was smaller than me, much smaller. I could take him in a fight if I needed to. But he backed away. He put a steady finger up to his bandana-covered face and whispered, "Shhhhh."

Then he disappeared across the town square.

6

Dante's Shadow. That's what we'd started calling the person who risked their tail to speak their truth. I actually thought it was kind of cool, like we had a local superhero who fought with words. But Marion disagreed.

"I already told y'all." Marion waved his hand dismissively. "It's gotta be a white dude."

"Why do you say that?" I sloshed in my ice bath, the ice cubes clanking against the metal siding as I turned toward him. The movement woke up the cold, and I shivered. "Dude, just get in your tub. The sooner you do, the less likely Coach will dunk you."

He danced along the edge of his container, shaking his head.

"Marion's right," Darrell said. "White people can protest all they want without fear of having a gun pulled on them. But us?" Darrell held up a finger gun and pointed at the cinder block wall.

"Silence is violence?" Marion repeated the words on the flyers with a shake of his head. "More like silence is safety. I'm telling you, you gotta be white to get away with that shit."

That struck a chord with me. My policy was to keep my head down and my mouth shut because nothing good ever came from speaking up. People like Bradley Simmons could be outspoken and obnoxious, could live without fear. But not us. Maybe Marion was right. The Shadow was probably a white guy.

"Dude," Terrance piped up from the training table nearby. We all jumped when we heard him speak, since we thought he'd been sleeping. "What if *Ms. J* is Dante's Shadow?"

"Don't be foolish." Darrell splashed his water toward him.

I shook my head, remembering the height and build of the dude in the shadows. "Whoever it is, they're small. Ms. J is way too tall to be the Shadow."

"Should we tell Reynaud?" Terrance asked innocently. For someone as smart as him, he could really ask some ridic questions.

"Are you crazy?" Marion said.

"We don't know anything, didn't see nothing, don't want no trouble." Darrell pointed to each one of us. "That's what my dad always says, and I'm gonna stick with that."

The clock above the door ticked just past two o'clock. I was supposed to meet Gabby in an hour to work on our project. I slapped the edge of my tub, eager to catch the trainer's attention. "Ms. Duval, can I head out?"

She skidded to a halt, then poked her head into our room. "How long have you been in?"

"About twenty minutes." I checked the time, then nodded to confirm.

"All right, out you go." She slung her thumb over her shoulder. Then she turned to Marion, pursing her lips as she looked at the ice melting in his bath. "Now, how can I get this guy in the tub?"

"You could make it about twenty degrees warmer," I said, sloshing out of mine.

"Or I could just call Coach?" She folded her arms, clearly not amused.

"No, miss. Please." Marion clasped his hands together as if in prayer. "I'll do it."

His jaw seized as he dipped his toe through the bobbing ice cubes. Before Ms. Duval could push him in, Marion slid in, his elbows knocking the sides as he immersed himself. He howled in agony, but we were too busy laughing to care.

"I'll catch you later." I grabbed my duffel bag from the counter. "Picking up that part from Gabby."

"I can guess what part that is." Darrell wiggled his eyebrows.

"Don't start that up again." My jaw tightened as I took an angry step toward him.

"Dude, Rus. Chill. Sorry."

I rinsed off quickly, then changed into my sweats. The hallways were empty as I scurried to my car, which was baking under the Saturday afternoon sun. By some miracle, I'd gotten the Civic to start this morning.

The bigger miracle would be if Gabby Dupre actually wanted to talk to me.

The Dupre warehouse sat at the edge of their thirty-acre property on the corner closest to the highway spur, near a cluster of smaller, weatherworn houses. The workhands who maintained the Dupre fields lived in some of them, although one or two looked abandoned. I turned down their dirt road, wondering if the dilapidated outbuildings were a sign Henry's grocery storage business was in trouble.

That thought was quickly dispelled as I pulled up the slope and parked in front of a two-story barn that looked like it was painted in a fresh coat of brick red. With large windows lining the front of the barn and a row of rattling AC units along the side of the building, it looked like one of the finest structures in all of Monroe.

Business must be real good to keep the place up like this.

I grabbed my bag and jogged to the front door, checking my phone on the way to make sure I wasn't too late. I opened the door and was hit with a wall of cool air. "Hello?"

My voiced echoed off splashed concrete floors in a cavernous great room. It didn't look like any barn I'd ever seen— not a bale of hay or horse stalls in sight. I craned my neck to check upstairs, which had an open, wraparound walkway that overlooked the main floor. Seeing no one, I looked around at the segmented areas of bagged grains, baskets of okra and green beans, and a packaging assembly line toward the back. I scooted past the wooden crates near the entrance and peered into an office window nearby. I jimmied the door handle, but it was locked. I was walking over to try the door on the other side of the room when a tiny head poked out from behind a stack of packed canvas bags.

"He's here!" a little boy near the back door screamed. I rounded the corner to find him standing on the bench of a wooden picnic table. He bounced on the balls of his feet, his bony elbows bobbing at his sides. "You're Russell Boudreaux, right?"

"That's me." I reached out to give him a high five, and he slapped my hand with so much enthusiasm that he nearly toppled off the bench. I gripped his tiny arm, steadying him. "And you must be Gabby's little brother?"

"I'm not that little. I'm actually tall for my age." He tilted his head and wiggled his freckled nose as he looked me squarely in the eyes. I instantly saw the resemblance to Gabby—that same piercing gaze. He raised his eyebrows as he sized me up. "Wait, how tall are you?"

"Six-three on a good day." The side door unlatched, and I looked up just as Gabby stepped in. She joined us, tucking her little brother under her elbow.

"Okay, that's enough out of you." She ushered him back to the table by giving him a pat on his backside. "Sorry, he's pretty chatty."

"But you promised if I finished my homework, then I could talk to Rus." He stuck his lips out in a pout.

"And when you finish, you can. Come on, Clayton. I only see half that worksheet done—the same half I left you with before I went outside."

"Ahhh so the genius gene hit everyone in the family." I looked over the mass of homework spread across the table.

"There are no geniuses here. Just hard workers." She smelled like herbs and honeysuckle, like she'd been gardening out back. It was a familiar scent—the trumpetlike flowers grew like invasive weeds all over Louisiana. But on Gabby that scent was something else, and I couldn't help but lean toward her.

In a whisper she asked, "I hope it's okay for him to talk to you after we're done? He's a major football fan, so you're like royalty to him."

"Sure. He's a real cool kid." I smiled as his little fingers grabbed a pencil. He couldn't have been older than seven.

Propped against the wall behind our table, a large trifold presentation board stood in a sea of printouts and clippings scattered on the surrounding floor. "Whoa, someone's been busy."

"I started on it, if that's okay." She squinted guiltily, the freckles around her eyes bunching up. How could I be mad at a face like that? "What did you think of the book?"

"It was a lot. But it was pretty good." I grabbed my notebook from my backpack and opened it to the *Beale Street* packet, thinking about some of the gut-wrenching scenes I'd read this morning. The main characters in the story, Tish and Fonny, were a young couple, full of promise, only to have their relationship strained by a false accusation that sent Fonny to jail. The descriptions of the couple talking to each other through plexiglass haunted me. It was sickening to read about the power a crooked cop had over an innocent man's life. "It was hard to read sometimes."

"I know what you mean. But I kinda like that Ms. J isn't afraid to challenge us." Gabby grabbed the corner of my printout and rotated it to face her. She looked up, her light eyes gleaming. She pointed to my packet, marked up with yellow and green highlights. "Ms. Jabbar would be proud of this."

I inwardly fist-bumped myself for having something to show for my efforts. I wanted Gabby to see I cared.

But I'd also gotten into the story. I'd cracked open the book last Thursday—the same day Ms. J had handed them out. Before I knew it, I was reading late into the night about Tish and Fonny, about their fractured family and fight for justice.

"So, what do you think of centering the project around this quote?" She swung her legs out of the bench and made her way to the poster board, her flip-flops clapping against the cement floor. She heaved it up and held it closer so that I could see.

"Neither love nor terror makes one blind: indifference makes one blind."

"I like it." Something about it seemed very familiar, like I'd seen it before. "Have you seen the new Dante Maynard posters popping up around town?"

"Hasn't everyone?" She set our project on the table, scooting some of Clayton's papers over to make room.

"They say Silence is Violence. Maybe we could paste one of them on the board?"

"That's actually a cool idea."

My conversation with the guys seeped into my mind. Marion had me almost convinced that Dante's Shadow was white—that Black people didn't have the luxury of protest without retribution. But I couldn't help but think about MLK, Kaepernick, and Baldwin. They were Black and outspoken against injustice. James Baldwin's *If Beale Street Could Talk* was a perfect example.

The excerpts from the story were chilling—a Black boy wrongfully accused of a violent crime who had to serve time in prison, spending years looking at the love of his life and his family through plexiglass. It was heartbreaking. But what really angered me was that the story was set in the 1970s, yet wrongful accusations were *still* happening to Black people—

innocent people were still falling short of their potential because of forces beyond their control.

"I don't care if Dante's Shadow is white. He's channeling Baldwin, so I guess he aight."

"Dante's Shadow?" Her eyebrows rose. She leaned forward, clearly intrigued.

"That's what we call him—the dude who's putting up the Dante flyers." I looked up just in time to catch a sly grin flash across her face.

"I kinda like that," she said, sounding amused.

She was in a good mood, so I decided now was as good a time as any to ask what happened last night. "You missed a good party."

"Yeah, sorry about that. I don't really go out." She gestured to her brother beside her. "Got my hands full, as you can see."

"But you—" Clayton popped up from his seat, but Gabby acted quickly, grabbing his shoulders and pushing him back to the bench.

"Clayton, sit your body down and finish your work," she said, her eyelashes fluttering.

"Oh, I see how it is." I looked away, embarrassed. Gabby was clearly trying to find a polite way to put me off.

"It's not like that. I..." Her eyes flitted away before she looked at me, a small smile dancing on her lips. "I was doing some paperwork."

"That's what Dad says when he has to poop." Clay dissolved into a fit of giggles, his nose scrunching up as he made fart sounds between laughs.

"God, Clay!" She tucked her curly hair behind her ear,

revealing a deep blush spreading across her face. "Seriously, though. How was the party?"

"Kind of boring," I said. "I was sort of hoping you'd show."

She looked down. "You know that's not really my scene."

And yet, I'd invited her, just like I'd invited her to that party three years ago. I needed her to see that I wasn't like the other ballers. I wanted to show her that I'd stand proudly by her side—anywhere, not just at a party—if she'd step out with me again. But I could see that I'd burned her badly. Maybe even more than I realized.

"You know, that party I brought you to freshman year… I know that wasn't the right move. I was young and nervous, and I'm sorry. But when you left early…"

Gabby snort-laughed. "*You* left first. You left me standing alone for the whole night. Of course, I got another ride home. Then the next day, everyone's talking about how you went home with another girl that night after you'd asked me out on a date."

"Oh, so it was a date? You never admitted that before." I smiled as a burning blush crept up her cheeks. She turned away, but this time I didn't let it fool me. She liked to hide her reactions, particularly from me. Maybe it was because she was afraid to reveal too much—maybe Gabby still cared about me. I leaned across the table, trying to reclaim her sharp gaze. "It *was* a date. And I messed up."

She shook her head, half annoyed and half amused.

"For real, though. If I could go back in time…"

Her phone dinged on the table, and she snatched it up before I could get a good look.

"I'll be right back," she said as she scurried to the back of the warehouse. "And I'll tell my dad you're here, so he can get started on your car."

But I had seen what I needed to see.

The person texting her was named Dave.

7

Coach Fontenot tapped me on the shoulder and nodded over to Marion, who stood at the front of the tunnel leading onto the Westmond field. I called to him, and he weaved his way through the throng of players, all suited up in Jackson's away-game uniforms and ready to play our second game of the season, this time against our fiercest rival.

Westmond High School.

By the way Coach's mustache was twitching, he had something special planned for this Friday night. He lowered his voice to talk strategy.

"Listen, we gonna do things differently tonight. If y'all win the coin toss, choose to receive, okay?"

"Coach, I thought you always said to go for the kick so we can receive in the second half," I said, confused.

"You see them boys?" He ticked his head to our teammates shadowboxing in the concrete passageway. "They're fired up. We gotta start hard and strong. This is our chance for redemption and revenge." The vein on his forehead pulsed with each pump of his fist. "They took the title away from us last year. Who's gonna show them how big of a mistake that was?"

"We are," I said a little louder than intended. But I was amped up, ready to rise to the challenge. I clenched my jaw thinking about Marion's dislocated shoulder, Brad's slurs, and Pops's trashed truck.

This was the chance for payback I'd been waiting for.

Fontenot clapped his hands, signaling everyone to follow him. We barged onto the rain-soaked field, so charged up that we welcomed the jeers of the home crowd. Darrell and Marion waved their arms at the Westmond stands to rile them up even more. The stadium flooded with boos and calls for us to go home.

Not tonight—not before we got that payback.

I scanned the packed bleachers for my parents. The floodlights bored into my sockets, but I blinked the brightness away, squinting as I skimmed through each row. There, near the middle of the center section, my parents stood clapping. Mama made eye contact with me and bounced up and down, tugging on Pops to turn and wave at me. I blew her a kiss before looking away.

Karim rolled his sleeve up and kissed his newly minted tattoo of his mother before flashing it to the stands. With a halo of black and white sunbeams radiating around her black afro, the ink of Ms. Williams posed as Mother Mary—complete with a bowed head and hands folded in prayer—stretched from the top of his shoulder to the crook of his elbow.

He pounded his fist above his heart then turned to bump chests with Marion. They collided with a thud, making our fans roar. It drowned out Westmond's new mean-spirited chant.

That's all right. That's okay. You're gonna pick up trash someday.

They were cocky, and it pissed me off that they had reason to be. Even though we were just down the road from the dinky Jackson Jackal field, we were in a different world. The bright lights reflected off their shiny new bleachers and gourmet concession stands. Still, I took consolation in the fact that money alone couldn't buy them a win.

Our drumline beat a rhythm that held the crowd captive, and the cheerleaders were in full swing, shaking their pom-poms as they twirled like dervishes. This might not have been our turf, but we claimed our space with every trombone blast.

Westmond High jogged in, bursting through a blue-and-white booster club banner with their mustang mascot emblazoned on it. They lined their benches and took off their helmets so that we could see the white lines painted across their cheekbones—white paint suspiciously like the color of the letters I scrubbed off Pops's truck last week.

My nostrils flared as I stepped forward. Marion elbowed my side.

"Imma say what you always tell me—save it for the field." He extended his arm to hold me in line just before the announcers asked the stadium to rise for the anthem.

The guest singer, dressed in a sequined dress, stepped onto the field and belted out a slightly off-key version of "The Star-Spangled Banner." I mumbled the words, my mind dead set on payback for Westmond's dirty tactics.

I wanted to win more than ever.

Coach swung his headset microphone up and yelled down the line of players. "Russell, Marion, go on. Remember what I said."

Marion and I stepped forward and walked to the center of the field where the head referee stood with the Westmond team captain and his second.

"What's up, homeboy?" Brad asked. His summer tan had started to fade, but his stupid sneer remained the same.

"I ain't your homeboy," I said with a growl.

"He's right, dude." Lawrence, the Westmond team captain, grinned. "Don't *egg* him on."

"See y'all found a better use for that paint," Marion said. He grumbled under his breath, something about hoping it was toxic.

The referee cleared his throat to point our attention toward the task at hand. "Jackals call it." The coin flew above us, deciding our fate as it turned in the air. But we didn't take our eyes off the Westmond players. They didn't tear their eyes away from us either.

"Heads," Marion and I said in unison right before the ref slapped the coin down on his arm. He lifted his hand to reveal our victory.

"What's it going to be?" he asked us.

"We'll receive," Marion said with a tiny wave at the opposition. Brad and Lawrence raised their eyebrows, clearly surprised by our choice to change up our usual formula. I smiled as Marion and I turned our backs on them, satisfied that we'd caught them off guard. Anything that threw Westmond off their game put us one step closer to that W. We whispered strategies to each other, Marion running bold plays past me, but we were interrupted by Brad's shouting.

"Whatever. It doesn't make a difference," Brad called after

us. "Gonna end up cleaning toilets, just like yo' daddy was cleaning mine last night."

"Shut your mouth." I turned and shoved a finger in his direction. "I'm coming for you once that whistle blows."

"Come on." Lawrence stepped forward, his hands extended between Brad and I. "Be cool, my nigga."

I inhaled sharply, covering my mouth. Marion whipped around, his eyes squeezed tightly shut as he massaged his temples.

"What he say?" His voice climbed three octaves as he gripped the sides of his helmet. "Please, tell me this dude did not just drop that word."

"So what if he did?" Brad yelled over Lawrence's shoulder as he puffed out his chest.

My lips smacked as I tried to find words, but I came up with nothing—I was in shock. This white dude, who probably listened to gangster rap but interacted with zero Black people, thought the N-word had somehow slipped into his domain. He thought that it was his for the taking. Just like white people felt entitled to *everything*.

No. I had to draw the line somewhere, and it was here. He couldn't say that word.

"Just chill." Lawrence shook his head at us, and I could tell by the casual way he stood, the relaxed parting of his lips, that he didn't think he'd said anything wrong. In fact, he thought he was diffusing the situation. "We cool. Let's play some ball."

But we weren't cool.

"Ref, you heard him say the N-word," I said to the referee standing beside us. "That's an automatic game suspension."

The league rules were simple—no racial slurs on the field.

And that went for all players, even the Black ones. *We* weren't even allowed to drop the N-word, let alone egg people's cars and call them garbage.

"Listen." The head referee stuffed the game coin into his back pocket before putting his hands on his hips. He looked at Lawrence, nodding his head toward the exit. "If I hear that word again, you're off the field."

The ref stepped between us, which garnered murmurs from the crowd. Something was brewing, and fans on both sides could sense it.

"That's not fair. They ain't allowed to say that word." I stepped closer to the fray. "If you heard it, he's gotta go."

"You know what? We straight, ref." Marion stepped so close to Brad that his chest came into contact with the referee's outstretched hand. "'Cause this dude gonna drop the ball as soon as he catches it. Like he always do. And we'll shut it down from there."

My chest rumbled through a laugh as Marion held his hand up for a high five. Then, with the same hand, he waved at the Westmond captains. "Buh, bye."

Brad slapped Marion's hand away from his face, then shoved him backward with both hands. The force sent him tumbling to the ground, taking me with him. My teeth chomped on my bottom lip.

Pain shot through me, and my eyes snapped shut as I breathed through the sting. When I touched my lip, I drew back bloody fingertips. I must have bitten straight through.

The referee blew long and hard on his whistle, frantically waving his arms in front of him, but it was too late for that. Brad had drawn first blood, and if I couldn't get this bleeding under control, the league wouldn't allow me on the field. Marion scrambled to his feet, a look of shock and anger on his face.

"Oh, you tryna get hood?" He pushed Brad into Lawrence. "Trust me, you don't wanna go there."

Brad lunged for Marion, grabbing the front grating of his helmet. He dragged him forward and thrust his knee into his gut, making him collapse to his knees. Marion grabbed Brad's legs, bringing him to the ground too. The two of them tousled on the ground, growling.

"Get your quarterback off mine!" I shouted at Lawrence through the side of my mouth. Blood dripped through my fingers.

The other referees ran across the field, blaring their whistles too. A medley of yellow and white flags spurted from their pockets in the direction of our scuffle.

A few of the game security guards charged full tilt toward the site of our failed coin toss, hands hovering over their firearms. Officer Reynaud brought up the rear, huffing as he sidled up next to me. My chest caved. He was the *last* person I wanted to see in an already tense situation.

He wasn't dressed in his police uniform, instead wearing the green polo shirt that all of the security guards wore, but off duty or not—he was still a cop. And now we were surrounded by them.

"Get 'em up." He waved to the two green shirts beside him. One pried Brad from on top of Marion while the other two hooked their hands beneath Marion's armpits and dragged him to a standing position. Red-faced and winded, Reynaud stepped in front of Marion. "You lost your mind, boy?"

"You should be asking him that." I pointed a shaky finger at Brad, who stood next to the officer who'd nabbed him. Brad wasn't restrained. But Marion was. "We didn't start this fight."

"I saw it all." Reynaud held his hands up. "And you better watch yourself, or you're going to the station too."

"The station?" Marion wiggled in the grasp of the security guard holding his arms back. "You're seriously trying to arrest me? I didn't do anything!"

His eyes widened as a zip tie tightened around his wrist. The officer muttered the Miranda rights, but Marion wasn't focused on them. Instead, he looked to me, tears pooling in his eyes.

"You should be arresting Brad!" I gestured to Brad, who stood with his head bowed, pretending to be sorry. I turned to Lawrence. "Tell him who started this fight."

Lawrence looked away.

Marion stopped squirming, and his shoulders slackened with the click of the second zip tie, a resignation to the inevitable.

"All right, come on, son," Officer Reynaud said, flicking his fingers to Brad. Obediently, he walked to Reynaud's side—still without his hands bound. But at least he was being taken to the station like Marion. Reynaud put his arm around his shoulder and turned to me. "Get on home and don't start no more trouble, ya hear?"

I whipped my head around and saw my team retreating into the tunnel in the corner of the field. The league must have postponed the game. My breath hitched. We wouldn't be playing tonight.

"We'll handle this, I promise!" I shouted as the guards

guided Marion to the gated exit on the far side of the field. I wasn't sure how we'd get him out or pay for a lawyer, but I wanted Marion to know that we'd be there for him. That I had his back, as his teammate and his best friend. As his brother. "I promise," I repeated to his retreating back, even though I knew he could no longer hear me.

8

Don't start no more trouble—Mama kept repeating it, each time with even more acid on her tongue. She mumbled it under her breath as she prepared another ice pack for me.

"That old fool." She grunted under her breath and paced our tiny kitchen. She shook her head as she leaned against the faded yellow wallpaper. "It's the fools you gotta watch out for, you understand? They the most dangerous."

The bag of ice cubes hit the counter with a *clunk* as she leaned forward, her gaze locked on the TV screen in the living room. The local news was on; at the top of the hour, they ran through the headlines. And the Westmond/Jackson High School fight was at the top of the list.

Shaky camera footage from someone's phone served as the visuals. In it, you could see Marion and I scrambling on the ground, me clutching my face while Marion grabbed Brad's knees and brought him to the ground.

Then the camera panned out to show the rest of our team bristling on the sidelines. Coach Fontenot and the assistant coaches were holding their arms out as wide as they could, making sure no one stormed the field. Coach's mouth chomped up and down, barking orders so loudly that the audio picked it up, "Stay back! Hold the line!"

I remembered that the Westmond coaches had the same struggle keeping their players off the field. But the video didn't show that. To the casual observer, the video kinda made Marion and our team look like the aggressors. I hoped *Fox 5 News* would get a better video—one that showed Brad starting the fight.

A painful bruise smarted against my rib cage just above my stomach. I switched out the semi-melted ice pack for the new one, wincing as I pressed the hard surface against my side. I teetered on my barstool, gripping the edge of the kitchen island for support as I breathed through the pain. But it was my lip that hurt the most. Mama held it between her fingers, studying the teeth marks.

"Almost went straight through," she said as she squinted, leaning closer. "Scoot over under the light."

I slid my barstool into the center of the kitchen, right underneath the four-pronged brass light. I winced as Mama pressed my lip again.

"Oh!" She held her hand over her mouth.

"Mama, don't." I put my hand on her knee, begging her not to cry again.

"You sure the trainer said it didn't need stitches?"

I nodded, remembering Ms. Duval's gloved hands giving me a once-over.

"Well, we're taking you to the doctor in the morning." She shook her head, planting her arms on her hips. Looking around the kitchen, she sighed. "I know you hungry. I'll see what I can fix that you can eat. There's gotta be a can of soup or a box of pudding buried in the pantry."

I wanted to tell her that I wasn't hungry, but it was strangely comforting watching her fuss around the kitchen. Adrenaline coursed through my body, making me jumpy, fidgety. My thoughts were far from food. Instead they were still on the field, embroiled in images of the fight.

Coach had already texted the team the league's verdict. In the absence of definitive proof of fault, both teams would be put on probation, but allowed a rematch. That meant that we weren't suspended from playing the rest of the season, but we were on thin ice. One more misstep and our season would be over. It was suspicious that the referee had not provided proof of Westmond starting the fight, but I couldn't even think about that. All I could think about was Marion sitting in some dirty jail cell. I hoped Pops would call from the police station with an update soon.

I should have let Lawrence's and Brad's comments slide. If I had walked away from Brad's taunts, had ignored Lawrence, maybe Marion wouldn't have been hauled away in handcuffs.

But I couldn't escape the nagging feeling that maybe I hadn't done *enough*.

I didn't share any of this with Mama. She seemed to relax as she channeled her energy into gathering supplies. Her eyes glazed over as she poured pudding packets into a mixing bowl and poured water into a saucepan. Then she looked out the window and gasped. She stepped away from the sink, wiping her hands on her jeans as she rushed for the door.

I hobbled to the sink and shut the water off, gazing through the kitchen window to where Marion was stepping down from my dad's truck. He swayed and Pops put his arm around him, guiding him up the porch stairs, where he crumpled into Mama's waiting arms. His shaky voice traveled through the single-paned window.

"I'm sorry, Mama. I'm sorry. I didn't know who else to call when my stepdad didn't show. And with my mom gone…"

"You did the right thing. Hold your head up. Let me see." She choked when Marion stepped into the light. The lighting on the porch was too dim, and the glass was too dusty for me to see up close, so I shoved off the kitchen counter and ran to stand behind Mama at the door, just in time to see her gently lift Marion's chin with the tip of her finger.

His eye was swollen shut, and his cheek was puffy. When tears started trickling down Mama's face, I couldn't hold mine back anymore. I covered my mouth, hiding my trembling lip.

"Look at what they've done to you. To both of you." Mama grabbed his arm, then reached behind her to grab mine. "My babies."

"Let's get him inside." Pops put his hand on the small of her back and ushered her through the front door.

"Eli, I got it." She waved his helping hand away before sinking into the chair, rocking back and forth as she shook her head. "I just don't understand how they could keep him till damn near one a.m."

"They said I had to wait for processing." Marion sank to the couch with a sigh.

"They the criminals." Mama gripped her knees. "Keeping high school boys in a jail cell."

"Oh, wasn't no *boys*. It was just me." Marion took the ice pack from my outstretched hand and brought it up to his face.

"Brad's dad showed up twenty minutes after we got to the station, yelling at the cops to release him, or he was going to get his lawyer involved. Then they disappeared. Brad never came back to the holding cell."

Silence claimed the room as we tried to understand. Marion shrugged, offering a half-baked explanation.

"Maybe he got out on bond like I did." He tilted his head up to my dad, who stood near the edge of the couch. "Thanks, Pops. I swear I'm gonna pay back every last cent."

"Baby, you don't worry about that." Then in a softer, hushed tone, she leaned over to Pops and asked, "How much?"

"Three racks." Pops looked to the side, over at the AC unit that rattled against the wall.

Mama braced herself. We were packing lunches and keeping our spending under control, and money was still tight. I couldn't imagine pulling our purse strings any tighter, but a loss of three thousand dollars from my parents' bank account was going to require some serious cuts.

"And I'll pay you back," Marion said, barely loud enough for us to hear. "I promise."

"You don't worry about that, sweetie. You did right calling us. We'll get that money back soon as you show up to court, whenever that's gonna be…" Mama's cheeks reddened as her gaze drifted to the corner of the room. I could almost see the wheels turning in her head—it could be *months* until they set a court date for Marion, meaning that three grand would be tied up until then. She blinked, bringing her eyes back into focus. "Ed should be ashamed of himself, not showing up when you called. As many times as he's called everybody this side of the parish to bail him out."

"What are they trying to charge you with?" I asked, crossing the room to take the other side of the couch.

"They're throwing everything at me—disorderly conduct, assault, and resisting arrest."

"I can't believe this." I slid my hands over my face as if it could make this mess disappear. "You didn't start that fight."

"I wish I'd had my phone taping it." Pops cussed under his breath as he stormed down the hall.

"So what are you going to do?" I asked Marion, searching his bruised face for answers.

"I'm going to fight it." Marion set his jaw tight. "I have to."

9

"I promise it looks worse than it is," I said to Gabby the following Monday. I tilted my head back at her outstretched hand. She opened the door of her locker wider so that I could see my swollen lip on her magnetic mirror.

In the morning light, I could see a lump jutting out from the right side of my mouth, exposing the inside of my bottom lip. Surrounding the brownish scab where my teeth had pierced the skin was a yellowish pocket, swelling that the nurse at the emergency clinic assured me would go down in a few days. I rubbed the knot of scar tissue with my tongue, hoping that it would heal quickly.

"It looks nasty." She hissed, reaching to touch her own lip. "Vicious, even."

"I'm fine." I ducked away from her locker, hoping she wouldn't press it. Students stole glances at my face as they scurried down the hall. Some had been at the stadium the other night and had seen the fight firsthand—witnesses to the miscarriage of justice. Others had heard about it from the news or social media. By now, everyone had seen Marion in handcuffs being escorted off the field like a criminal. It wasn't right.

"I shouldn't have taken the bait." I shook my head as I lost myself in the memory of the fight. *Silence is Violence.* That's what the posters around town said, and maybe I let that influence me. But where had it gotten me? Gotten Marion? "I shouldn't have mouthed off."

"Rus, this isn't your fault. They egged your dad's car. They busted your lip. You're only human."

I shrugged. "This is going to blow over."

"Rus, look… I'm not trying to be a dick, but I don't think it'll blow over." She bumped my side with her elbow, then looked up at me, her eyes still uneasy. "Marion really hasn't said anything since Friday?"

I shook my head. After Marion came home from the county jail, he'd planted himself in Mama's rocking chair, occasionally watching the local news Mama left droning in the living room. I didn't know when I'd dozed off, but I'd woken up in the morning to a crick in my neck and an empty room. And I hadn't seen or heard from him since.

"I guess that's good. I wouldn't talk to anyone but my lawyer." Gabby tilted her head. "Does he have a good one?"

"I think so. He's a public defender. He sounded aight by the way Marion described him."

"Hmm. My dad's friend in New Orleans is a lawyer. I don't think he specializes in criminal law, but he might be able to give Marion more time and research toward his case than a public defender can."

"It'll be fine. Marion mentioned he was pretty cool and would help him get some of the charges dropped."

Gabby snorted. "Yeah, by pleading guilty to one of the charges."

"Nah, he wouldn't plead guilty for something he didn't do." I thought of Marion's bruised face, his jaw set tightly as he said he would fight the charges.

Gabby sighed and dropped her backpack to the floor.

"Rus…that's how our justice system usually works. The prosecutors overload you with charges and make it seem like taking your case to trial is a death wish. Then they push you to take a plea deal."

I frowned. That didn't sound like justice to me.

"I have respect for PDs, but most of them are so overworked that they push their clients to take plea deals instead of going to trial. He's seventeen, but they're probably going to try him as an adult. That means he'd have a criminal record. Every school he applies to, every job interview he goes on—that record will follow him *everywhere*. Marion deserves more than that."

I nodded, letting it all sink in. Everything she was saying sounded convincing. I wanted to prevent Marion from paying for this for the rest of his life. I'd told him we'd take care of this, that I'd help him in any way I could. But hiring a fancy lawyer from New Orleans was out of my reach.

"We can't afford a lawyer." I bent my head low. There was no way Pops had anything left in the bank after posting Marion's three-thousand-dollar bail.

"Then we'll beg him to take Marion's case pro bono. I'll ask my dad for his friend's number, and I'll give him a call tonight. If he agrees, I can pass your number along, if that's all right?"

"Seriously?" My eyes glazed with tears, but I blinked them away. "You'd do that?"

"Sure. We're friends, aren't we?"

My heart swelled, my breath catching. A few weeks ago, Gabby and I were *nothing*. Now, we were *friends*. I couldn't help but wonder where we might be in another three weeks. My lips throbbed, and not just from the pain from my bruise. But I shook it off, regrouping.

"It's going to be tough to find time for Ms. J's project with everything going on, but I think I have time tonight, if you're free?"

"Look, Rus. Don't worry about the Baldwin project." She exchanged her morning books for her afternoon ones and shut her locker. Her face was soft as she tilted her head up to me. "Seriously, we finished most of it last weekend, and we still have a few more weeks until it's due. You should just focus on—"

"My face?" I sputtered a chuckle. It surprised me, but it felt good to be able to laugh. I nodded toward the other end of the hallway, inviting her to walk with me. "I'm fine. Really—you should see Marion's face."

"I know." She shook her shoulders as if trying to ward off a chill. "He looked pretty banged up when I saw him."

"Wait." I turned quickly, searching her furrowed brows for answers. "When did you see Marion?"

"Just a few minutes ago." She paused, looking confused. "In the breezeway."

As we approached Coach's office, we found a crowd huddled on the edge of Fontenot's window. Muted yelling came through the panes. Standing head and shoulders above most of the students, I didn't have to fight for room to see Marion hunched in a chair across from Fontenot, looking defeated.

"You can't do this to me." Marion cried from the seat opposite Coach. "Please. I'm begging you."

"Let me get through, y'all." I elbowed my way past the knot of students until I filled the doorway.

"It's not up to me, Marion." Coach Fontenot sank to his elbows. "You know I'd do anything for you, but my hands are tied here."

"What's going on?" I asked, closing the door behind me so that the whole student body couldn't eavesdrop.

"I'm just telling Marion—"

"Coach says I can't play no more," Marion cut him off, his gaze wild as it darted between me and Coach. I felt like the wind was knocked out of me. Playing a game without Marion would be like sending me onto the field without my right hand. And for Marion… I couldn't even imagine what it would feel like to have to sit the bench, this season of all seasons, when it mattered the most.

"Now, I didn't say that." He raised his hands in surrender. "This is coming from the *league*, son. I just got off the phone with them this morning." He turned to me, his eyebrows slanted in appeal. "If it were up to me—"

"No. No. I can't… This is all I got." Marion rocked back and forth in the chair opposite coach, rubbing his bruised temple. "Just call the league back."

"I tried everything, but the rule book states plainly that players charged with violent crimes can't suit up." He shook his head slowly, like he'd tried to find a loophole but come up short. "Best we can do is get this cleared up so we can get you back on the field."

"And how long is that gonna take?" Marion gripped the front of Fontenot's desk, his arm trembling. "The public defender said this process could take months, even a year to get resolved. So, all I'm asking is for you to *call them back*. We gotta appeal this."

"He's right, Coach." I stepped forward, placing my palms against his desk. "Marion *is* this team. We can't lose him because of something he didn't even do."

Coach's hair tangled in his fingers as he hunched over his desk. "Boys...the rules are clear here."

"Call them back!" Marion sprang from his seat, his arms outstretched. "Rus, tell him."

"There's no wiggle room?" I asked, desperation hitching my voice up a few notches. "Maybe he can agree not to suit up for the rematch. Then he can play the other games."

I thought my reasoning was fair, but before I even finished, Coach's head was swinging left to right. I saw it in his eyes; he'd obviously been on the phone all morning trying to iron this out.

Marion's suspension was set in stone. And it was for more than just the one game. He could miss the whole season, if his case took as long to get resolved as the public defender thought.

I turned slowly, afraid to meet my best friend's dewy eyes. "Marion..."

"Don't, man." He held a hand up, and a gasp escaped his lips. It was followed by another, then another, until he was doing something I'd never seen him do. He was crying. Through a jumble of sobs, he said, "I can't get recruited from the bench. My life is fucked!"

He barged out of the office, and I scrambled after him.

"Come on, Marion." Darrell touched Marion's shoulder, but he ripped his hand away.

"Don't!" he shouted, making Darrell cower away. His chest heaved with ragged pants as he barreled down the hall. "Move out the way, y'all."

"Marion." I jogged after him, desperate for him to take a breather. But he didn't turn around, instead choosing to break into a jog down the breezeway.

"Don't follow me," he called over his shoulder.

I froze on the spot, fighting the urge to run after him. But it didn't feel right. It was the first time in a long time—maybe ever—that something bad had happened to me or Marion, and we weren't going through it together.

It was late, well past dinnertime, and Marion hadn't turned up. He wasn't answering my texts, not even my parents' calls. But I knew where to find him.

The football field was quiet when I rolled up, the only sound the hum of the floodlights towering above. A silhouette with dreads stood next to a canvas bag of footballs. As he reached to grab another ball, he stumbled but found his footing and sent it flying to the back corner of the field. Marion could always perform under pressure.

He suffered at home, where his stepdad beat him and his mom frequently abandoned him, and at school, where his teachers talked down to him. The field was the only place where he was on top.

And now that had been taken away from him.

"What part of 'don't follow me' didn't you understand?" His body rumbled through a burp.

"It's just me, man." I held my hands up, walking slowly.

He threw another ball across the turf, then staggered up the steps to one of the bleachers, where he'd tucked a forty under the bench.

"You got every right to be pissed."

"Pissed don't even cover it, man. Pissed is when my step-dad throws a beer bottle at my head. Pissed is when I ain't got enough money for a Coke. But this? Nah, this is beyond all that. It's another level, man."

I edged closer, careful to give his anger the space it needed. I sat on a bleacher below him.

"And you know the really fucked up thing? I keep thinking it could be worse." He hopped down with a hysterical laugh. "Like, at least he didn't shoot me."

"Don't think like that." My chest tightened at the thought. This was bad, but…his comment reminded me that it could be *so* much worse.

"But you know what? Reynaud might as well have shot me. Because he just took my life away." When Marion turned to me, his eyes were bloodshot. "Ed always said I'd end up in jail. Are those the only choices we have? Jail? Shot in the street? The system is rigged. I ain't never getting out of here."

"Marion, we can still fix this." I stepped up to his bleacher and sat next to him, touching his shoulder. "Look, I've been talking to Gabby, and she thinks—"

"Y'all talkin'?" He slapped his knees. "Shit that's how it'll be from now on. Everybody's changing, moving. And I'll be stuck here."

I wanted to tell him he was wrong, that I'd never leave him behind to rot in this town. But I didn't let the lie slip from my lips. Deep down, I knew he was right. If he didn't have a chance to play his senior season in front of college recruiters, he would be stuck here like Homegrown Gary and Ed—washed-up ballers who got sucked back into Monroe.

"Where is she?" Marion buried his face in his hands, his shoulders slumping as he sniffled. "I thought with all this press, she'd come back. But look."

He unlocked his phone, then slid the glowing screen toward me. Every outgoing call was to Mrs. LaSalle—dozens of unanswered calls.

"Her phone don't even ring anymore. It says the line is disconnected. So, I guess I'm on my own." He twisted his mouth, squinting his eyes like he was fighting back more tears. "She ain't coming back this time."

"Marion." I ran my hand over my scalp, searching for another way to reach him. A lump caught in my throat. "Look, man. I'm sorry—"

"Don't apologize, Rus," he slurred, his voice thick with sadness. "You go get another W, get into college and all that shit. And I'll get started on the life I was born to live."

He snatched up the bottle of Olde English and took off across the field, his figure fading into the shadows as he left the glow of the floodlights.

10

Marion didn't show up to school the next day or the day after that. Or any day that week. Four days passed without me seeing or hearing from him—our longest stretch of radio silence since we'd known each other. Jackson High allowed eight unexcused absences before the school notified a truancy officer to look for the student. And Marion certainly did *not* need another officer coming after him.

He'd promised to fight these charges, not run from them. And I'd promised to be by his side. Where was he?

By Friday night, as the team packed into our bus for our third game of the season against Shreveport, I was feeling queasy—sick with worry and doubt, wondering if Marion had disappeared for good. But it was game day, and with or without my best friend, I needed to keep my eye on the prize.

I gripped the vinyl seats of our rickety bus, swaying through its turns as I made my way down the aisle. Crouching down, I tapped Ricky on the shoulder. "Remember what we practiced."

The second-string quarterback nodded.

"I really need you to land that throw." I pounded my fist into my hand.

"I got it, Rus. Don't worry."

But I *was* worried—really worried. Tonight we were playing Shreveport High School, ranked second in the league just behind Westmond. They were a well-funded white school like Westmond and just as formidable, with a deep bench who could play starting positions at *any* school. It was also where Dante Maynard had gone to school.

This was going to be a rough night.

We were about to go up against one of the top teams in the state without our starting quarterback, without the anchor of our team. My stomach twisted into knots, and not just about the hard match ahead. Marion's tough situation also occupied my thoughts. But I hadn't seen or spoken to him since our late-night talk on the field. Marion was a ghost. He wasn't answering his phone, and I was concerned—we *all* were. How could we focus on the game when one of our own was suffering off the field?

As we trickled out of the bus, clusters of reporters descended on us. I'd seen clips of star ballers on ESPN—the very cream of the high school crop who were being recruited by every D1 program in the country. But the lens had never found its way to our small pocket in the backwoods of Louisiana. My teammates' eyes were wide with shock. Coach held his arms up, asking the group to step back. He wasn't interested in participating in the media circus, but they were relentless. A woman in a red suit approached me with a cameraman behind her.

"Hi, Russell Boudreaux? I'm Lauren Peters with *Fox 5*

News. Could we have a moment?" Before I could answer, she thrust her microphone beneath my chin. "We just have a few questions. How are you feeling going into tonight's game?"

"Pretty confident." I'd never been on TV before. I couldn't tell if I was supposed to look at her or at the camera. Instead, I looked at the wall of Shreveport's stadium. "Our guys are ready. Hope to take home another W."

"Even without quarterback Marion LaSalle?" She held the mic closer.

I nodded.

"You were there when LaSalle struck Bradley Simmons—"

"Hold up." I held my hand up, cutting her off. "That's not what happened. We were both pushed to the ground first by Brad."

The reporter regrouped, catching her breath before launching into a different question. "LaSalle faces some pretty serious charges, including assault. His stepfather also did time in Stanwell Prison for aggravated assault and battery. Do you think that influenced—"

"That boy Marion should be in jail. Y'all both should be," a random Shreveport fan said from nearby. He spat on the pavement before adjusting his red baseball cap. "You can't treat them good Westmond boys like that." The hateful gleam in his eyes hit me with full force.

"Sir, could you please—" The reporter shifted closer to me, trying to block the agitator from getting in the camera frame.

"I hope they lock him up," he yelled over her shoulder. He ripped his hat off and pointed it toward the camera. "Give him time to screw his head on straight."

"All right, all right." Coach held his arms up to the camera crew. "Show's over. Come on."

He wrapped an arm over my shoulders and steered me toward the locker room. I couldn't help but look behind me at the reporter feverishly typing on her tablet.

"Don't let them get in your head," Coach said gently.

"Did you hear the stuff they're saying about Marion? What happened to getting your facts straight?" These people hadn't bothered to research the whole story. They'd spun it into the story they wanted, and we'd be the ones paying the price. I wanted to grab the microphone out of her hands and speak the truth for everyone to hear, but it would be a waste of breath. They'd just edit my comments, twist my words until the point was lost or I became the villain somehow. I longed for a way to get my message across. To be heard above all the interference and noise.

"I know, but there's nothing we can do about any of it," Coach said. "You focus on the game."

"Settle down." Coach shoved his way past the bulk of players, parting the waters so he could claim the center of Shreveport's state-of-the-art guest locker room. But there was still a lot of quiet murmuring, everyone still ruffled by the reporters outside.

Coach clapped his hands to get everyone's attention. "Y'all better not test me. I said, settle down!"

The assistant coach rounded the circle, making sure everyone's mouth stayed shut tight. Silence fell in the room, allowing Fontenot to speak softer. "Come in close, y'all, and take a knee."

I stepped forward, knocking shoulders with my neighbors as I joined the huddle. Kneeling to the floor, I sucked in a deep breath to steady my nerves.

"Y'all have a right to be upset. Hell, I am plenty. But y'all ain't going nowhere to get no revenge. Not on my time. Not when we still got work to do."

Normally I would agree. *Get even on the field*—that's what I always told Marion. But that hadn't worked.

"Coach, how we supposed to beat Shreveport without Marion?" Terrance asked. He shrugged his shoulders at Ricky, our second-string. "Sorry, dude."

The truth was splashed across all our faces. Ricky was good, but he wasn't Marion-good. Without Marion, our season was at risk, and that meant each of our scholarship opportunities had shrunk from small to smaller. And without scholarships… I sank my forehead to my knee, hiding the panic in my eyes. Marion's future wasn't the only one at stake.

"Shreveport's gonna be just as bad as Westmond. Did you hear them yelling at us?" Darrell jumped up, hopping on the balls of his feet. Coach snapped his fingers, bringing Darrell to his knees again.

"We'll show them who we are," I said. It was more to convince myself than Darrell. "We'll get what's ours on the field."

"Russell's right, y'all understand?" Spit escaped Coach Fontenot's lips, and I knew he was barely containing his anger. "Look, we're on probation. That means the league will be keeping a close eye on us. Watch your personal fouls, and don't mouth off at players or refs. They're going to try to get a rise out of you, so remember to keep a level head at all times. They want you to fail. Don't give them what they want."

He slapped his clipboard with his fist, cussing under his breath, but he got ahold on himself by taking a deep breath.

"Let's play like we got somethin' to say. Now, they have a lot of star players from last year. But they lost their season opener to Belson. They're looking for a comeback. Let's not be the one to give it to 'em!"

We filed out of the locker room, an eerie quiet among us. Coach gripped my shoulder, holding me back.

"Keep your teammates in check. I don't want any funny business, you hear?" He raised his eyebrows above his glasses. Leaning forward, his eyes gleamed conspiratorially. "But give 'em hell."

In the dim confines of the stadium tunnel, the team lined up, buzzing with that familiar pregame energy as we prepared to enter Shreveport's turf. The jeers echoed down the tunnel before we even got on the field. We poked our heads out of the passageway to get a better look.

"They're fired up tonight, bro. Shhh." Terrance pointed to the stands. "Listen."

Lock them up! Lock them up! Lock them up!

My mouth slackened as I leaned forward, shocked and a little rattled. A white-hot chill rolled up my spine as the chant echoed in the stadium.

"You see that dude's sign." Terrance pointed to a man with the word *CRIMINALS* smeared onto a poster board. "They tryna lynch us for real."

"I'd like to see you try!" Darrell yelled out of the tunnel. "I hope he runs into my cousin Gary in the parking lot later. We'll see how bold he is then."

"Don't let them rile you up." I tugged him away from the crowd. "Stay focused."

The words rang hollow. They didn't have any conviction behind them, because the crowd was getting under my skin.

Coach's whistle sliced through the air, signaling for us to run to our sidelines. I had an overwhelming sense of apprehension as the hot lights of the field beat down on us and the home crowd showered us with insults. I tried to block the crowd out, but it was hard. They were *so* charged up. And there was something more—a sense of hatred vibrating in the air, so thick I could almost touch it.

I bounced on the balls of my feet before jogging down the track, trying to stay loose, focused. It was the perfect opportunity to search for my parents in the stands. I craned my neck to look for them, but the stands were fuller than usual.

A curly mane of honey-brown hair stood out from the crowd. Gabby stood with her little brother, Clayton, near the corner of the field. I blinked, making sure she was really there. When they caught my gaze, they both waved. I jogged toward them.

"You came to a game?" I reached up to grab Gabby's outstretched hand. I stared into her light brown eyes with a mixture of gratitude and disbelief. "I thought you hated football."

"Clay begged me to take him." She smiled down at her brother, whose toothy grin grew wider by the minute.

"What's up, little man?" I waved to Clayton, who was jumping up and down next to her.

"And to be honest—" Gabby looked at me, her smile growing shy "—after our conversation the other day, I felt like you might need some friendly faces in the crowd. I wanted to be here for you."

I didn't know what to say, I was so touched. Gabby saw me—*really* saw me. The way her eyes softened when we spoke, I could tell she was listening to me. She cared about me.

"Gabby, quick." Clay thrust his phone into her unsuspecting hands. "Take a picture."

"Okay. Okay. *So bossy.*" She waved for us to get in the same shot, then snapped a few pictures. She gave a thumbs-up, then handed the phone back to Clay. He sank onto the bleacher and flipped through the images, his gap-toothed smile growing wider. "I didn't know these games drew such big crowds."

"They usually don't. Not like this." I poked my head around the corner, viewing the packed crowd. My breath rushed out of my lungs, my chest tightening. "Have you seen my parents?"

"Yeah, they're back there." She pointed behind her.

On the edge of the announcers' tower, my parents were crammed into a packed row of Jackals fans. I waved to them, and Pops nodded then flicked his head to the field. He looked from me to Gabby, probably wondering why I was getting cozy with her when I should be falling in line, focusing on the game ahead.

But how could I focus on anything but this angry crowd? In this court of public opinion, the Jackson Jackals had been convicted by an angry mob slinging slurs. With every offensive chant and sign, they tarred and feathered us. In their eyes, we were criminals. Not just Marion, but *all* of us.

"I wish I had a sign," Gabby said, turning her attention to the crowd on the Shreveport side, which was getting more riled up. Cupping her mouth, she crowed, "You're all hypocrites!"

"What are you doing?" I leaped up and grabbed the railing, brushing my fingers against hers. "They can't hear you anyway."

"That doesn't mean I shouldn't speak up. That Bradley dude wasn't even *charged*. And Shreveport is picking Westmond's side?" She gripped the railing and strained her voice through another scream. "It's because they're all racists."

"What?" I gawked at her, struggling to find words. *"Seriously?"*

"Yeah, the prosecutor let him off." She flared her nostrils. "Silence is violence, right?"

The whistle blew, and I turned my back to her just as she screamed at Shreveport again. The urge to join her, to scream at the top of my lungs, threatened to overwhelm me. Brad was the one who started this whole mess, and he'd gotten off scot-free, while Marion was going through hell. I thought of what Marion had said the other night under the glowing lights of the field.

The system is rigged.

I came to a halt at the front of the line, tuning out the crowd. I turned my back to them and focused on the field. I didn't watch Shreveport tear through their booster club banner, didn't listen to the announcer as he introduced their star players. I kept my head low, occasionally glancing down my row of brothers to make sure they stayed cool.

"Please rise for the national anthem," the announcer boomed.

A creak echoed through the stadium as onlookers rose from

their seats. This time a local boys' choir took the stage, and they began to sing the song with an upbeat tempo.

O say can you see by the dawn's early light.

I clutched my chest as I waded through the familiar words of the anthem. I stole another glance to my right, where Darrell and Terrance silently seethed as they mumbled along to the words of the song. Rage rippled off their shoulders, and I couldn't blame them. I felt it, too, settling deep in my belly. I felt helpless, and that only fueled the anger even more.

What so proudly we hailed at the twilight's last gleaming?

I could almost see the plots of revenge forming in their minds. With their jaws clenched and heads shaking, they wanted any kind of justice they could find, and Homegrown Gary offered them that. His offer to help take care of our difficulties rang in my mind: *Westmond wannabes, cops—you name it. I got your back.*

And by the gleam of his eyes and the gesture to his pistol, I knew he'd meant it. But that wasn't a road I wanted to travel. Blood feuds like that led directly to jail, and that wasn't where any of us belonged—including Marion.

Whose broad stripes and bright stars through the perilous fight.

My mind wandered to Gabby, her head held high, shouting for justice. I wished I could join her in the stands and shout until my voice grew hoarse. I had to do *something* other than sing this stupid anthem for a country that obviously didn't care about *us*—a country that might take away a promising boy's future, all because of the color of his skin.

I thought of Kaepernick's protest to take a knee—to bring awareness to racial violence and injustice in the country. Right now, we were at Dante Maynard's old school in a town that refused to investigate his *murder* at the hands of police. And Shreveport was calling us criminals? Why? Because we stood up against racist white kids? Something was seriously wrong with this country.

Dante deserved better. So did Marion. All of us did.

I understood how Kaepernick must have felt when he could no longer recite the words of a broken promise for a country who made criminals out of innocent boys. If we were criminals, it was because society had already decided that. And that was something I wouldn't stand for. My hand slackened, then fell limply to my side. I turned to look around the stadium, instead of at the flag. A fresh wave of boos and hisses rippled through the crowd, but I didn't care.

O'er the ramparts we watched were so gallantly streaming?

My legs twitched, but I pulled back at the last moment. I could feel Pops's eyes boring into my back. He'd say to keep my head down and not start something. He wouldn't be happy about this, but if I'd already been found guilty, why not do what I needed to do?

Gabby had called the crowd hypocrites at the top of her lungs, and she was right. Everyone who sang the praises of a system that bulldozed people like Marion was complicit. *I* was complicit in continuing the cycle if I stood for the anthem. I'd made my choice, but it wasn't really a choice at all.

And the rocket's red glare, the bombs bursting in air.

My legs bent and I sank to the ground, feeling the crinkle of grass beneath my shin as I took a knee.

11

My heart hammered in my chest, and my hands were shaking well after *the home of the brave* echoed through the stadium. My legs trembled so fiercely I was afraid I wouldn't be able to get up. I pushed off the ground with both hands, willing my strength to return. Darrell gripped me underneath my elbow and tugged me up the rest of the way.

"You done it now." He grabbed my arm tighter as he gazed at the opposing stands. They were frothing with more rage than before. Security guards rushed to the other side of the field, where a Shreveport fan was trying to breach the gates leading to the turf. Other men stood behind him, red-faced and energized as they waved their fists at us.

Coach was livid. The vein in his forehead throbbed as he threw his headset on the ground. A muffled curse escaped Darrell's lips before he spat on the turf. When he saw Fontenot making his way toward us, his eyes grew wide. "Incoming."

"What in the Sam Hill?" Coach barked as he rumbled down the line. "Russell, have you lost your damn mind?"

"Have *I* lost *my* mind?" I gulped but managed to hold my

chin up. I pointed to the stands, at the police reinforcing the left gate with their bodies. "Listen to them, Coach!"

Lock him up! Lock him up! Lock him up!

"We can't let them get away with what they did to Dante Maynard or to Marion. This system is—"

"Unfair?" He lifted his eyebrows and let out a humorless chuckle. "Hell, we all know that. But I said keep a low profile. I said don't give the refs a reason to rain fury down on us. I told you to lead by example. And you just made things a *lot* harder for yourself. You're cutting your team off at the knees!"

He wiped his brow with his forearm and looked across the field, his eyes flitting in panic as he watched the head referee and the opposing coach gather in the center. My teammates packed in close, encircling us. Some of their faces echoed Coach's frustration, and I was afraid to look them in the eyes. I hung my head.

"Ain't no room for personal agendas in the game." He rammed his finger toward the bench. "Ain't no way you're going out on my field."

My jaw slackened as I failed to find my words. Coach was taking me out of the game before it even started. My eyes burned with bitter tears as I stepped over the painted line on the grass separating the field of play and the sidelines. First Marion's disappearance, then Shreveport's heckles, and now *this*?

Sinking to the bench, I bit the inside of my cheek to keep my lip from trembling. Indignation and shame swirled in my belly, settling into an anger that smoldered as I continued listening to the crowd's jeers. They could crucify us, and Coach was punishing *me*? I thought he would understand since he was Black, but I was wrong. I buried my head in my hand, frustrated with my own powerlessness.

After kickoff, our backup quarterback jogged to his place on the field. Dwarfed by the meaty linemen on Shreveport's side, Ricky was clearly much smaller and younger than the majority of the senior players. He called a huddle, and the Jackals on the field gathered around him. I prayed he could hold his own. A quarterback needed to have a firm lead on the play.

I should be out there. Marion too. It's so unfair.

The huddle broke, and the formation set. My nails dug into the bottom of the wooden bench as I gripped the edge harder. At the blare of the whistle, the two sides collided for the first play. One by one, the Jackals succumbed to tackles by Shreveport, who had obviously anticipated Ricky's play. Unable to find an open running back, Ricky panicked and tried to run the ball himself. His small legs were no match for the defensive lineman, who snaked his arm around his waist and threw him to the ground. Ricky hit the ground hard, a true sack.

"Come on, Coach!" I hopped off the bench instinctively, hoping that Coach Fontenot would finally let me play.

"Sit down!" he yelled from down the line. By the way his eyes narrowed, I knew he meant it.

Darrell tossed his receiving glove at me, and it hit me right in the chin.

"Bro, sit your ass down." He frowned, beads of sweat running down his face. "You can't fix this tonight."

I caught Clayton and Gabby in the corner of my eye, and

for a moment, my clenched muscles relaxed. Gabby's natural hair bobbed with the wind as she jumped up and down and clapped in my direction. She didn't know a thing about football—probably didn't know we were playing like crap tonight. But she was still excited, still on my side. It was ridiculous enough to make me smile. But only for a minute.

The sacks happened again and again—every play we ran ended incomplete. It ended with an embarrassing fumble of the ball that the other team caught. Watching my team fall apart against Shreveport was torture. Every time one of their players ran to the other side of the field, my stomach churned like I was gonna puke.

And if there were any recruiters in the stands, I could only imagine what they thought of us. There was no way any of us would get Division 1 scholarships playing like amateurs. And I sure as hell wouldn't be noticed from the bench.

But there was someone who would see me—Pops.

I didn't want to look, didn't want to see his face, but I could almost feel his cold, steely eyes boring into my back. I turned around, looking to my parents' seats beside the announcer's stand, and my chest tightened. They weren't there. Another pair of spectators stood in their place, as if my parents had left the game and given up their spots.

Oh, shit.

As much as it usually embarrassed me, Pops was always rooting for me—screaming louder than anyone else in the audience. Of course, his enthusiasm often got him into trouble. Coach said he was sometimes *too* involved in the game. I couldn't remember a time when I'd looked to the stands and hadn't seen one of my parents. Now, in the wake of his silence, I felt more alone than ever.

Had they left because I took a knee? Or because I was benched? Either way, it wasn't good, and I wondered what I would face when I got home.

In the locker room after the game, I knelt to untie the laces on my cleats. They were clean and tidy, the mark of an unused player—a benchwarmer. I wanted to throw them against the wall, I was so angry at not having played. But I kept my cool. That was expected of a team captain.

I peeled off my pristine uniform, unblemished from an evening of sitting and watching. I'd never ended a game without a mark on my uniform. And I'd never ended a game feeling so fractured with my teammates.

I set my cleats on top of Darrell's duffel bag straps—an honest mistake in such close quarters. But his blood was hot from a rough game, and his rage was searching for release. He snatched his bag straps from under my shoes.

"Sorry," I mumbled. I knew what a hothead Darrell could be and wanted to douse his temper before he got started.

"Yeah, you should be." Darrell slammed his fist on the metal grating of his cubby.

"What'd you say?" I whipped around, irritated at his level of disrespect. I narrowed my eyes, warning him to tread carefully.

"You heard me." He stepped forward, his fists clenched at his sides. His chest heaved as he breathed deeply. "You *should* be sorry for costing us the game."

"Oh, so your interceptions are now *my* fault?"

He lunged across the aisle, hands outstretched. He collided with me so hard that my back banged into my locker.
I shoved him back, and he stumbled over the locker room
bench. I crouched, ready for his next move but hoping he
would leave it there.

Darrell had a right to be upset, but so did I. I'd lost big
tonight—in more ways than one. But I wasn't going to take
this lying down. I was prepared for a fight…but Terrance
stepped between us.

"Ain't gonna be no more drama tonight." Terrance held
his arms out. He looked from Darrell to me to make sure we
heard him.

"No. Let's lay this all out on the table." Darrell shook his
head, then turned to the rest of the team. "This fool cost us
tonight's game."

"Shut up, D!" I stepped forward, pushing into Terrance's
outstretched palm. "Westmond cost us the game last week,
and we *still* payin' for it."

Our game this week was lost the second I was called a
nigga by a white boy who received *absolutely no discipline*—
while Marion took those punches and ended up in handcuffs.
Meanwhile, we'd been deprived of our most valuable player.
But Darrell wasn't hearing any of it.

"You ain't fool nobody. What you did was selfish as hell.
You knew *exactly* what would happen. You knew Coach
would be pissed off. You knew that would rile Shreveport
up. And you *still* did it." He pressed his index finger to his
temple. "Think about it. You could have written an Instagram

post. You could have talked to the reporters after the game. You could have done literally anything else, but you weren't thinking. So, you realize this is your fault, right?"

"Are you forgetting what happened to Marion? He was jailed by the same cop who shot and killed a kid *five weeks ago*." I raised my chin so that my voice carried to the far corners of the vast locker room. "Have you ever stopped to think how scary that must have been? And you're over here talking about how terrible losing tonight's game is. Shit. You could lose a whole lot more. Dante did. Marion did. Who's it going to be next?"

"You could've given us a heads-up," Terrance said, letting his role as mediator fall to the wayside. "We could have chosen another time."

"Yeah, why you do this when we're down a member?" Darrell flared his nostrils, bobbing his head to the side. "You the captain. Supposed to think about the team."

"I am thinking about the team. And the team should think about its members. Or have y'all already written Marion off?" I stepped toward Darrell, daring him to contradict me. "I don't know about y'all, but I'm not about to stand quietly while a murderer is policing our streets and while those white people are yelling to lock us up. Man, y'all are trippin'."

"All I'm saying is that tonight we were down two players!" Darrell paced in the small space along the line of lockers. "You think you 'bout to save us from the system? Man, you didn't do nothing but make things worse."

I wanted to call them cowards. I couldn't believe they were turning against me like this. But I left it there because it was overwhelming to feel my team—my *family*—turn against me when I needed them the most.

"Whatever, dude." I waved a hand dismissively. "I can't with you right now."

I snatched my bag off floor and barreled toward him, clipping his shoulder before making my way down the hall. Alone.

12

The Jackson Jackals bus dropped us off at our school, and I quickly shuffled to my car, doing my best to avoid Darrell. I flipped my hoodie up and turned the keys in the ignition, eager to put distance between me and football for a while. The Civic's headlights whipped through the spindly trees, which looked almost bald without all their leaves. The weather was shifting, the wind picking up. I cranked the heater to full blast, fighting the early crispness this September night promised to bring. The vents blew out cool air—exactly the opposite of what I needed.

Nothing was going right tonight.

Darrell's words taunted me, demanding my attention. I gripped the steering wheel so tight, my knuckles turned white.

You realize this is your fault, right?

In the confines of my car, separated from my anger toward Darrell, I let the wave of guilt rush through me. Part of me was mad my brothers had turned against me, but I could not deny the doubt that had settled in my heart. Had I *really* done the right thing?

I feared the truth in Darrell's statements—I had acted alone and impulsively, and those actions had spoiled our team's chances to win against Shreveport on their home turf. Then I unearthed a deeper worry, something I'd allowed myself to bury deep within myself.

Was Marion's arrest my fault too?

I'd been standing right next to him when Brad and Lawrence provoked him. I could have deescalated the situation instead of getting angry at Lawrence's call to a *nigga*. I could have held him back when Brad kneed him in the gut. I could have bowed and backed up and apologized for things I didn't do or say or mean, because that's what a Black man in America was supposed to do. But I hadn't done any of that.

I wasn't about that life.

At the few stoplights Monroe had to offer, I resisted the urge to check my phone, which was too quiet. After a game, I usually heard from people at school—classmates from study hall, random kids from my classes, teammates texting about an after-party. I usually got *something*. But tonight—*nothing*.

And still nothing from Marion.

My car's tires crept over the loose gravel of my driveway until I was parked right behind my dad's truck. The lights were on in the kitchen, and Mama milled about, as if she was in the middle of cooking. They'd clearly been home for a while, confirming my suspicion that they'd left the stadium early. Still, I touched the hood of my dad's truck just to make sure. It was cold. They must have left the game hours ago.

Foolish—that's what Pops thought about Kaepernick, and he probably thought I was foolish too.

If I had more faith in the Civic, I'd have stretched the drive longer—maybe stopped at the diner for food. Anything was better than walking into the white-hot anger of Pops. But I was here now. I knew they'd heard me pull up. There was no turning back.

I took cautious steps up the porch, wondering if I could handle another tongue-lashing. Darrell had let me have it. And I expected nothing less from Pops. But before I could reach for the handle, a clatter drew my attention to the corner of the house. I approached with caution as I rounded the corner.

The light was on in the shed, a makeshift workshop my dad used for storage and odd projects. I tapped on the cloudy glass and received a grunt in response.

"Pops, you in here?" I leaned my ear closer and received another grumble. My forehead sank to the windowpane. "Look I—"

"Don't wanna hear it." His voice was followed by another clatter against the wall.

I pushed the door open, wondering what was making that noise. Nails dotted the workbench along the wall and the surrounding floor. Dad had a careful, steady hand when he did his work. He was obviously rattled enough to spill a can of nails. My actions tonight had unnerved him.

"Tread carefully," he said, glaring up at me, and I wasn't sure if he meant to watch out for the nails on the ground or the splinters in his voice. Maybe it was a little of both, so I stayed on the other side of the threshold.

"I'm sure you heard we lost the game." I tossed my bag on the ground, imagining it was my whole football career. I was still on the fence about kneeling, my confidence shaken by the team turning against me. It didn't quite feel like the right thing to have done, especially now that I was facing my dad's disappointment.

It didn't feel right to be silent either.

I kicked my duffel, feeling defeated—feeling like I could do nothing right. My dad's head popped up so fast, it startled me.

"You know what I see when I look at that uniform? When I look at your duffel you tossed on the ground and kicked?" He wiped his hands on his gray work clothing and stepped closer. "That's years of overtime in that bag. That's my bad back from leaning over toilets."

"I know you've sacrificed a lot for me." I inhaled sharply, unsure what to say. Countless times I'd heard the front door squeak open late at night, the sound of Pops's work boots shuffling down the hall to my parents' room. He took every call, every job he could get to keep the lights on. "Believe me, I know."

"Do you?" He raised his eyebrows, then walked to the workbench and picked up a crumpled piece of paper. "Eleven years of football and *hundreds* of dollars a year, plus the cost of at least a dozen cleats along the way, plus various other expenses."

"So what? You think that was a waste of money?"

"It didn't look like a good investment tonight."

My lips clamped down on the silence. I was unable to find words. I wanted to offer to pay him back every cent. But I couldn't.

I'd made a snap decision on the field, and through the course of the evening, I was coming to terms with the consequences of that choice. I'd jeopardized my senior season and maybe my chances at a full ride to college by taking a knee. But my season had been upended the moment Marion was barred from playing. I played my best when I was surrounded by the best. I'd knelt for myself just as much as I'd knelt for Marion.

Pops didn't see it that way.

"You don't just owe it to yourself to finish big. You owe it to *me*." Pops looked to the side, as if he could barely look at me. There were conditions to his good humor, and I'd evidently crossed the line. "But you're throwing it away."

"I'm sorry you feel that way." I staggered backward, grabbing the doorframe for support. The old shack wobbled under the weight of my grasp. When I had firm footing, I held my head up, jutting my chin out as I decided to stand by my protest. I deserved better than to be labeled a criminal. Dante deserved better. Marion deserved better. And no one was going to do anything about it until people started pushing back on the silent compliance.

People needed a wake-up call, and I'd just given it to them.

"I'm not sorry for what I did tonight."

I gritted my teeth, thinking about all the summers in peewee I'd committed to football instead of camp—all these years in varsity I'd overworked my body to the point that I got full-body cramps. I remained as committed as ever. I wasn't throwing away *anything*. This country was throwing away boys like me and Marion—discarding us like garbage.

"Excuse me?"

"I'd do it again." My stance was more calcified than hours ago when I'd stood in front of Darrell. I squared my shoulders, raising my chin higher. "My only question is why no one supported me. Why can't you be on my side?"

"Don't take that tone with me. Not in my house," Pops boomed. "If you can't respect me, I swear to God—"

"Enough!" Mama yelled from behind me. She brushed me aside and stepped into the shed. "Ain't no need to wake the neighbors over something we can fix. They're an acre over, but I bet they can hear all this fussing."

"And how's that, Cheryl?" Pops dropped his hammer on the table and folded his arms.

"First thing Monday, Rus can apologize to the league. Isn't that right, baby?" She grabbed my hands, her worried eyes searching for agreement in mine. "Then we can appeal their decision to allow Marion to play."

"Mama, we tried that!"

"Well, we gotta try *again*. We've got no power here." She blew a breath through her tight lips, sending her bangs into a flutter. "Ain't nothing but prayer and perseverance gonna work."

My stomach curdled at the sound of her suggestion. I was doubtful that prayer and perseverance would save us. Those words sounded so familiar—exactly like the speeches local officials gave after Dante Maynard's shooting, like what Coach had told me after Marion's unfair suspension.

Our thoughts and prayers are with them.

I grabbed my stuff, turning to look at the front door of my house—a house I was no longer welcome in. Darting around the shed, I headed to the darkness beyond—to a refuge tucked deeper into the woods.

I stormed across the backyard and dipped behind the tree line. My arm caught on a thorny bramble, and I winced through the pain as I pushed farther into the night. Under the blanket of darkness, I couldn't see the blood on my fore-arm, but I could feel it pooling. It was too dark to see much of anything on the overgrown path, but I knew the way to the old tree house by heart.

An acre behind my house, where the bedrock sloped to-ward the bayou, the tree house floated twenty feet up in the branches of an old oak tree. It had been years since I'd made my way back there, a forgotten part of childhood. But it was the only escape I could think of.

I leaned against the tree, stopping to collect my thoughts. Silence swallowed my breaths, and then the cicadas and crickets resumed their nightly calls. I stood frozen, allowing the night to swallow me whole. It was the closest to disappearing I could get—a way to escape my upside-down life.

I pawed in the dark, feeling for the rope ladder, but I couldn't find it. I slammed my fist against the tree. I should have known the tree house wouldn't be intact. It had liter-ally been years since I'd been out here, but this was the only escape I could think of. But of course, *nothing* was going my way tonight. Nothing.

Shuffling sounds came from above, and I stumbled back-ward, startled.

"Hello?" I called up, unsure if it was an animal or a squat-ter. No one had been here for years. It would be the perfect place for someone in hiding to claim.

"Rus?" a familiar voice whispered through the night. "Is that you?"

"Marion?" I frowned and looked above me, blinking rapidly so that my eyes could focus on the entrance above. I couldn't see anything past my nose, but I knew it was him—the voice

of a ghost who had disappeared for the last few days. "Throw the ladder down, will ya?"

The mangy rope ladder spilled from the bottom of the tree house and grazed the forest floor. I slung my bag across my shoulder, tightening the strap to secure it. Grabbing the ladder, I set a tentative step against the weathered rope. Would it hold my weight? It'd been a while since I'd used it, and I was probably eighty pounds heavier. The last thing I needed was to end my football career by hurting myself falling out of a tree. I wasn't sure the ladder could take the strain, but if it had held Marion, it would hold me.

Please don't break.

I repeated that prayer over and over as I clung to the ladder, taking the rungs slowly and methodically. A dozen unwieldly steps later, my head popped through the opening. There, in the corner of the tree house, an eerie glow came from Marion's phone on the floor. I pushed my bag over my head, then grabbed the wooden ledge to steady myself. My broad shoulders grazed the sides of the opening, but I managed to squeeze through.

"I do *not* remember that climb being so wobbly. Remember how we used to zip in and out of here like it was nothing?"

"I don't know. I guess." He shrugged. And for a split second I wondered if I was intruding on him.

Maybe I should go back.

But I looked out the tree house door, down the twentysomething-foot drop to the ground, and I thought about Pops's anger that awaited me at home. If this was Marion's last option, it was mine too. I didn't have anywhere else to go either.

I sat with my legs dangling over the edge, catching my breath as I took stock of the childhood fort we'd built so long ago. The tan paint we'd so lovingly applied was now flaking in several large spots, revealing old, mealy wood underneath. And the roof sloped to one slide, creating a sizable gap between the high beams and the sideboards. It was a lifetime ago when we'd holed ourselves up here, convinced we'd be safe from the world in our fortress. Now it didn't look so sturdy. From what I could see through the dim light, our stronghold was ramshackle—just as that dream of safety was.

Marion clicked a yellow flashlight on and set it against a corner so that the light reflected off the walls. He brushed crumbs off his sleeping bag, I guessed in an attempt to tidy up. He grabbed a plastic bag from the top of a pile of snacks.

"Want some jerky?" Marion held it out to me.

It was such a normal thing for him to do. I sputtered a laugh but then buried my head in my shoulder, gulping down tears I'd been holding back all night.

"Long day?" He set the bag down at his side and sighed.

"Long week." I wiped my nose on my sleeve, thinking back to when this all started—back to the point when life seemed to get harder. "Actually, it's been a long *month*."

"I know what you mean." He leaned forward and grabbed his phone. The hushed voices of the local news channel were barely audible over the sounds of the cicadas outdoors. "I'll turn this off."

"No. I wanna hear it."

The news showed angry fans still congregating in the parking lot, angry about Mr. Boudreaux's disrespect of the flag and our troops.

Earlier tonight, he refused to stand for the national anthem. Now there are calls for the league to pursue disciplinary action against the player. The Jackson Jackals are no strangers to controversy. Just last week, quarterback Marion LaSalle was arrested for brawling on the field with Bradley Simmons and Lawrence Perkins. This comes on the heels of the police department's manhunt for a masked vandal who has been defacing property with protest flyers demanding police accountability. Clearly a town in the grips of turmoil—

"Disrespect to the troops?" A string of obscenities escaped my lips as I listened to reporters and angry fans hijack my protest, just like they had with Colin Kaepernick. I remembered reading that he'd even met with veterans while planning his protest. But that still hadn't stopped the president and other powerful people from framing his protest as an act of aggression. "Why do they even report this stuff? This isn't news. They know full well I wasn't kneeling against the troops. Man, turn that shit off."

In the absence of the news, we heard music from Pops's workshop drifting through the air, making its way to our perch in the trees. Marion pursed his lips, looking at his lap.

"He's been out there for hours." He looked up and studied my face. "He came home before the end of the game, so I knew something was going down."

"You heard?" It was a stupid question to ask. If we could hear Pops's music all the way out here, then Marion had definitely overheard our argument.

"I've never heard him pop off like that. But I kinda get where he's coming from." He nodded, then sighed deeply. "Dang, Rus. You took a knee?"

I clenched my jaw, prepared for another scolding. "And I guess you have something to say?"

"I'm sure you got enough from the guys. I can see it on your face. And shit, dude. I know you got it from Pops too."

I sat back, relaxing from my defensive hunch. Marion's opinion was what meant the most to me. But his response—although comforting and nonjudgmental—wasn't supportive either. A part of me wanted to know whether or not he approved. Ambivalence wasn't enough. Between Darrell and Pops, I needed someone firmly on my side. But I didn't want to draw a hard line. Not tonight. I focused my attention on a discarded fast-food wrapper.

"How can you live out here?" I looked around the rickety fort. It wasn't a full house with all of the things a person needed to get by. "Where are you charging your phone?"

"There's an outlet behind the shed. No one goes back there, especially when y'all are gone for the day." Marion shrugged and looked at his lap, a tinge of embarrassment on his quivering lip. "Pops don't ever lock the shed, and there's a bathroom in there. Some snacks in the minifridge. It's enough for now."

"Enough?" I asked, my voice small. I didn't want Marion to hear the worry behind the words, but this base level of subsistence was not *enough*. I thought of the bathroom in the shed, which had no lights and was a tight squeeze, of the sink that ran only cold water. And the junk food my dad kept in the fridge and on the countertop—it wasn't enough to live on. With the weather turning cooler, Marion couldn't have been comfortable out here. "Have you been up here the whole week?"

"Nah, I went home for a few days." His voice hitched on

the word *home*. Because that wasn't his real home. It hadn't been for years. "Came up here last night, because…"

"Ed." I knew it before he said it. Ed was dangerous on a good day, but seeing Marion brought low by being kicked off the team—Marion must have taken a beating. "Why not just come to our house instead of hiding up here?"

"Same reason you ain't in the house right now. I can't face them." He waved his arms toward the house, where the lights were still on. Mama was probably worried sick about both of us. "I can't face anyone. I'm so…embarrassed."

"You have nothing to be ashamed of. *They* do." I pointed to the phone, to the newscasters and angry white people calling for young boys to be locked up.

"Jail? Three-thousand-dollar bail? Getting suspended from playing?" Marion's voice shook, his lips smacking as he struggled to find the words. "I can't even think straight."

"Me neither." I shrank into the opposite corner, tucking my knees to my chest. "Coach didn't let me play tonight. After I took a knee, he lost his shit."

"Rus…" He hid his face in his hands, swinging his head back and forth.

"Pops thinks I jeopardized my spot." I said it quietly, not wanting to breathe life into those words.

It was a real danger. Coach had discretion to play whomever he wanted during any game. If he was still angry, he could bench me again. Then there was the league—they could slap me with disciplinary action, pull me from play for the next few games for violating their code of conduct. That's *if* they believed all the bullshit about me *publicly disrespecting the troops* by taking a knee. I gulped. As ridiculous as that sounded, a *lot* of people on the news saw it that way. Maybe the league did too.

"Shit." I clenched my jaw, feeling my stomach churn.

"You think they'll really take you off the team?" Marion's eyebrows turned upward.

"I don't know." I shrugged and let out a deep sigh. "All I know is that I gotta do what I gotta do."

"You heard the news. The league's been talking about sanctions and disciplinary actions, about making standing for the national anthem mandatory." Marion shifted his weight so that he sat on his knees. His dreads grazed the roof of the tree house. "So, we're both gonna be out the game? Our senior year? Man, this is a mess."

"Have you called that pro bono lawyer Gabby found for you? What's his name—Mr. Samuels?" I waited for a while for Marion to respond, but he finally nodded. "What did he say?"

"Same as the other lawyer. That my case will take time. And time is the one thing I *don't* have."

The crickets filled the silence, so loud I almost couldn't hear Marion continue.

"What happened to me, man. It was fucked up. Not as fucked up as what happened to Dante. But, Rus." He shifted in his sleeping bag. "Pops and Coach and the guys—they're right. Ain't *nothing* you can do about my situation. And the kneeling thing—I get what you're trying to do, but that ain't gonna change anything."

I clenched my jaw and snatched one of Marion's pillows from the middle of the floor. He tossed me a throw blanket, and I recognized it as one of Mama's—the one she always set out for him when he came to stay.

Propping my head against the far wall, I reached for the flashlight and clicked it off, feeling shutdown and defeated. Once my eyes adjusted to the darkness, I could see the stars through the gap in the roof. The sheer vastness of the night sky was overwhelming—maybe we *were* helpless in the enormity of what we were up against.

It was easy to lose myself in the thousands of tiny lights in the sky, and I began to drift, thinking about Marion's assertion that nothing we did could change our fate.

No. No, I don't believe that.

The thought comforted me long enough to release me from wakefulness.

13

The crinkling of leaves woke me up shortly after first light—small careful footsteps. I propped myself up with the wall and scooted toward the window, rubbing my neck as it pinched with pain. I'd slept restlessly, waking up periodically throughout the night to reposition myself or just lie on my back and listen to the crickets chirp as I blinked into the darkness. Deep thought came easily. Sleep did not. And comfort was hard to hold on to.

I poked my head out the window. Mama cautiously dipped her toes in the thick leaf litter, her foam rollers bobbing as she hopped from spot to spot, no doubt thinking of all the bugs that hid below the rotted rug of leaves.

When she looked up, she caught my sleepy gaze. With a shake of her head, she put her hands on her hips. Her eyebrows tightened, and I thought she might scold me for not answering her calls. Instead, she waved for me to come down.

"Time for y'all to come home," she said. "I got work aplenty for you."

* * *

Pops leaned forward in his recliner, sending biscuit crumbs flying as he watched the Dallas Cowboys line up for a field goal in New Orleans Saints territory. A superstitious sports fan to the core, he wiggled his fingers in front of the flat screen as if he could affect the outcome of the game.

"Booga-looga-wooga!" He rocked back and forth in his recliner, mumbling hexes of his own making. "Get outta there!"

I frowned as I surveyed the mess of crumbs on the carpet—a carpet that I'd *just* vacuumed. I wondered if Mama would make me do it again, which seemed unfair given that I hadn't made the mess. But I was grounded.

Fairness didn't matter.

I leaned over the kitchen island, displacing some of Marion's homework papers as I craned my neck to catch a glimpse of the game. The Cowboys versus the Saints was one of the biggest matchups of the season, a game I wouldn't dream of missing on a normal day. But as part of my punishment, I was not allowed to watch any TV.

Until I say otherwise.

That's what Pops had said when I asked him how long I was to be punished. And he hadn't spoken to me since.

How could my parents expect me to miss one of the biggest rivalry games in the NFL?

Pops howled in frustration as the Cowboys' ball soared through the goalposts, dead center. It was a solid field goal, a predictable outcome. It was rare for a professional team to miss a kick. Their error rate was definitely far less than that of a high school football team like the Jackson Jackals. From our unreliable kicker to the second-string freshman quarterback we'd played last night, my team was in tatters.

Then there was me and my silent protest. I hadn't helped the situation. I shook my head, trying not to think about it.

Pops straightened in his chair and turned slightly, catching Marion's eye. He gave a curt nod in commiseration, then caught my gaze. He blinked furiously away, pretending like he didn't see me—like I wasn't until recently the center of his pride and dreams. But I knew he'd seen me. In that fleeting moment, as his eyes tightened and watered, I could see worry and fear, a carryover from his anger last night.

I wanted to talk to him, but I didn't know what to say. Striking up a probing conversation on the merits of peaceful protest seemed impossible. So the tension remained intact, and avoidance was the best strategy.

I bent my head, escaping his scrutiny. I didn't want to betray my hurt feelings either. The silence between us stretched further.

"Quick, your mama's coming." Marion looked over his shoulder, then snapped his head back toward his English book as the shuffling sounds of Mama's slippers drew nearer.

Abandoning the TV, I scrambled to the back counter and aimed my attention to the blob of dish towels that floated in the sink. My nose crinkled at the smell of bleach. I swirled the cloths around, waking up the putrid smell. This was definitely my least favorite chore on the long list my parents had cooked up.

They said their reason for grounding me was simple: football was my job, and my promising career was my contribution to the family. Since I'd taken a knee, my spot on the team was jeopardized. So until my starting spot was normalized, my contributions would be chores.

I thought it was a little premature. I mean, we didn't know for sure if Coach was going to bench me in the next game or if that was just a onetime punishment. But remembering his blistering red face, there was a good chance he might still be angry with me.

"You about done with those?" She put her hands on her hips and cocked her head to the side. "Rinse 'em off real good and then hang them—"

"Over there," I said, cutting her off. I huffed under my breath, trying not to sound too frustrated. I was in enough hot water as it was. I didn't need to add mouthing off to my list of wrongs. "I got this, Mama."

"You do that load of laundry yet?" she asked.

I stopped twirling the dish towels in the bleachy water as blood drained from my face. I'd totally forgotten the laundry.

"Yes, ma'am, he did," Marion said from his barstool. "He switched it over to the dryer an hour ago."

Relief washed over me. I'd owe Marion a favor for helping me out. I wiped my forehead with my sleeve.

"Good, it oughta be about done." She bustled out of the room, humming softly under her breath.

"You didn't have to do that," I murmured. He shouldn't have helped—Mama had made it abundantly clear that he wasn't grounded. He hadn't done anything wrong. I'd wanted to argue the *I* hadn't done anything wrong by taking a knee, but they wouldn't have listened to me.

"I kinda had to. The struggle is real." He extended his leg

from behind the counter, wiggling his big toe through a hole in his sock. "This is my last set of clothes."

No amount of washing would fix the holes in Marion's clothes—I'm sure he knew that. But there was dignity wrapped into his cleaning. He might not have the best, most complete wardrobe, but he needed to take care of what he had. Still, I was sure we could do something more for Marion.

I shook my head, a grumble escaping my lips. Every day brought new worries, challenges that needed solutions. When would life slow down?

My brows furrowed as I wrung the towels under the faucet. I hung the last of the dishcloths on the edge of the sink, then held my fingers close to the sunny windowsill. In the light, I studied the slimy, slick coating of bleach on my fingers.

"Ew," I grumbled as I rubbed them together. Everywhere my fingers had touched the bleach was slippery.

A low chuckle came from over my shoulder. Marion brought a fist to his mouth and tucked his lips between his teeth, stifling another laugh.

"Keep laughing." I gritted my teeth as I ran my bleached fingers underneath the cold water.

"Why you think your mama put those gloves on the counter?" Marion raised an eyebrow.

"What's so funny?" Mama blew into the kitchen with an overflowing laundry basket in her arms. She took one look at my fingers and shook her head with a sigh. "Russell, what am I gonna do with you?"

Her eyes crinkled at the edges as she glanced past me at the yellow gloves on the counter. By the tone of her voice, I got the sense she was asking beyond the chores. She looked through me, straight to my stubborn soul. Then, as quick as her curious concern touched her eyes, it was gone. She cleared her throat, resuming the avoidance—the part where we weren't actually talking to each other about important things.

"Use apple cider vinegar. That'll do the trick." She sidled past me and opened the kitchen pantry. Her eyes scanned the shelves until she located what she was looking for. She waved a bottle of cloudy vinegar in front of her with a knowing smile. She was clearly amused at how I kept getting myself into sticky situations. "Next time, use the gloves."

I complied silently, my stomach roiling from the smell of bleach and vinegar mixing in the small space.

Marion hopped off his barstool and jumped at the chance to get some clean underwear from the laundry basket.

"You need more clothes, baby?" Mama lifted her chin toward Marion's duffel, which was deflated and empty in the corner of the living room.

"No, ma'am." His lips turned downward and he shook his head, trying to be casual.

Mama tilted her head, opening her mouth like she was going to say something like, *How many times do I have to tell you? Call me mama.* Something to make him feel like he was home. But the truth was, this wasn't his real home with all of his belongings. His stuff was at Ed's house.

"I'm fine." He shrugged. "I really appreciate all that y'all have done for me. I can make it work."

"We could drop by your house." I stepped closer to their huddle in the living room. "We could pick up another bagful."

"You ain't going nowhere." Pops slapped the arm of his

recliner, his lip quivering. He didn't make eye contact with me. Instead, he looked toward the TV, his eyes unfocused as he said, "You're grounded, remember? That means no car. Period. End of story."

First the TV, and now the car??

"Really, Pops?" My nostrils flared. "How am I going to get to school? Or practice? Are you seriously gonna keep punishing me for doing the right thing?"

"That's enough." Mama held her hands up as she stepped between us, neutral territory between two hot spots. She pursed her lips, her eyes narrowing as she shook her head at me. It was a warning to tread carefully. "Now, you listen to me. The both of you."

Her gaze darted to Marion, making him freeze on the spot too.

"I don't want you boys *anywhere* near Ed's trailer, you understand? He's been running his mouth around town about you and Marion, saying nasty hurtful things. I'm not even going to repeat them. Just stay away from him, you hear?"

"Yes, ma'am." We both nodded vigorously.

"Your dad and I will figure something out." She pressed her lips together as if trying to formulate a plan. "We'll get you some fresh things at the store today."

Marion clenched his jaw. He flared his nostrils and shook his head slightly, like he was fighting the urge to contradict her.

"And, Eli," she said, turning her attention to Pops. She stepped forward, advancing on his space with a stern brow. "Russell may be grounded for what he did on the field, but it won't interfere with his schoolwork. That comes first."

Her glare deepened as she looked toward me.

"You can use the car for school and football only." Then she took a menacing step in my direction. "Don't make me regret this."

I shook my head, knowing she meant business.

"Good. Now grab the keys to the truck. You're coming to the store with me."

There was only one grocery store in Monroe, and that was Rick's Supermarket, just off Main Street. There wasn't anything *super* about it—just eight aisles crammed full of whatever they could fill them with. Mama put her foot on the gas, barely making a yellow light.

"You missed our turn." I looked out the window, watching Main Street whiz by.

"I know where I'm going," she said as she drove down Calumet. She eased to a halt at the light in front of the interstate, the line that separated Monroe and Westmond. "Fresh Horizons has a sale on firewood. Got the coupons in my bag."

She patted her purse on the other side of the console, then pressed the gas when the light turned green. We crossed over the freeway into Westmond territory—the *last* place I wanted to be. But I was grounded, and my mom needed help carrying firewood. I didn't have a choice.

Fresh Horizons Market was larger than our strip mall grocer. It had all of the expensive organic stuff but had some pretty good deals too. Mama preferred shopping on our side of town where there were less stares at her brown skin. But she'd venture across the freeway for a good sale. When you were living paycheck to paycheck, deals were all that mattered.

As we pulled into the parking lot, Mama skirted a delivery truck near the entrance. The side of it read Dupre Produce Delivery. My heart ticked up a few beats. The last time I'd seen Gabby, she'd been howling at the Shreveport stands, calling them all hypocrites. If anyone approved of my kneeling, it would be Gabby.

And right now, I needed an ally.

We parked then crossed the lot, Mama rummaging in her purse to find her coupon booklet. I craned my neck to see around the truck, searching for any sign of Gabby, listening for the confident tenor of her voice. A deliveryman with gloves heaved a crate onto a hand truck, then leaned against it to catch his breath. He raised an eyebrow when he saw me looking, and I quickly scampered after Mama, who had already made it to the shopping cart bay.

I pulled out a cart while she flipped through the pages and mumbled under her breath.

"Ah, here's one." She ripped a page and stuffed the book back in her pocket. "I'll look for underwear and socks while you load the cart with firewood. The stacks should be in the back of the store."

I nodded, yawning widely. I was still exhausted from my restless night sleeping on the hard wood of the tree house.

"You need socks too?" Mama tapped another deal in her booklet, just waiting to be ripped out.

I shook my head. "I'm good."

"All right, then. I want you to get twenty bundles of wood." Mama double-checked her coupons. "Yeah, that should do it."

"*Twenty?* Mama, come on. It ain't *that* cold." I'd slept outside just last night, and while it had been a bit chilly, it was not cold enough to keep the furnaces burning.

"It's not now, but it will be. And this firewood is cheaper than running the heat."

She pursed her lips, letting that sink in. Our finances must have been tighter than I thought, and Mama was already looking to winter, trying to keep us warm during the leaner time of year when the substitute teaching jobs dried up and Pops's plumbing business was the only thing keeping us afloat.

"I'll meet you back there after I grab Marion's things," Mama said as she pulled another cart from the bay. Then she bustled through the sliding glass doors and turned in the direction of the pharmacy, where the miscellaneous and personal items were.

By the time Mama made it to the back of the store, I'd taken a good chunk out of the woodpile. My fingertips ached with the sting of splinters as I loaded the last few bundles into Mama's cart. Watchful white eyes tracked us as we wheeled the two heaping carts to the register.

"Y'all having a bonfire?" the cashier asked as she smacked her gum.

"Nothing wasteful like that," Mama mumbled as she handed the woman the coupons she'd ripped from her booklet. She leaned over the counter to look at the screen, making sure every item was scanned and discounted correctly.

The cashier handed Mama the receipt with a strained smile, likely annoyed at Mama's micromanagement. Mama gave her sweetest smile, but double-checked the receipt.

"We good, honey." She nodded at me. "Hold it steady."

I followed slowly after her, my feet dragging after a long

night and even longer day of physical labor. I was *tired*, and I hoped this was the end of my day of chores. I stumbled over my feet as I surrendered to a massive yawn.

That's when a sign on the glass window caught my eyes.

HAVE YOU SEEN THIS PERSON?

Sketched in black-and-white was a drawing of a hooded figure, their face cast in shadow, their features indiscernible. At the bottom of the poster read: "Wanted for repeated acts of vandalism. If seen, notify the police department immediately."

The police were looking for Dante's Shadow.

The sketch was similar to the figure I'd seen slinking in the shadows the night of Terrance's party. All I'd been able to make out was a black hoodie and a messenger bag stuffed with flyers. It could have been anyone in that alleyway with me. If this was the only image the police were working with, they were just as clueless as I was.

I couldn't help but smile at the thought of the police scrambling to find this guy.

"They're never gonna catch him," I said to Mama, pointing at the sign on the glass. "I've seen him, and he's *fast*."

Mama flared her nostrils, inhaling sharply.

"Well, don't broadcast it to everybody." She gripped the front of the shopping cart and heaved it toward herself. "Keep moving. Ain't nobody need to see us next to that wanted sign."

"It's not like I'm the guy on the poster," I called after her, pushing my cart. She moved surprisingly fast for having a cart full of firewood, but I guessed she was feeling motivated to get out of Westmond as soon as possible. We stuck out like a sore thumb with our discount firewood, our brown skin,

and my bulky six-foot-three frame. I wondered if people recognized me.

I wondered if they were afraid of me. After all, I was part of
the brawling football team who'd attacked their quarterback.

I rushed to catch up with Mama, squaring my shoulders as
I skidded to a halt at the truck's tailgate.

"Do you agree with him?" I raised an eyebrow at her. She
tilted her head and looked at me like she didn't know what I
was talking about. "Are you mad at me like Pops is?"

"No, baby. No. But it's complicated." She sighed, putting
her hands on her hips. "Look. I understand why you did what
you did last night. Someone needs to answer for what happened to you and Marion—to what keeps happening to boys
on our side of the parish line."

"Why can't Pops see that?" My shoulders slumped as I
thought of his face last night, of the anger he'd spewed in the
shed. "Pops don't understand."

"Don't worry about him. He'll come around. But a word
of advice—you've said your piece. No good can come from
you continuing to stick your neck out. I don't want you to
get hurt." She nodded toward the wanted poster on the glass
door across the parking lot. "Stay away from whoever's running these streets, putting up flyers. There's only one place
they're gonna end up, and that's in juvie. Or worse—prison.
The law doesn't see you as a child."

She leaned against the back of the truck, running her hands
through her hair. Usually Mama didn't like to have a hair out
of place, but right now she seemed too distressed to care. She
let out another heavy sigh.

"I want you to get out of here. Look at what happens to

Black boys here. Shot dead. Kicked off a team. Futures ru-
ined." Her eyelashes fluttered, picking up her unshed tears.
She wiped her face with the back of her wrist. "I support you,
but I also want you to get out, Russell. Or else this place will
swallow you whole."

I slumped against the truck, watching Mama's retreating
figure as she walked the cart back to the front of the store.
Mama had confirmed it—kneeling had been the right thing
to do, but it would have a cost. She just hoped it wasn't me.

I still had my sights set on leaving Monroe. I hoped I hadn't
jeopardized my shot.

Mama rubbed her eyes with her sleeve as she made her
way back to the car. Behind her, the doors to Fresh Horizons
opened, and Gabby strolled out with a clipboard in her hands.

She scribbled something on the page, then paused in front
of the wanted poster. I shoved off the truck, prepared to
cross the lot and talk to her, but Mama told me to get in the
truck. I checked out Gabby one last time before I got in and
buckled up.

She looked right, then left, as if checking to see no one
was looking, then she ripped the wanted flyer off the glass.
She crumpled it into a ball and shoved it in her back pocket
as she walked to her dad's delivery truck.

I smiled, intrigued.

14

I yawned so hard, it stopped me in my tracks. It was only lunchtime, but I was *so* tired. This was going to be one of *those* Mondays. I leaned against the wall of lockers and surrendered to exhaustion, letting another yawn overtake me. I'd barely slept over the weekend. Between the unforgiving wood floor of the tree house and doing two full days of chores on top of homework, quality rest had been hard to find.

Still, the night spent aloft in the tree house had been weirdly fun. It was such an unexpected interlude to the higher stakes of my life, and even though I felt like crap, I was grateful for the experience. All this time, while I'd been searching for Marion, worried that he was still looking for answers in bottles of malt liquor, he'd been in the woods behind my house. And just when I needed him the most, he'd been right where I was headed.

We never had decided what our next step was, content to sit in silence, play cards, or walk in the woods. The chances of Marion rejoining this football season were growing more distant by the day. I worried about him, now more than ever.

And now my spot on the team was in jeopardy. The words from the newscaster preoccupied my thoughts.

There are calls for the league to pursue disciplinary action against the player.

I knew all too well the kind of *justice* the league doled out. It was the kind that saw one football player barred from the field and the other released without a slap on the wrist. A league that housed referees who remained silent on the subject of who'd started the fight. A league that hired crooked cops like Officer Reynaud—a murderer and a liar.

I didn't need to wait for the league's disciplinary action. Their justice was rigged, and not in my favor.

By the sneers Darrell kept throwing at me from across the hall, I knew I had not been forgiven for Friday's loss. The jury was still out with the rest of my classmates. Some gave me the regular high fives they always did, but they were fewer and far between. Without the prestige of football and winning, I wasn't the hero of Jackson High. I was just a six-foot-three dude, hunching into his locker, trying to make himself less conspicuous in the wake of disgrace.

The chatter of the lunchroom sapped me of energy before I even made it to the door. Instead of entering, I ducked into my homeroom classroom halfway down the hall. Thankfully, it was empty.

Flipping my hood over my head, I picked a random desk and sank my forehead to the hard surface. My shoulders slouched, my body relaxed, and my mind eased as I allowed it to go blank.

I didn't know how long I drifted, but I was brought back to the surface by the soft sound of knuckles rapping against my desk. I lifted the corner of my hood and saw the threads of a lumpy sweater.

"I thought that was you," Gabby said softly. Squatting on the ground, she rifled through her backpack. I groaned.

"If this is about the project, can we talk about it later?"

"It's not about the English project." She set something hard on my desk. "Here, you need this more than I do."

Curious, I sat up, squinting at the room's brightness. When my eyes adjusted, I saw a Red Bull sitting inches from my fingertips.

"Thanks," I said, popping the cap. With deep gulps, I guzzled the tart soda. It landed with an acidic splash, causing my stomach to gurgle. I looked at Gabby apologetically. "Didn't eat lunch."

"Obviously. You look worn *af.*" She threw her head back and laughed. "I have a veggie stir-fry if you want?"

"You're not going to eat it?"

"I'm not really hungry." She shrugged as she set the stir-fry on my desk. She zipped her bag up and slid into the desk in front of me. She leaned her elbow against the back of her chair. "Today has been *loud.* I can only imagine what you're feeling."

Every kid in school was either talking about the Westmond fight or my protest during the Shreveport game's national anthem. I could feel the words of the newscaster in every stare I got. I couldn't change what I'd done on Friday. I wasn't sure I wanted to. But the negative attention was wearing on my nerves, making me edgy and anxious.

That anger sent another gurgle through my stomach. I opened the lid of Gabby's Tupperware and dove the plastic fork into the food. It was surprisingly not terrible for cold veggies. But after a while, it lost its luster. I shoveled it into my mouth just to stop the hunger pangs from roiling through my stomach.

We let the silence draw out. I was grateful for the companionship. It reminded me of my weekend with Marion…until I overheard students talking about me in the hallway. Their gossip and giggles echoed down the hall.

You heard what he did, right?

He took a knee.

Yeah, during the anthem.

It was wild.

I slammed the fork on the desk. "You know what really pisses me off?" I flared my nostrils. Gabby's eyes narrowed. "I was listening to the news over the weekend, and they're all focused on the wrong thing. I'm *disrespecting the troops*, the Jackals are a *bunch of upstarts*—how can they focus on that without looking at Officer Reynaud? Without looking at Marion's bullshit charges?"

"I know," Gabby said in little more than a whisper. "It *is* bullshit."

"What else can I do?" I shrugged so high, my shoulders grazed my earlobes. "I guess I gotta fall in line and keep my mouth shut while the white people of this region be wilin' out?"

"Well, I wouldn't say *that*. Silence is violence." Gabby shook her head. "We can't stop until people listen. If you ask me, maybe we should turn up the heat."

"Turn *up* the heat?" I choked on a laugh, my head spinning. "Like you did at the store this weekend?"

"What?" Her eyebrows flinched.

"I saw you yesterday at Fresh Horizons." She raised an eyebrow, a challenge. I liked catching Gabby off guard. It made her careful facade falter, allowing me to see her vulnerability. I leaned over the desk, a smile tugging at my lips. "I saw you tear down that sign with the description of the Shadow."

"Did anyone else see?" Her cheeks turned a bright red.

I shook my head.

"Good. I don't want that to affect my dad's business." She folded her arms and slouched into her desk chair. She lifted her head, looking relieved. "The way I see it, the police are looking for the wrong person. That's why I tore down the poster."

"Nah. I've actually seen the guy, and it was a pretty accurate description."

"No, I mean the cops shouldn't be wasting their time searching for...the *Shadow*." She smirked at the nickname we'd given the guy who was putting up Dante flyers. "They should be spending their time investigating Reynaud and all the other officers responsible for the shooting of Dante Maynard."

"Well, you can keep dreaming about that. If they haven't taken Reynaud down yet, they're not gonna."

"Says the guy who just took a knee in front of a stadium full of people." She leaned forward and put her elbows on her desk, so close I could count her freckles. She grinned, nodding slowly. "Now *that's* turning up the heat."

I choked on a laugh, my head spinning. I felt like I was in the deep end of life, treading water against the tides of parental punishment and football expectations. If anything, I was interested in turning *down* the heat.

Still, it was gratifying to know that Gabby approved of my protest. I felt a little less alone.

I smiled, my lips twitching nervously as I tried to avoid eye contact. "I'm in a *lot* of hot water over the kneeling. I'm grounded. I'm probably benched too. To be honest, I'm pretty stressed out."

"Sounds like you need a break."

"Like you wouldn't believe." I leaned forward, drawn in by her shy smile. "Do you have something in mind?"

"Maybe? It's not exactly a break, but we still have the rest of our Baldwin project to work on. We could finish that. And... I could come over." She tucked her hair behind her ear, stopping momentarily to twist the ends with her finger.

My jaw dropped, but I recovered quickly by covering my mouth with my fist and pretending to cough.

Did Gabby just ask me out?

"I thought you didn't want to give the boys anything to talk about?"

"Oh, you're right," she said with a slight stammer. "Well, I only suggested that because you're grounded. And I thought maybe you'd want to hang—I mean, do the project there. It was a weird suggestion. Sorry."

I fought to restrain my smile—I didn't want her to think I was laughing at her. Because I wasn't. In fact, I was pretty flattered. The world was on fire, but Gabby was warming up to me. And that warmth felt wonderful, especially since it was coming at the same time that people were giving me the cold shoulder.

I tried to picture Gabby at my house. All I could see was my parents being nosy, watching our every move while they eavesdropped on our conversation. It wasn't exactly the break I needed.

"It wasn't a weird suggestion. I promise," I said, reaching across the table to tug on her lumpy sleeve. "You're right. I do need a break. Mind if we meet at your dad's warehouse again? It'll have to be after practice, so anytime after six."

Mama had promised that I could use the car for school, and this technically was for school. It was the perfect opportunity to get from under my folks' watchful gaze.

"Sure." She sighed, then looked me squarely in the eyes, a smile tugging at her lips. "What day works for you?"

We spent the whole lunch hour together, then walked to English class, our arms occasionally brushing against each other. The closeness felt natural, even though Gabby shied away every time it happened. When she slid into her seat in the classroom, she kept looking across the aisle with her mouth turned up in a smirk, and I think it had something to do with our plans to hang out later.

Sure, I wished it was more of a real date—something normal like showing up at a party together or going to the movies. And I wasn't super thrilled about finishing a paper on the many forms of racism in Baldwin's *If Beale Street Could Talk*. I was already drowning in racism. But I'd suck it up if it meant acing our project and spending more time with Gabby.

Ms. J stood in front of the class, her shoulders confidently squared, as she clapped her hands.

"As a reminder, your 'Olaf' papers are due next week—

not this Friday but next—and your *Beale Street* team project is due on October 21." She clasped her hands. "Now is an opportune time to examine the vilification of unarmed Black men, the incarceration of them, and the curtailment of their futures and potential. If you can't stand for that…then take a knee and pray on it."

I was certain I saw her wink in my direction. It warmed my heart but made me nervous at the same time. I squirmed in my seat. Was that a reference to what I'd done Friday night?

Ms. J moved swiftly to the next subject, picking up her lesson plan from her desk. She recited the first few lines of one of our readings, "Still I Rise" by Maya Angelou, while barely looking at the lines on the page.

"You may trod me in the very dirt
But still, like dust, I'll rise."

"Who is Angelou implicating here?" Ms. J held her arms open as she scanned the class for a volunteer. "Who is she talking about?"

"Haters," I mumbled under my breath. Ms. J heard it, earning me a raised eyebrow.

"That's a good start, Russell. Can anyone be more specific?" She looked at Gabby.

"She's talking to people in privilege. People in power."

"Ahhh, the *powers that be*. My absolute favorite." Laughter rippled through the room. We all knew the struggles Ms. J had with the school board regarding her curriculum. She tapped her pages with the palm of her hand. "And yet she draws her power from within, despite what?"

"Despite people wanting to see her fail," Gabby said before anyone else could answer.

"Raise your hand." Ms. J smiled proudly at Gabby. "But yes, I think you're onto something. Listen to this."

She paced the room, her eyes fixed to the page as she read the next stanza. She paused, taking a deep breath before looking at the class.

"The writer is describing the two worlds she lives in. One is a power dynamic she cannot control. It's designed to make her feel small. The other reality is hers by right. It's her pursuit of liberty and happiness."

Ms. J walked the aisle, likely checking for our markings in the margins. One of the new transfer students sitting a few rows over didn't have a packet on his desk. Ms. J frowned at the naked tabletop.

"Unless you have the excerpt memorized, Michael, you'll need to get out your packet."

"I don't have it," he said, his cheeks reddening.

"Where is it?" She folded her arms. "Your locker?"

"It's—" He looked down at his lap. "My parents said I didn't have to read it. Said it was garbage."

Ms. J walked behind her desk and sat in her chair. It was unusual to see her seated. She preferred to roam through the aisles or sit on top of her desk, right on the edge where she could hop off at any time. She'd told us that separating herself from her students didn't feel right, that it hindered engagement and she wanted to be as close to us as possible. But not this time. She slouched in her chair, sinking to her elbows.

A kid next to me pulled out his phone to record the scene, but Ms. J was fuming so much she didn't seem to notice.

"Garbage…" She said it over and over again, as if trying to make sense of it. Finally she scoffed in disbelief. "So you—what? Threw away the words of Maya Angelou?"

"Yes, ma'am." Michael nodded, still avoiding her eye contact. "They think—"

"Oh, they *think*?" She slapped the desk, like she was shocked to hear thought had gone into this nonsense.

"They think that kind of stuff riles people up."

"Art *should* rouse the senses," she said, raising her voice a few octaves. "Poetry *should* pierce your soul. It should stick with you after you read it."

"Yeah, but…" Michael squirmed in his seat. "We've been reading a lot about anti-war, civil rights, and revolution. It's like you got some political agenda."

"Would you have tossed Wordsworth in the trash?" She held up a hand before he had time to answer. "Don't answer that."

She got up and paced in front of her desk, her nostrils flaring. Gabby looked across the aisle and mouthed, *This is bad.*

"Those readings were approved, as is everything I hand you these days. I'm so sick of my curriculum being dictated by a bunch of small-minded folks who don't know anything about culture." She scowled at Michael, who had slouched beneath his desk as far as he could. Her outburst was directed at him, but I got the sense that it was about so much more. She looked to the clock on the wall. "Class dismissed."

"But—" Gabby opened her mouth, then closed it again, clearly struggling to find a response. I guessed she was going to mention that we still had twenty minutes before the bell rang, but in a rare act of censorship, she kept her opinion to herself.

I waited for my classmates to trickle out before I approached Ms. J, who stood on the far side of the room, her hands on her hips. She heard my footsteps behind her and whipped around.

"Oh, it's you." She looked away, her eyes dewing with tears. I imagined her job was a thankless one. Teaching the same lecture, several times a day, hoping to get through to us on a deeper level than what Instagram offered—it must be frustrating.

She slumped against the windowsill and stood there, cradling her head in her hands. "I'm sorry y'all had to see that. I rarely lose my temper like that."

"I just wanted to say that I enjoyed the reading. It really helped me." As with many of Ms. J's assignments, it had snuck up on me at just the right time. I'd read Angelou's poems in bed last night, feeling a kinship with her struggle. That same empathy extended to Ms. J. "I also wanted to say that…well, I know *exactly* how you feel right now."

"I bet you do." She broke out in a genuine smile and stood up straighter. "If it's any consolation, I'm really proud of you. I bet you inspired a lot of people last week."

"I don't know…" I shook my head, that kernel of doubt growing larger in my mind.

"Oh, yeah." She pressed her lips together, nodded earnestly. "I know it."

In a lot of ways, Ms. J had as much to lose as I did. If kids talked too loudly about what happened in class today, she would likely be disciplined for her outburst. And given that her curriculum had already been rebuked by the school board, she was already on shaky footing with her job. But she still took a principled stance in the midst of all that risk.

"Do you ever regret being so vocal?" I asked.

"Sometimes," she admitted, her smile faltering. "But regrets are kind of pointless, don't you think?"

I shrugged.

"It's okay to question your motives and to review your actions, Rus. You *should* do those things." She leaned forward, her signature grin returning. "But sometimes you have to trust your gut and not look back. That's how I try to live my life. I invite you to do the same."

15

Crouching, I waited for the whistle. When it sounded, my muscles hitched and I darted right, setting the edge, just like Coach had asked. I held my hands up, waiting to catch Ricky's pass. The football soared several feet over my head, then disappeared underneath the bleachers, out of bounds.

"Y'all are playing like a bunch of gosh darn amateurs! This ain't peewee football." Coach tooted his whistle, slapping the clipboard on his side. He wound his hand in a circle. "Again!"

My legs felt like lead as I walked back. I'd lost count of how many times we'd run this play—must have been at least a dozen. Each time Ricky overshot his mark, Coach's face got more and more purple. He wasn't a patient man on a good day. And ever since Marion got kicked off the team and I took a knee, there weren't a lot of good days.

"When I'm finished with y'all," Coach Fontenot said, straightening his visor, "you're going to *wish* the league had chosen to discipline you instead of me. I said run the dang play again."

He said it to sound tough, but I knew that deep down, Coach was relieved the league had chosen not to pursue disciplinary action against me. He couldn't afford to lose another player.

Of course, he was still plenty sore about Friday's fiasco and the ensuing loss. My decision to protest during the anthem had left him reeling.

Because Mama had insisted, I'd submitted a lukewarm apology to the league. I didn't want them to sanction the team or smack me with disciplinary action. The apology was short and to the point.

"I'm sorry if my actions distracted from the game."

It wasn't exactly a lie. I was sorry for the effect I'd had on my team. But I had been very careful not to admit any wrongdoing. I hadn't done anything wrong. Ms. J was right. Sometimes you have to trust your gut and not look back.

Coach hadn't been impressed. He'd wanted me to go all in—tell the league I *deeply regretted my actions*. But to our relief, it had worked.

I walked to the back of the formation, deep in the pocket where Ricky stood. Sweat pooled around his tired eyes, the salt making them red and irritated. His chest rose and fell quickly as the pressure to fill Marion's shoes mounted.

"Before you call for the snap, be sure to call the play again." I wiped my neck with my gloved hand and pointed to Karim, who was inspecting his new tattoo instead of getting ready to set the play. "Make sure Karim actually sees you, because if he doesn't, that's when he opens up a hole, and you get flushed out the pocket. And swivel your stance with your waist as much as you can. You don't need to walk around too much—that wastes time."

"Thanks, Rus." Ricky grabbed my shoulder pads and tugged. "I'm trying, man. I swear."

"You can do this." I clapped my hands, grabbing my teammates' attention as I found my spot on the right side, hoping I'd sounded convincing. I'd played with Marion for years, watched him refine his craft with every coach and every opposing team. He'd be the first to tell you he wasn't the best quarterback out there—that he really had to work for his spot on the field—but that was horseshit and he knew it. Hell, everyone knew it. Marion was a phenom with a football. Ricky had a long way to go if he wanted to catch up.

I lowered to a squat, my fingertips brushing the freshly mowed grass. At the whistle I was off like a flash. The throw was high, but I managed to catch it. I took off toward the goal line, hoping this would end Coach Fontenot's endless practice session.

Darrell's long legs chomped at the yard lines as he closed in on me. He managed to grab my jersey at the torso, but I shoved him off, making him tumble onto the green. When I made it to the end zone, I slammed the ball to the ground and bent over my knees.

"Finally!" Coach jumped up and down. "Was that so hard?"

A cramp pinched my side as I walked back to the center of the field. I needed water or electrolytes—something to keep my muscles from seizing up. Darrell was catching his breath on the ground, right where he'd fallen. I held my hand out to pull him up, but he brushed it aside.

"You've helped enough." Darrell scrambled to his feet, losing his balance slightly.

It was normal to play rough in a practice. In fact, it was our duty to rough each other up. Coach Fontenot said it was better for us to feel the full wave of brute force in daily practices than experience it for the first time on game day. It made us stronger, tougher. But I couldn't help but wonder if Darrell had taken my push differently. His scowl made me think so.

Coach blared his whistle. "Line up and give me twenty touch 'n' turns."

My heart sank. Touch 'n' turns was a hard drill, requiring us to sprint from one end zone to another and then back again, over and over until we could barely breathe. Coach said it was to test and fortify our endurance, but we knew what it was.

Punishment.

"I've made my thoughts known, but let me reiterate." Coach Fontenot cupped his mouth, following our progression as we ran the field. "We are here to play *football*. Nothing else! Now, keep working off Friday's sorry-ass game!"

I gripped my side to squelch the cramp, running as fast as I could under the circumstances. I was a sloth masquerading in a uniform, trudging through every yard like it was harder than the one before. My brothers felt the same, no doubt. Their feet dragged as we jogged the field, heads bowed as they huffed through the drudgery.

Ms. Duval had set up a table at the far end zone with water bottles and plastic cups filled with Gatorade. When Coach had his back turned, I stopped and squirted a sports bottle of water into my mouth, closing my eyes as I guzzled as much as I could between panting. Darrell and a few players stopped to do the same.

"Y'all can thank Rus for this," Darrell said in a breathy groan. "Thank him for bringing this on us."

I didn't do him the disservice of contradicting him. This was payback for my kneeling. Payback for Marion getting kicked off the team. Payback for Ricky not being good enough.

"Thanks, Rus." Karim jogged breathlessly past me, water dripping onto his jersey.

"Yeah, thank you, Rus," Bobby said as he lifted his uniform to wipe his face.

I'd never felt more like an outsider in my own world as players rounded the water table and thanked me for the pain and shame I'd brought upon them.

It was like that all week. Extra-long practices coupled with extra-long drills. By midweek, my teammates and I were exhausted. If the purpose of those drills was to make us stronger in the face of the opposition, we had been welded into ironclad steel.

But I was flailing in my academic life. I couldn't keep up. There were only so many hours in the day, and getting home after seven o'clock didn't leave enough time for homework and sleep.

On Thursday, after another grueling practice, I knocked on the Dupre warehouse door, unprepared to dive into my Baldwin project with Gabby.

"Come in!" she yelled from the other side of the glass.

I entered and walked to the picnic table behind the packing crates. My tired legs wobbled as I scooted onto the bench.

"You look tired," Gabby said, scooting her papers aside to make room for me.

"I am *beyond* tired." I struggled to keep my eyes open, to give Gabby the attention she deserved, but it was hard. My body had been moving nonstop since this morning. Now that I was seated, my muscles relaxed, making me hunch over my backpack. I resisted the urge to use it as a pillow.

Gabby, on the other hand, looked refreshed. Her cheeks were flushed as she smiled at me, her eyes bright behind her tortoiseshell glasses. "You look nice."

"Really?" She raised her eyebrows, her mouth open. She looked surprised yet flattered. "It's officially ugly sweater season." Gabby squealed with glee as she pushed out of her seat. She pulled her sweater taut so that I could see every detail. It featured a busy Halloween motif with a haunted house, a full moon, and a jack-o'-lantern. Her sleeve had a felt bat sewn onto the shoulder. It popped off the sweater as if to say *BOO!*

It was breathtaking in a weirdly cute way.

"My mom just sent it to me. She lives near this funky thrift shop in South Beach and…wow, right?"

Her enthusiasm was infectious, and I couldn't help but laugh along with her. But as soon as I opened my mouth, a yawn slipped out.

"Sorry." I shook my head, trying to stave off the exhaustion that kept creeping in, then rifled through my backpack. I brought out the Tupperware container she'd lent me during lunch the other day. "Before I forget, I wanted to give this back to you."

"Thanks." She set it on the bench beside her. "I thought we could combine our written portions for the presentation. I've written the introduction and the synopsis of *Beale Street.* Can I see your portion?"

I shut my eyes, inwardly cussing at my lack of preparedness.

"Mine is…rough." I pulled out my notebook, eyeing Gabby's printed pages. There were no scratch-outs, no bullet points like my paper. Hers looked like a complete and polished draft. Reluctantly, I handed her my draft as I skimmed through hers. It was solid—definitely better than mine.

"Rus, this is due in a few weeks." She exhaled as her gaze darted across my pages. She looked at me over the rim of her glasses, her lips pursing. "If you weren't ready to meet, you could have just told me."

"I did come ready to work. Look, I even brought printouts." I flipped to the folder in the back of my binder and pulled out a stack of paper. "They're from the color printer—the one the librarian never lets anyone use."

"Now we're talking." She pushed my notebook aside and sorted the pages between pictures of Baldwin, images from the movie, and quotes from the book. "I've tried begging the librarian to let me use color, but she never budges."

"The perks of being a football player." I smiled, but after a moment, my lips faltered and turned downward. I used to love the game and all the status that came with it. Now it seemed like a burden. Football was kicking my ass right now.

"Sometimes I wish I could call in sick, you know? Take a break from it all for just one week."

"Can't you? I mean, you play against Jasper High tomorrow night, and then you play against Belson, Alexandria, and then Cary before your rematch with Westmond during the bye week."

"Whoa." My eyebrows shot up at the sound of her game roster knowledge. She had my attention. "Look who's keeping track of football."

"I'm not." She straightened in her seat, tucking her curls behind her ear. "I hear stuff from Clay, that's all."

I shook my head. Gabby couldn't fool me with that hardened facade. She might not have cared about football, but she cared about me… I was sure of it.

"Stop looking at me like that." She squinted at her page, making sure she glided her scissors precisely along the outline of James Baldwin's face on one of the printouts. She was avoiding eye contact, and that made me want to smile even more.

Suddenly, I found a second wind.

"Okay, fine." She dropped her scissors on the table, a reluctant grin sweeping across her face. "So, maybe I am following the games a little closer this season."

"That's what I thought."

"To be honest…" She searched my face for a moment. "I can *see* the stress in your eyes. You need a break. A *real* one. Our project is due in two weeks, and it's our midterm grade. Do you *promise* to finish your draft of the presentation by next week?"

"I swear I'll have it done."

"Okay, then. I trust you. Now for that break." She swung her legs over her bench and hopped up, then beckoned for me to follow her as she crossed the room. She shoved the warehouse door open and yelled over her shoulder, "You coming?"

"Wait up," I said, scurrying to my feet. My sneakers squeaked across the concrete floors as I scrambled after her. When I got outside, Gabby was already walking down the dirt road that bisected her father's fields. "Where are you going?"

"Here is as good a place as any." She panted, her nostrils flaring as she looked out onto the rows of corn. "Scream at the top of your lungs."

"What?" I scrunched up my face, shaking my head. "I'm not gonna yell. Your dad might hear me."

"Oh, he's used to it." She grinned widely. She stepped into one of the rows and sank to the ground, crossing her legs. She patted the space across from her, encouraging me to sit on the dirt. "I used to come out here all the time when my parents got divorced and I had *all* the feels. I went to the back fields and screamed it all out. My dad even joined me a couple times. And you know what? It helps."

"You're crazy," I said, my heart rate quickening. Ripping the top off my anger and frustration was against my nature. My folks, the team—they were all telling me to fall back, to keep my mouth shut. But not Gabby. She was encouraging me in a way no one else had. She wanted me to speak up more—to literally scream at the top of my lungs.

I took a step closer to her and to the edge of the field.

"You know you wanna try it." Her eyes narrowed, a challenge. When I didn't budge, she threw her head back and howled into the setting sun. "GAHHHHHHH!"

A surge of adrenaline rushed through my veins as I watched her scream into the void. I wanted to feel that release.

"AHHHHHHHHH!" I emptied my lungs until my voice cracked. I inhaled deeply and cupped my hands over my mouth. "FUUUUUUUUUCK!"

"That's the spirit. Feels great, right?" Gabby giggled into both hands.

We roared into the wind until the sun dipped below the horizon and our voices gave out.

16

I shut the front door and rounded the driveway, where Pops and Marion were tinkering with my car. When Marion turned the key in the ignition, the Honda wheezed, coughing and spasming while he pumped the gas. Pops leaned over the open hood, one hand on his hip while he tried to locate the source of the sound.

I checked the time on my phone. I had thirty minutes to get back to the high school before the game bus departed for Jasper. It was a short half hour drive to their stadium, but Coach liked for us to arrive together, as a team.

After a week of grueling practices, we were ready to erase our shellacking against Shreveport. We had no choice but to win against Jasper tonight. We *had* to. Otherwise, our chances of making the playoffs were in jeopardy.

"That doesn't sound good." I leaned over Pops just as Marion revved the engine again. The Honda protested with another *whirr*.

Since Mr. Dupre had fixed my battery cables, like the aging senior it was, the Civic had developed more health complaints.

It hiccupped and sputtered to a stall, sounding more ominous than ever. Pops brushed his hands on his pants, then held one hand up for Marion to stop.

"Looks like it's the alternator." Pops wiped his brow with his sleeve.

Marion crawled from behind the steering wheel and gave me a shake of his head. "That's exactly what we didn't hope for." He joined Pops near the hood and gestured for me to take a look. "Probably gonna be three or four hundred dollars to replace."

Pops spat on the gravel and rubbed his stubble. "Lemme check one more thing."

"I've gotta get to the stadium some kinda way." I studied the smoking hood, feeling nervous. "Can I take your truck?"

Pops grunted as he dove headfirst into the Civic, his body contorting to follow the wires deep into the bowels of the car. He was still not talking to me. How long was this going to last?

"Or we can ride together? You know, instead of y'all catching a ride with Karim's mama later." My voice thickened, but I coughed it away. "You're coming tonight, right?"

Pops grabbed the sides of the hood and pushed himself up, his lips pursed, eyes averted. "We've got plenty of work to do over here." He looked at Marion instead of me, as if searching for corroboration—for an excuse to not attend the game.

"What about you?" I asked, afraid to look Marion in the eye. But I held my chin up, even though I wanted to bury my head in my hands. "You coming?"

"Nah." He shook his head and looked at his phone, scrolling through his social media feed, seeming more interested in other people's lives than ours.

I slumped. Marion was a part of the team. Even though he wasn't suiting up with the rest of us, he should be there. Maybe part of my question was also selfish. His presence would bring unity to the team—something I'd been unable to accomplish this past week. Marion would be able to squelch some of the discord Darrell had sown.

There were two team captains for a reason. Flying solo during this shitstorm was beyond my abilities. But my co-captain had made up his mind, and I felt the chill of isolation like I never had before. I tightened my hold on my duffel bag and stormed off in the direction of Pops's truck. I didn't have keys, didn't have faith. But I couldn't look at them anymore.

"Rus, wait up." Marion called after me.

"For what? You to give up? Nah, I'm straight." I blinked toward the sky, breathing in as much fresh air as I could. It stilled my nerves, if only for a second. "The league said you couldn't suit up. Not that you couldn't come to the stadium and support your team."

"I can't sit on the sidelines." He put his hands on his hips, shaking his head. "You know how hard that is."

I knew all too well. And even though Coach said he'd play me tonight, there was no guarantee that would happen. If yesterday's drills were any indication of his mindset, Coach was *still* angry at me for kneeling.

I needed Marion's help. Couldn't he see that? Or was he too busy gearing up for a life without football, one where he would put on a different kind of uniform and do manual labor under Pops's tutelage? Plumbing was a decent profession, one that put food on the table and a roof over our heads. But Marion had so much talent as a quarterback. How could I drill that into him?

"You said you would fight," I said, remembering the night Marion came home from jail, bloody and battered. I hadn't conjured that moment since it happened. I knew it was painful for Marion to look back on that day—the night *everything* turned upside down for him. For all of us. But I didn't know how else to get through to him.

"I know what I said."

"So then, *fight*. Show up tonight. The team needs you." Marion and I were the glue that held the brotherhood together. Without him, the team was splitting apart. There was no cohesion.

Marion nodded as he continued to scroll through his phone.

I waved my hand in front of his screen. "Hello? Are you listening?" I frowned. This was important.

"Holy shit." Marion held his screen closer to his face. "Look what Aysha just DM'd me."

"Aysha?" I raised my eyebrows, startled. "You two talk?"

"It's not like that." Marion bit his lip, looking uncomfortable. He'd always admired Aysha, but he'd never chat her up without telling me.

Would he?

"Before you pop off, take a look at this." He shoved his phone into my hands. "One of her friends posted a Latergram of the Westmond game. This video is different. *Look*."

The shaky video was of someone filming their friends, then excitedly panning the field...to capture the beginning of Marion's argument with Brad. You could see Brad slap

Marion's hand away, see him push us to the ground. I'd yet to see a camera shot of the beginning of the fight when my face hit the ground, busting my lip. But from this angle, you could clearly see me chomp the turf—the moment Brad drew first blood. Marion pushed him next. And that's when Brad grabbed his helmet to steady him enough so that when his knee snapped up, it hit him squarely in the gut. I covered my mouth with my hand.

Holy shit! He's saved!

"They'll have to drop the charges now!" I bounced on the balls of my feet, ecstatic.

"I can't believe this! I'm sending it to my lawyer." Marion's fingers flew across his screen as his fingers typed rapidly. When he looked up, he had a twinkle in his eyes. "I might just be able to play the tail end of the season."

"That's great, Marion! We need you. Seriously, we're not going to make it to the playoffs with Ricky." As much as I liked our second-string replacement, he did not bring out the best in me. "You *have* to come to the game tonight. We can share the good news with the team."

"I don't know." The lightness left his eyes. "Coach can't let me ride on the bus. Remember, I'm off the team until the charges are lifted."

I nodded and looked behind me. Pops was wiping his hands on an oil-stained rag as he walked toward us. He slung the cloth over his shoulder, then handed me the keys to his truck.

"This is a hard fix. Go on and take my truck." He looked me in the eye for the first time all week. "This is only for tonight's game. And I don't want to see any new scratches or dents when you bring it back."

Marion's gaze moved to the small dent on the driver's side door. I shook my head at him, a warning not to bring it up. Pops's head would explode—just when we were *so* close to getting our lives back on track.

Shut up, dude.

He looked away, hiding his smile. Pops didn't know a thing about the vandalism, and I wanted to keep it that way. We'd washed the mess away and scraped the word *garbage* off the back window, but the pain still lingered. Brad had done a lot of damage to us in the past few weeks.

Soon, Brad would get what was coming for him. With the emergence of new video evidence showing him as the aggressor, he was going to be in hot water, and Marion would be in the clear.

For the first time in weeks, I felt my jaw muscles unclench.

"Thanks, Pops. We'll bring it back in one piece."

"You decided to go?" Pops raised his eyebrow at Marion.

"Yeah." Marion nodded slowly. He slapped my shoulder, then clasped it tightly. "Yeah, I'll go."

17

Darrell peered at my phone screen while he rewatched the video of the fight. He brought his fist to his mouth and winced when Brad slugged Marion in the face. Terrance leaned over the back of his seat and snatched the phone out of Darrell's hands. He pressed Play, leaning closer to Karim so they could watch it together.

"So, they're gonna drop the charges?" he mumbled, looking up from the video.

"They have to," I said, holding my hand out for my phone. I didn't want the battery to die. I'd need to check back with Marion after the game to get a ride home. "Does that look like disorderly conduct and assault?"

"Hell, nah. And I don't see him resisting arrest neither." Karim turned around to wave at Marion through the back window. I turned in my seat as well and looked at Marion, driving Pops's truck, trailing the bus as we made the short trek to Jasper.

"See? The whole kneeling thing wasn't even necessary." Darrell's eyes tightened as he grinned at me, an accusation still lingering behind his playfulness. "He'll be back on the field by our next home game."

"Let's hope so." I smiled, too excited about the prospect of Marion playing with us on our home turf next week to let Darrell get under my skin. "But I stand by the knee."

"Forget you, man." Darrell waved a hand at me, sinking back into his seat.

We still didn't see eye to eye on this.

Coach wobbled in the aisle, his eyes hooded as he ran his gaze around the school bus. His hefty figure swayed as our thirty-minute bus ride ended and we pulled into Jasper's stadium. He chewed a wad of gum as his nails dug into the seat's green leather. I could see the pulse throbbing in his neck. This was our first game since I'd taken a knee and ripped the cap off Shreveport's stadium. Anticipation laced with apprehension was in the air.

As we rounded the south end of the stadium, right near the concession stands, we caught sight of a bevy of reporters gathered near the entrance. Coach cussed under his breath.

"I guess this is going to be the new norm." He straightened his baseball cap and set his jaw tight. "All right, remember what I told y'all. Head straight to the locker rooms. You don't need to talk to them."

His eyes narrowed, and he looked at me as if his message was meant specifically for me.

I bristled. Still, Marion's new surveillance video had soothed my nerves, helping me hold my tongue. A clear and complete view of the fight from start to finish would speak *volumes* to the prosecutor. It was only a matter of time before the charges against Marion were dropped and he was back on the field. That made me smile.

Marion turned into the visitor lot, away from the pool of reporters along the side of the stadium. At least he'd avoid the minefield. My smile grew wider.

The bus screeched to a halt. Coach Fontenot grabbed his clipboard from the first row, then gave the driver the nod to open the doors.

"Don't let this zoo rattle you," he said over his shoulder as he stepped down the stairs.

As soon as the doors opened, a barrage of questions and camera flashes filled the bus. Coach swatted them away. He mumbled "Git!" as he charted a path for us through the crowd. They only circled tighter around him.

I tried to follow Coach, but the reporters closed in around me too. I squinted as camera flashes exploded. Karim grumbled behind me about wanting to get a move on, but I think he was secretly grateful not to be in the limelight. Coach muscled his way back to our cluster in front of the bus doors.

"Coach Fontenot, are you losing control of your team?" A reporter from KILA ABC 11 held a microphone above the heads of her colleagues.

"No, ma'am." Coach rubbed his short hair, a cocky grin on his face. Sure, Coach had told us we didn't have to talk to reporters, but he obviously wanted to set the record straight on his coaching abilities. "We've issued a full apology for last week's incident. Now, we just came to play some ball."

"Do you condone kneeling? What are your thoughts on the NFL's policy on this issue?" another reporter yelled.

"I have nothing more to say, except that we love our country, and nobody meant to disrespect the flag." He shook his head.

"Will you be looking to take a knee today, Russell Boudreaux?" The Channel 11 reporter pointed her microphone over Coach's shoulder toward me.

Cameras pivoted upward, along with dozens of eyes and microphones. Coach bit the side of his cheek. I stammered, warring between speaking out against the blatant racism that existed in our towns and keeping my mouth shut in the interest of the team. Coach's glare seared into me, and my teammates behind me fidgeted nervously. Feeling trapped, I shut my mouth and looked away from the cameras.

"Like I said. We are confident that justice will be done for our suspended player." He held a hand up. "We just came to play ball. And nothing else. Excuse us." He shimmied past the masses, making an avenue wide enough for us to follow him.

Confident that justice will be done.

Coach's words struck me, but I didn't know why. They bounced around in my head through the press swarm, all the way to my cubby in the guest locker room. It took me a long time to realize why his words stuck with me. Did I have any confidence in the criminal justice system?

Absolutely not.

Marion still couldn't play. The prosecutor had overwhelming evidence to exonerate him, and I was more hopeful than ever. But the criminal justice system still had its hooks in an innocent Black man. That was far from justice.

Those hooks could be there for *years*, through trials and probation. I didn't understand why Coach was so oblivious to the enduring trauma of police brutality—he was a Black man. Maybe he was so broken down by the system that he'd lost the will to fight for what was right.

And what about all the other Marions out there—the ones without video evidence or a good lawyer? The ones who ended up in jail or worse—dead in the streets. Where was their justice?

If this was justice, then maybe I didn't understand the meaning of "liberty and justice for all." I suited up in silence, determined to take a knee and continue speaking out for all of us who were in danger of the same fate as Marion.

"This is your moment, y'all." Coach pointed to the locker room door. It was almost time to run through the tunnel and line up on our sideline. He pointed that finger at his chest. "It's not up to me. I ain't gonna win this game. Y'all will. Understood?"

"Yes, Coach."

"I said, y'all are gonna go out there and win!" Coach shouted, sweat dripping from his temples. "And I mean win *big*. Tick the scoreboard sky-high and take no prisoners!"

The team erupted, the baritone of deep cheers reverberating off the metal lockers. Sufficiently pumped up, we grabbed our helmets and started jogging down the stadium tunnel. I followed, but Coach sidestepped me, blocking the exit.

"Russell, let me talk to you," he said from the threshold of the locker room. He looked over his shoulder, waiting for the stragglers to be out of earshot before turning back to look at me.

I pressed a palm against my chest, hoping that the pressure would slow my heart rate. His tone sounded serious. I hoped he wasn't going to renege on his promise to let me play tonight.

"I spoke with Jim Regan." He leaned forward with a knowing look. "You know, from Clemson. He called this morning."

And then my heart *really* started hammering. Clemson University had one of the greatest football programs in the nation. They'd won every game they played last year, and with the way they were playing this year, they'd do it again.

"Head Coach Jim Regan?" I asked, but I didn't need to. I knew *exactly* who he was. And if the head coach had taken the time to call our tiny football program to ask about *me*, it could mean only one thing—a scholarship.

"He had a lot of interest in our program, particularly with regards to you." He jabbed a finger into my shoulder pads, chuckling under his breath. He slapped the doorframe. "What did I always tell you? You've always had a rare talent at this game."

"Clemson wants *me*?" I gripped the edge of the nearest locker to steady my balance. Clemson was the reigning NCAA football champion. Clemson was the *dream*. "Did he really say that?"

Coach Fontenot erred on the side of wishful thinking when it came to his recruitment process. A form letter became a lifeline, assured interest from a top school. He'd make it a point to tell the whole team that the college in question was *definitely* interested in scouting us. But they weren't—not *really*. We hardly ever had recruiters come to our games or follow up with us.

Needless to say, I was suspicious of Coach's recruiting call with Jim Regan.

All of my insecurities about the team record this season flared up. We were out our MVP, playing a second-string quarterback, had one loss under our belt, bad press in part because of me, and serious team cohesion problems. A top-five school was unlikely to be sniffing around a small-town team like Jackson, especially with all of *that* going on.

But Coach's face remained steady, firm in his conviction. This was the real deal.

Clemson was actually interested in me.

"Regan said he watched your tape three times, and he's impressed." Coach nodded proudly. Slipping his thumbs in his belt loops, he rocked back and forth on his heels. "He'll be in the stands at the end of next month, and he's coming here to watch you play."

"That's the rematch against Westmond." I swallowed hard, wishing Regan was coming for a different game. Westmond was our toughest competition. I hoped Marion would be back on the team, so I could impress the recruiter.

"That's right. And if you keep playing like you've been playing, you're set."

I'm set?

I stood there, unmoving except for my heaving breaths. I let the news sink in, trying to accept this new reality. If I finished the season strong—like I did every year—the prize at the end of the tunnel would be a Division 1 scholarship to the best football program in the country.

I'm set! This is what I've been working toward!

Coach held his meaty hand out, and I took it, shaking it firmly as he beamed at me. His eyes watered, and I felt mine tearing up too. The only thing missing was my family. My parents would be thrilled—this was the realization of an impossible dream. And Marion—what would he think?

I couldn't have caught Clemson's attention without an equally talented counterpart. I didn't have to look at my highlight reel to know that 90 percent of the balls I'd run were because of Marion's phenomenal aim. If a Division 1 scholarship was truly within my grasp, Marion should be getting one too.

My hand faltered, my grip slackening. I wasn't prepared to claim victory until both of us could. I scrunched my nose and looked at the empty surroundings. I should be on the field with my team.

Something felt *off*. Coach could have given me this news earlier. Why was he telling me now, right before the game?

The notes of the anthem blared down the concrete tunnel. I released Coach's hand, understanding. He pursed his lips unapologetically.

"I couldn't let you do it. Not with Clemson sniffing around." He leaned forward, so close I could see his pulse thump through his veiny forehead. "I couldn't let you kneel."

18

Heat waves bounced off the asphalt of Calumet Street, blurring the street lines as they wafted upward. I stood across the street from Marion, too distracted to throw the ball back to him. I had mixed feelings about my conversation with Coach Fontenot, and it was all I could think about. Marion clapped his hands, snapping my attention back to our makeshift practice. I lifted the ball to my chest then sent it flying across the lawn.

"Of course, I'm grateful for the opportunity to showcase in front of Regan. I mean, that's big-league shit." I yelled across the road at Marion, who stood below the porch steps—so close to Mama's flower bed that if I'd thrown the football harder, he might have fallen into it. "But he had no right keeping me cooped up in the locker room during the anthem."

"I don't know, Rus." Marion pawed the football in his hands, shaking his head. "He's just looking out for you."

"But it's the way he told me." I was still ticked off.

It had been smart, dangling Clemson in front of my face. I'd give him that. And Coach had wasted no time clueing

Pops in. The two of them were prematurely patting them-selves on the back. I could see it in the bounce in his step—Pops felt vindicated. He'd squeezed my shoulder and gruffly apologized for missing the game. The conditional strings of love were back in their rightful position. I was redeemed in his eyes.

It made me even more annoyed.

I looked over Marion's shoulder at Pops, who had loudly cleared his throat. His brow furrowed as he tinkered with a suction motor outside the shed, but I knew he was only pretending to work. When he thought I wasn't looking, he stopped and watched our makeshift practice. But I was a sea-soned football player, trained to have eyes in every direction as I covered the field. I saw him.

"Yo, dude." Marion cupped his hands around his mouth, his hips cocked to one side. "Do you want to practice or not? I thought you were going to help me get back in shape."

"Sorry," I said, and it wasn't just an apology for being a crappy throwing partner. It was also an apology for talking to Marion about the Clemson recruitment. I was starting to feel like an asshole for even bringing it up again—especially since Marion was still suspended. "Any word from your law-yer about the video?"

"He sent the newest video to the prosecutor. Now we wait for him to do the right thing." He shrugged.

"Gimme one down there." I pointed down the street, hop-ing to catch a running pass.

My tennis shoes chomped at the pavement as I ran down the hot asphalt, anticipating a long pass from Marion. The ball whizzed to the right, but it fell short and dipped to the grass long before reaching the road. It wobbled and came to a halt near the sidewalk.

"Damn it." I cussed under my breath as I leaned against my knees, hands sweating, slipping against my skin. I winced, flashing back to the game last night. Ricky couldn't make the accurate throws Marion could. And when he couldn't make the passes, I couldn't do my job. I wished Marion was back on the team, but now *his* throws were faltering too.

"I'll get it on the next one." Marion slumped against the porch railing, squirting his water bottle into his mouth. "But it would help if you just *chilled*. Y'all won the game last night. Even Ricky did all right. And Coach held you back to tell you some seriously great news. No harm done, right?"

"I guess." I wiped my forehead with the back of my hand and stepped onto the neighbor's grass to allow a car to pass. Maybe it was time to let the kneeling thing go.

I ran across the front lawn and down the sidewalk before I threw the football at him. Marion had barely straightened out of his slouch, but he easily caught it. Even on his worst day, he was decent with a football.

We'd done drills out here for as long as I could remember—since we were kids. That was how we'd become so attuned to each other's playing style. I *needed* Marion to slip into his familiar groove. He flicked his head, signaling me to run right.

The ball soared, spinning tightly, and landed it my outstretched hands—a perfect pass.

"That's what I'm talking about!" Marion pumped his fist in the air. He kissed his fist then pointed to the sky, as if sending God a little prayer. He waved his fingers, asking for the ball again. "Mark my words, Rus. I'll be back on the field in no time. And we're going to crush it."

I threw the ball, wanting to believe him, praying that the prosecutor would do the right thing and fast. Our Westmond rematch was in two weeks, and I needed Marion in the game.

The screen door snapped shut on my heels as I carted the trash to the bin. I slung it over my back, feeling the elastic band dig into my shoulder, then breathed in the muggy night air. I was grateful to have an excuse to come outside, even if it was to take out the garbage. Our tiny house made for tight quarters, and it didn't seem big enough to hold the chill between me and Marion *and* my parents.

Things were supposed to get back to normal.

A clank came from the porch, and I looked up. Pops was sitting on the far end with a glass of amber liquid perched on the table next to him. For a moment, he held my gaze, and I froze. I'd gotten used to Pops not making eye contact with me, but that had changed since the Clemson news. He continued watching me, even as he drew his glass to his lips.

Breaking his gaze, I shoved the trash bag into the black garbage can and shuffled back to the front door. I kept my head down as I took the stairs two at a time, looking at my shoelaces instead of the complicated eyes of my dad.

"Son, I want to talk to you," he said, and cleared his throat. He leaned forward, reaching behind him to fish something out of his back pocket. When he pulled it out, he had my car keys in his hand. "Managed to fix up that alternator. The car should start now."

"Thanks." I edged closer, wondering why he was telling

me this. I was in a suspicious state of mind, unable to trust anyone, particularly Coach and Pops. "I can't really use the car. You know, because I'm grounded."

"Well, I don't know about that." He leaned back in his chair, his bottom lip jutting out as he looked to the rafters. "Spoke to Fontenot last night. So… Clemson? They've thrown their hat in."

"Yes, sir. Marion and I will practice up. Hopefully he'll be back on the team when Regan comes to watch me." I shuffled my feet, feeling weird.

This wasn't how I'd imagined talking with Pops about a potential Division 1 scholarship. In my dreams I'd run home to tell Mama and Pops the good news, and we'd jump up and down in the living room, crying and laughing about the long journey it'd taken to get to the dream school. That's how I'd always pictured it. Instead, I was hunched against a porch column, awkwardly avoiding eye contact with my dad.

"Well, if I can help with the drills, let me know." He squinted and chuckled. "I'm as invested in this as you are."

I tucked my chin closer to my chest and fought the urge to roll my eyes. Pops had played ball in the '90s. He'd gotten injured, missed his final season, and found his second chance in me. But I wasn't living my life for *him*. That meant I needed his support even when I wasn't tracking in his exact footsteps. I could have used his support after the Shreveport game, not after the dust had settled. I wished he could see that.

"So, here you go." Pops dangled my keys in front of him, but I hesitated to reach for them.

"What's the catch," I asked, tilting my head. For the past few weeks I'd been strapped with a heap of chores big enough to keep me busy late into most evenings. Surely, Pops had something up his sleeve.

"No, catch." He shook the keys, stretching his arm farther into the space between us. He winced in pain. "Come on, Rus. My back is barking."

"Fine." I shoved off the support beam and snatched them from his hand. They were the same rusty keys to the same busted Civic—a car that gave me more grief than pleasure most days. But at least it was mine again. I looked up. "So, that's it? No more punishment?"

"What did your mama and I say last week?" he asked, his eyebrow sharply raised. "We told you that football was your job, your family contribution. And you're back on the field. It looks like you're in the hunt at Clemson. So…no point in you being grounded anymore, I guess."

It was true that football was my duty to the family, so when my place on the team was in jeopardy, I expected the backlash. But that wasn't the *true* reason behind my punishment.

"And if I kneel again?" I clenched my teeth, setting my jaw into a tight line. That was the real reason Pops had been angry beyond words. It was why he hadn't spoken to me for almost two weeks, why he could barely look me in the eyes.

To my surprise, he threw his head back and let out a cackling laugh. He slapped his thigh, then locked eyes with me.

"I ain't worried about that." He caught his lips between his teeth, as if he was holding back another burst of laughter. "With Clemson on the line—and God knows what other top schools are interested—I am *not* worried about you taking a knee during the anthem."

"Marion's still suspended, and Officer Reynaud is still roaming free. There's still a reason to fight."

"Yeah, and this corner of the world is really messed up. Ain't it?" Pops shook his head, his smile faltering. "But you got a ticket outta here, don't you?"

I opened my mouth to refute it, but I couldn't bring myself to. The truth in his words hit me deep in my chest. He had a point.

My biggest fear was being stuck in Monroe like Homegrown Gary, a washed-up baller with untapped potential. Even Pops lamented being in Monroe. He wished he'd left, played ball, and gotten a better education. As much as I hated the pressure Pops put on me, and as much as I hated the feeling of him living vicariously through me, I was hopeful about the opportunity to play at the top. I'd always wanted something different for my life, and now I had a *real* chance to leave this town.

I intended to take it.

I was willing to stand against injustice, but not at my expense. I'd made the sacrifice of kneeling, and that hadn't gotten me anywhere but in *trouble*. As much as I felt salty that Coach Fontenot had stalled me in the locker room during the anthem last night, a part of me thought he'd done me a favor.

A Division 1 scholarship wasn't a hypothetical now. It wasn't some distant, impossible dream. It was within reach, so close I could almost taste it. Was I willing to throw that away for another failed protest?

I...didn't think so. Circumstances had changed.

Maybe it was time I started thinking about *me* when I was on the field—not all the problems that needed fixing in the world. Maybe it was time I fixed my sights on Clemson and didn't look back.

Pops sat back in his chair, donning his smug smile again. "See? I ain't worried about a thing."

19

Gabby leaned over my notebook, her head resting on her hand as she read my biggest contribution to our English class project—the written portion. She'd asked me not to watch her while she read.

It'll throw me off my editing game, she'd said with a devilish grin.

But I couldn't help it. She was so interesting to watch.

The red pen in her hand hadn't moved an inch since she'd started reading. I finished cutting out more clippings for our already crowded poster board collage—an attempt at busywork. I couldn't help but sneak glances at her progress. Every sigh, every shift in her seat had my eyes snapping in her direction.

If I'd been working on my own, I would have written a perfectly adequate essay—something guaranteed a passing grade with enough wiggle room to spare. I was no slouch in the classroom, though I certainly wasn't a genius like Gabby. But if I was being honest, I'd spent much longer writing this paper than I had on anything else I'd ever done.

I eyed the notebook, reading my handwriting upside down. She was on the last page. I fidgeted across from her, wringing my hands underneath the table as I awaited her verdict—and hoped for her approval.

It wasn't just that I was hungry for acceptance since I'd been deprived of it lately—although, it would be seriously cool if my teammates got off my case. No, I wanted *her* approval. I wanted to earn it, even if I had to rewrite the whole damn thing.

"Well?" I asked anxiously, folding my arms.

She held a finger up, urging me to be patient, then bit the end of her red pen. After a while, she looked up through her lashes.

"Well," she said with a sigh.

My insides churned, and not in a good way. Maybe she didn't like it. I was prepared to hide my face in embarrassment, but she cleared her throat and said, "This is good."

"Really?" I said, my breath coming out in a rush.

"Rus, I mean *really* good." She flipped back a few pages and read a line from the beginning. "A life unencumbered by prejudice is a life worth living, worth demanding, even worth fighting for."

Her dewy eyes widened and she gulped down a swallow.

I'd been hoping for this very reaction—Gabby's wide-eyed wonder. If I could, I'd make sure she felt that sort of joy and inspiration every day of her life. If she'd let me. Because that's what she deserved.

But my confidence wavered. I'd written a draft of these words before Clemson popped onto the scene, before I'd discovered a hard truth—social justice would have to take a back seat to my budding football career. Would Gabby look

at me the same way if she knew I had no intention of kneeling again this season?

I studied the way her freckles looked darker in the bright
light of the warehouse, and the dimple in her left cheek that
puckered when she was concentrating hard on something,
hoping that I could just tell her—

"Is there something on my face?" she asked, snapping me
out of my thoughts.

"Nothing." I shook my head, afraid to meet her gaze again.
It would reveal too much, and I wasn't ready for her to know
about the deal I'd made with Coach and Pops—my deal to
not take a knee again.

Maybe I was a coward. But I accepted that.

"It's kind of poetic." Gabby thumbed through the pages.
"Couldn't have said it better myself."

"Thanks," I said, sitting up a little straighter. I inwardly
fist-bumped myself for looking up words in the thesaurus a
few nights ago. "I guess I thought…"

"What?"

"I thought you'd say that you wrote something better." I
pursed my lips, jutting my chin out. "And you already had it
typed up, and that it would be easier to just use your thing
for the project instead of mine."

Gabby's cheeks reddened, and she hid her face in her hands.

"I knew it!" I jabbed my finger on the tabletop. Gabby
wouldn't leave anything to chance, *especially* one of her final
grades.

"I couldn't help myself!" She brushed her curls away from
her face. "You never know who will pull their weight in a

group project. And with everything going on in your life, I just figured..."

"You doubted me." The bitterness of having my world turned against me bubbled over, and I said it more harshly than I intended. "It's okay. I'm used to it."

"But I won't again." She nodded solemnly.

I nodded back, appreciating the fact that she took me seriously.

"What are those for?" My gaze settled on the far corner of the warehouse near the door leading to the Dupre greenhouse, where dozens of paper bags stood open on the floor.

"They're care packages for the homecoming this weekend." She strode over to one of the bags and rifled through its contents. "My dad usually sets up a table after the parade and hands these out to people who need them."

"You just give it away? For *free*?" I asked, walking to meet her by the bundles. I poked my nose in the bag, imagining what it would be like to give all this away without expecting anything in return. In this bag alone, there was easily fifteen dollars' worth of fresh produce—salad greens, tomatoes, and the biggest stalk of celery I'd ever seen sticking over the brim of the bag. There must have been a hundred bags lined up and ready to go.

I pulled a particularly misshapen tomato out of the bag— big and yellow with green shoulders bulging from its crinkled sides. I raised my eyebrow and Gabby laughed.

"Sometimes grocery stores won't take the ugly fruit. They want the uniform stuff." She grinned conspiratorially at me. "But if you ask me, the troublemakers are always the best."

She turned back to the table, but not before giving me a

knowing look. She made eye contact with me and lingered for a fraction too long, like she was talking about more than tomatoes. Sometimes I got the sense that there was more to her than she let on—a wilder, more rebellious edge that I'd yet to see.

The more I got to know her, the more I wanted...*more.*

I stepped forward, and words tumbled out of my mouth before I had a chance to talk myself out of it.

"Would you like to hang out? You know, at the homecoming parade?" My hands started to sweat, and I shoved them into my pockets. Our school couldn't afford more than one dance a semester, so the student body had opted to have a winter formal instead of a homecoming dance. So the parade next weekend wouldn't be a black-tie affair—nothing fancy like that. But there'd be a DJ and free food.

Maybe I could ask Gabby to dance between the hay bales after I finished riding on the Jackson Jackals float.

"What do think?"

"Yeah. That'd be cool." She tucked her hair behind her ear, a blush creeping back to her cheeks. "You know where to find me. Just follow the trail of the troublesome fruit."

20

"Line up five across." Coach spread his arms wide like he was conducting his greatest symphony. He yanked a crumpled-up water bottle from his back pocket and spat a wad of chewing tobacco into it before tucking it out of sight. He wasn't allowed to chew tobacco on school property, although I'd seen him slip a couple times. But here, it didn't matter—the homecoming parade was on *his* time.

An organizer for the parade interrupted Coach's formation instructions by holding his hands up, and I recognized Anthony Tillman—or Mr. Tony, as we all called him. In case you didn't know who he was, he had it spelled out underneath his official title: *Program Director*. He always took an active role in the parade because he had one of the nicest cars in town: a black Chrysler convertible. A Monroe parade didn't kick off without Tony leading the way. He wiggled his fingers in the air to get the team's attention.

"Actually, if we could have y'all line up three per row." He squinted and stepped forward, grabbing Darrell's forearm. He dragged him to the right so that he stood about five feet away from Karim, then nodded in approval. "There. That should do it. Let's keep the procession spread out."

He cupped his hands over his mouth and leaned closer to Coach, like he was about to say something privately to him.

"Gotta space 'em out. Give everyone a chance to look at the Jackson Jackals!" he said in a fake whisper, loud enough for the entire team to hear.

Darrell snickered under his breath in a way that made me think he was laughing *at* Mr. Tony instead of *with* him. He could make fun of the process all he wanted, but deep down I knew he was thrilled to be a part of the parade. We all were.

The homecoming parade was one of the town's biggest events of the year. And its pride—past and present football players of local renown—were the main event.

"Now." Mr. Tony clapped his hands. "Which players will be on the float?"

He nodded toward a shiny F-150 parked along the street in front of Emmett's Quick Stop. Attached to the back was a flatbed trailer with streamers dangling from the edge of the plywood. That was our dream-mobile.

Marion fidgeted next to me at the mention of *player,* clearly still uneasy about his place on the team. But he was suspended from game play, not from the team as a whole, and I wanted to make sure he felt confident in his place as co-captain. I nudged his side with my elbow, making his head snap up. I nodded, encouraging him to claim his spot.

"Boys, I—" Coach stepped forward, his gaze bouncing nervously between us and the rest of team and then back to us. "I been over this with y'all. The league hasn't lifted Marion's suspension. And I still haven't received word that the pros- ecutor's dropped the charges."

"My lawyer say he working on it." Marion's jaw tightened. It had been a week since he'd sent his lawyer the video evi- dence.

"He's part of the team," I said, backing Marion up. "We're not gonna be on the field. We're not suiting up for league play. He should be with the team, where he belongs."

"I'm here to stay." Marion took a step forward, looking at the rest of the team over Coach's shoulder. "That is, if y'all will have me back."

"Shit, man." Darrell spit on the sidewalk. "We been wait- ing for your ass to tell the league to go fu—"

"Language." Coach snapped his finger and pointed at Dar- rell. He crossed his arms as he turned to Marion. "Fine. You can come on the float, but no one is telling the league to eff themselves. Got it?"

Marion lunged forward and hugged Coach Fontenot, then pulled back, coughing through the awkwardness. "Um, thanks, Coach."

Then he sidestepped out of Coach's way and joined the team. Terrance engulfed him with his meaty arms and spun him in a circle. Karim tousled his hair while Darrell playfully punched his shoulder.

Marion was back.

"Well, it looks like we're decided." Mr. Tony clapped his hands and jumped onto the platform. He waved at Marion, urging him to join him. "We have room for two more play- ers. And then Coach Fontenot will be in the middle."

"Sure thing." Coach nodded and spat brownish liquid on

the pavement. He eyed me over his sunglasses. "Lemme talk to ya, son."

I took a cautious step forward.

"Listen, I don't want any funny business today." He folded his arms and jerked his chin toward Marion, who was now joined by Karim and Darrell on the platform. "If y'all are planning on kneeling or making speeches or something in between—"

"We're not," I cut in. "Coach, I spoke to my dad. You don't have anything to worry about." I held his stare, unflinching. "We're only interested in representing our team—*nothing else.*"

The subtext of my message was clear. There would be no more fights, no more protests, and no more making Coach Fontenot look bad. It seemed to convince him, because he relaxed his stance, and his eyebrow stopped its nervous twitching.

"That is exactly what I wanted to hear. I feel your frustration. You know I do, right? But we cannot afford to piss the league off any more." He lowered his head, running his fingers through his short coils. "Remember what I told you about Clemson?"

Of course I did. I'd thought of little else since he told me. How could I forget?

"They do *not* take kindly to the kneeling protest." He shook his head gravely. "Help me help you, Rus. Get that scholarship. Or your dad is going to kill me *and* you."

He snuck a glance down the line of parade cars, stopping at the small 1998 State Champions' float. There were only a handful of players from that year who still lived in the area and cared enough to show up for the parade. Pops squinted our way, likely noticing that we were having a heated conversation. Coach's body language was unmistakable—he was laying down the law. Pops nodded in approval, then turned his attention back to his float.

Tony Tillman blared the whistle hanging from around his neck.

"Okay, y'all have a little time to do whatever you gotta do—phone calls, bathroom breaks, last-minute changes to your float. You can use the bathrooms inside Emmett's, or you can hold it until after the parade." Mr. Tony drew his lips tight and tapped his watch. "But be back to your positions in ten."

Marion hopped down from the float and jogged over to me with a lightness to him that I hadn't seen in a while.

Terrance followed closely at his heels. "You coming?" He pointed toward the shop, his wide lineman frame pulling his shirt above his belt loops.

"You know I gotta grab some jerky." Marion punched me lightly in the shoulder. "You wanna split some chips?"

"I'm good." I waved them on. "I'll save room for the crawfish at Jean's booth."

They disappeared into the store, leaving me by myself in the parking lot. Last time I'd been here, I'd waited under the awning next to Gabby while her dad jumped my car. I'd been blown away by the floor-to-ceiling wall of Dante Maynard posters. I wondered if they were still there.

I looked over my shoulder, making sure Coach's back was still turned. His attention was on Mr. Tony and the final details of the parade. Our team was the grand finale, and Coach wanted to make sure everything was squared away. The coast was clear, so I made a run for it.

I darted around the side of the building and stepped back so that I could take in the entire wall. Only a few faded posters hung along the brick facade. Some looked like they'd been ripped off, leaving behind streaks of scrap paper.

I bet Brad Simmons had ripped some of them down. Probably Officer Reynaud too.

What remained on the wall were the weatherworn, faded eyes of Dante. The washed-out call for justice scrawled across the bottom, barely visible—Justice 4 Dante.

Where was Dante's Shadow?

Had they caught the guy in the wanted poster—the serial vandal who had rubbed the police department the wrong way? I hoped not.

Maybe it was a double standard, but I didn't want the Shadow to give up, even if I had stepped away from protesting. Dante deserved more than a few posters and a town's collective amnesia. Pretty soon, people would forget who Dante was, and it would happen again.

In a few more weeks, would people stop caring about Marion's charges? Would they forget what Officer Reynaud had done?

Dante's Shadow—wherever he was—needed to come out of retirement because this town was still in need of some *serious* justice.

21

The gleam from Homegrown Gary's gold tooth shone brightly in his rearview mirror as he rolled through downtown Monroe, just in front of our big finale float. His shiny red Mustang convertible definitely gave Mr. Tony's parade car a run for its money. He wrapped one arm around the passenger seat headrest, while his other arm waved to the crowd. I wondered how he was driving with both hands off the wheel, but that wasn't the only thing that made me curious.

"How the hell did Gary score *that* car?" I asked through tight lips. We were making our way slowly down Main Street, and I didn't want anybody to read my lips.

"You already know." Darrell turned his head slightly, and I could see his nostrils flare. "He knows people."

I tried not to roll my eyes. Homegrown Gary was, in his own words, in the *import-export business*, which was his fancy way of saying he had sketchy business dealings. However he'd acquired the car, I knew it wasn't strictly legal. There was a reason he carried that concealed pistol. Hopefully, he'd given his gun the day off.

Peppered in between the football flatbeds were various business owners. Jean's restaurant had a block of space between the floats, as did Rudy's Diner. There was even a small trailer with war veterans on it, retired and active military. For as long as I could remember, football and patriotism had gone hand in hand. It was why kneeling during the national anthem created such a firestorm. Respecting the flag was not up for interpretation for football folks.

I searched the crowd for familiar faces, which wasn't hard to do in Monroe. I knew almost everybody in my small town, and the whole town seemed to be on the streets. But I was of course looking for one particular face—Gabby's. She'd said she'd be here, but I hadn't caught a glimpse of her yet.

Our float crawled behind my teammates who were lined up shoulders-length apart in three rows, surrounded by the Jackson High marching band and our color guard—just as Mr. Tony had envisioned. The dancers threw their batons in the air in an intricate formation while I wobbled atop the platform next to Marion, Darrell, Terrance, and Karim in a V formation. Coach stood behind us on a small step so that he could match our height. Waving and cheering mixed with our band's beats, but I was still focused on finding her.

"Come on, Rus. Look alive!" Coach bellowed from behind.

I raised my hand higher above my head, exaggerating my wave to please Coach. Darrell's shoulders trembled against mine as he laughed at me. When I was sure I'd shown enough pep, I lowered my arm to a less conspicuous height.

The truck jolted to a stop so that it didn't slide into the marching band ahead of us. Craning my neck to look around the traffic jam, I saw Gary's convertible idling at the end of the street. He leaned into his car horn, soaking up the limelight for just a little longer. It was his last chance to be seen before he turned the corner into the unloading zone.

"Your cousin crazy, man." Karim shook his head at Darrell.

"Just give him a break." Terrance covered his mouth with his hand, concealing his words. We still had a few blocks to go before we reached the end of the parade, and all eyes were on us. "This is all Gary has to show from his time on the team."

A lump formed in my throat, and I turned away from Gary's enthusiastic waves. I didn't like that he forced me to confront the hard truth that had solidified in my gut—that I would do *anything* to make a better life for myself. Even if that meant swallowing my pride and keeping my mouth shut on the field. Even if that meant abandoning my pursuit of Marion's justice.

I snuck a glance at Marion, at his easy smile and bright eyes. The people on the sidewalks cheered him on, calling out his name as we passed. They had their quarterback *back*.

He waved exuberantly at the crowd lining the street, his chin proudly up like Gary's was. Gary hadn't gone further than winning the 2011 championship. He'd never finished his senior season, never went onto college. In fact, most of the people in the parade procession had similar fates.

I peered toward the beginning of the procession at the 1993 playoff finalists. They hadn't even won their game. Behind them was Pops's float, where he stood shoulder to shoulder with what remained of his 1998 State Championship team. Their biggest glories happened during their high school days.

Will that happen to Marion?

Pops's float rounded the last corner, disappearing down Elm Street. I held my hand up and waved at the folks lining the streets until our platform turned away from the town square. Downtown Monroe spanned all of five blocks. The parade was over before it even started.

A firm grasp on my shoulder rattled my frame, followed by Marion's happy timbre.

"So glad I came. Thanks for putting in a good word for me." He hopped off the flatbed and straightened his letter jacket. His eyes narrowed as he appraised me. "You okay?"

"Of course," I said, a little too eager. I didn't want Marion to know anything was wrong, and I didn't want him to catch the whiff of pity in my eyes.

"Dude, it was high time someone talked to Coach about Marion." Darrell stepped forward, his mouth pulled to the side. He looked at me, past his high cheekbones, his expression unreadable. Then he held his hand out. "We cool?"

"Yeah, man. We straight," I said, grabbing his hand. I tried not to look too happy—didn't want Darrell to know that his cold treatment had gotten under my skin.

"Last one to the table has to eat a crawdad eyeball," Terrance said, shoving his way past us. His hefty frame rumbled down the side street, his sneakers squeaking on the asphalt as he ran toward the town square.

"Oh, hell naw!" Darrell took off in a sprint, nipping at Terrance's heels in no time.

"Don't worry." Marion shook his head with a smug smile. "I'll beat them. I always do."

Then he took off down Elm Street, a wild laugh escaping his lips. If anyone could defy shitty odds, it was Marion.

But I couldn't help but feel a kernel of doubt.

Seeing the fallen titans of the town's football legacy had shaken me. Marion's fate still hung in the balance. He could end up stuck in Monroe. Our fractured team was on the mend, but we were not cohesive yet.

Even though Marion had told me not to worry, I did.

I strolled across Main Street and into the town square, my hands shoved in my pockets. Several people were carrying the familiar brown Dupre Produce bags, so I followed the trickle of patrons to the source at the center of the lawn, where dozens of people had gathered.

And that's when I saw her—my friend with the troublesome fruit.

Gabby dove beneath her booth and resurfaced with a bundle of grocery bags in each arm. When she set them onto the Dupre Produce Delivery booth, it shuddered under the added weight. And as soon as the stock was replenished, eager hands grabbed the handles, and the table was bare again.

She looked flustered, her cheeks flushed as she dove under the table for more bags. But I didn't try to step in. Remembering how she'd grumbled at my offer to help her with the jumper cables at the beginning of the year, I left her to do her thing. I walked to where the guys were congregating on the edge of the line of food tables, deciding to give her room to work. Because when she finished working, she was going to hang with me. As in…a date.

I hoped it was a date. I wanted more with Gabby.

"You got it bad, dog." Marion nudged me with his elbow,

breaking my trance. "Don't even try to say you don't like her like *that*."

"I'm working on it," I mumbled under my breath.

"When they gonna start serving? I'm starving." Terrance's nostrils flared as he eyed the tables' steaming pots hungrily. The smell of crawfish and potatoes filled the air, and I couldn't help but breathe it in. My stomach grumbled in anticipation.

"Negro, you ain't starving." Darrell poked Terrance's stomach.

"This a well-oiled lineman machine right here." Terrance's broad shoulders shook with a laugh as he pulled his shirt back down.

I laughed with them, but my attention drifted back to Gabby. She brought a hand to her forehead to shield her eyes from the sunlight, then scanned the crowd. My heart raced at the thought of her looking for *me*. Maybe she wanted more too.

I was standing in a group of freakishly large football players. It didn't take long for her to find me. I ducked my head as soon as we made eye contact. I didn't want her to catch me staring—stalking was definitely not a good look.

"Yo, is she waving at us?" Darrell squinted in Gabby's direction.

"Shut up." I elbowed him in the gut, regretting it the moment I did. I hoped he wouldn't take it personally. Our friendship was only just getting back on track.

To my relief, he held his arms up and laughed it away. "I ain't saying shit except *good luck with that*."

"Hey!" I yelled. Standing head and shoulders above most

of the people, my voice carried all the way to Gabby. I waved her toward us. "You hungry?"

She tapped her dad on the shoulder, then motioned to us. As soon as he nodded, she untied her apron from around her waist, then cut through the crowd on her way to our table. She threw her arms into the air when she saw Marion.

"You're *back*." She rattled her hands in the wind.

"It's good to be back." Marion bobbed his head from side to side. "Well, not *back* back. But soon. I'll be back on the field soon."

Gabby's arms sank, as did her smile. Her eyes shifted between me and Marion, and I mouthed the words: *Tell you later*. But there wasn't much to tell. Marion's future was still in limbo as long as the prosecutor sat on the video evidence.

"Y'all ready to eat?" Terrance's hungry eyes followed the gumbo-sized pots making their way down the rows of tables. He hiked up his long legs and squeezed them underneath the table. Tucking his napkin into his T-shirt collar, he asked, "Who's doing the honors?"

Gabby sheepishly raised her hand, and Darrell burst into laughter.

"You've got to be kidding me." He gestured to the ten-gallon pot. "That thing's bigger than you are."

"It's my favorite part, though, dumping everything on the table." She bounced on her toes, then rounded the table. "I wanna give it a shot."

Bracing herself on the edge of the table, she lifted the silver pot, her bony elbows wobbling as she attempted to pour its contents onto the red-and-white-checkered tablecloth. It was tradition to lay the whole crawfish boil directly on the

table—crawdads, sausage, red potatoes. No plates were re-
quired. It was a dig-in situation.

The pot wobbled, almost falling into Terrance's lap, so I
stepped behind Gabby with a steadying hand. It was the closest I'd been to Gabby since our childhood kiss. With my chest
touching her back, her hair skimming the bottom of my chin,
I could feel her breathing. Darrell brought a fist to his mouth
with a hiss, earning him a slap upside the head from Marion.

"Don't trip," he warned him, even though he also couldn't
help but laugh. He mouthed a little louder than a whisper,
"Slay the baller way."

Shit, just act cool, for the love of God!

Feeling their stares, we pulled away from each other at the
same time. I fell to the bench, taking her with me. Flushed,
Gabby tried to laugh it off. So did I.

"Terrance has to eat a crawfish eyeball," I blurted out. The
guys snickered across the table at my abrupt segue. But it did
the trick—our embarrassing tumble was soon forgotten.

Making fish lips and weird gurgling sounds, Marion waved
a crawfish between Terrance's eyes. I could almost see him
mentally kicking himself for even suggesting their racing con-
test from the parade floats. I chuckled, unfurling my napkin.
A small flyer slipped out of the folds.

"What is that?" Marion leaned over my arm to get a better look.

"Did you get one too?" I looked around me.

"Yeah." Darrell shrugged, shoving his underneath his soda.
He was going to use his flyer as a coaster without even bothering to read it.

"Maybe it's a flyer from the *Shadow*." Gabby winked at me

conspiratorially. My heart pounded against my chest. I was equal parts shocked and amazed.

Yeah, she liked me.

"Um, I don't think the Shadow would do this," I said with a shake of my head. The hooded vigilante was a street vandal who put up social justice flyers, not a member of the Monroe Homecoming Committee. That was just a bunch of old ladies who volunteered their time. "I don't see him rolling a hundred paper napkins."

"I don't know. This dude seems pretty mysterious." She wiggled her fingers in front of my face.

It was an intriguing thought, though. Maybe Dante's Shadow had come out of hiatus.

Murmurs swept through the tables as people discussed the flyer, which had the silhouette of a person with an afro, her fist raised above her head. The text scrawled across the image read:

It's time to UNITE!
Hear Charlotte Martin Speak
Central College Friday, Oct. 11 @ 9:00 PM

"Does anyone know who Charlotte Martin is?" I asked the table. Darrell and Terrance had already lost interest. D was trying to get Terrance to eat a crawfish eyeball, and Marion was digging into the spread like he hadn't eaten a decent meal for a week. Even Gabby was on her phone, seemingly disinterested. "Do you know who this is?"

"I've seen her speak before. She's all over YouTube." She shrugged and looked up, her bright eyes betraying interest.

"She's definitely got some big ideas about turning the heat up in the Black Lives Matter movement."

Turning the heat up.

I had a strange sense of déjà vu. That was exactly what she'd encouraged me to do after I knelt at the Shreveport game.

"I take it you'll be there on Friday?"

She looked around us, then leaned closer. "Maybe. Go with me?"

Wait. Did she *just ask* me *out??*

I blinked slowly, trying to work out in my head whether or not I'd be able to make an event on Friday night. That was game night—a time devoted to football. And then there was also the commitment I'd made to Coach, to Pops, to *myself.*

I had my sights set on Clemson, and social justice wasn't going to interfere with football again. That meant no more kneeling and no more protesting.

"Look, Gabby, I—"

A blush crept up her cheeks, and she looked into her lap. Her fingers tangled into knots. Before I could speak, I felt a familiar squeeze on my shoulder. I tilted my head back, finding Mama standing over me.

"Well, isn't this nice." She squeezed my shoulder again, bracing herself as she dove for a red potato on the table. Covering her mouth, she waved at Gabby and said, "Hey, baby girl. Haven't seen you in a good while."

"Hi, Mrs. Boudreaux." Gabby smiled tightly, her invitation still hanging awkwardly between us.

"I see y'all got those flyers. We did too."

"It's nothing, Mama. We were just throwing them away." I

scrambled to gather all the visible flyers on the table. I didn't want her getting any ideas about me protesting again.

"Did I hear y'all were handing out bags of groceries over there?" Mama redirected her attention to Gabby. She was clearly interested in something more important than the flyers.

When Gabby nodded, Mama smoothed down her edges, her hand moving slowly toward her bun. She was doing her best to seem casual. Only I noticed the tightness around her eyes.

"Do you have any extra?" She smiled self-consciously, and my heart clenched at the sight of her asking for free groceries in front of my friends. I'd known our finances were tight after paying Marion's bail, but I didn't know things were this bad.

"We should have a few bags left in the truck." Gabby's face softened, and she scooted her hand next to mine. Her pinky finger grazed my skin. "I can bring it to your car. Just point me in the right direction."

I could have told her I loved her in that moment, because her words made my mom visibly relax. She wouldn't be seen carrying charity groceries around homecoming. I don't know why Mama felt so embarrassed. There were plenty of people grabbing free groceries, and there was no shame in it—but Mama...well, she was a proud woman.

Mama took off in the direction of Pops's tuck, parked on the corner of Main Street and Elm. Gabby slid out of her seat, but at the last minute, I grabbed her hand. She whipped her head around, startled.

"To answer your question—*yes*." I nodded at the stack of flyers on the table. It was a spur-of-the-moment decision. Agreeing to go see Charlotte Martin speak at Central College existed in a gray area of the rules I'd drawn up for keeping football and activism separate. The speech wasn't on the field. It was *after* the game—on *my* time. And my time still belonged to me. "I may be a little late because we have a game, but I'll be there."

I'd meet Gabby *anywhere*.

"Save me a seat next to you."

22

Fresh off the heels of our win against Cary High School, I showered quickly, then ran to my car, praying to God it would start tonight. I was determined to meet Gabby at Central Community College on time—or as close to on time as I could.

This was a date after all.

I was panting by the time I made it into the auditorium. It was packed—more packed than I'd thought it would be. Most of the seats were filled, and the overflow spilled into the aisles and around the back of the room. A bundle of natural hair near the front row caught my eyes and I made my way down.

"Did I miss it?" I gripped the armrest of her chair as I caught my breath.

Gabby's smile widened, brightening the room. "It's just about to start." She removed her coat and purse from the seat next to her. "Saved you a seat."

The seat was a small wooden folding chair, barely big enough to accommodate Gabby's slight frame. I stepped as carefully as I could between Gabby's feet and the seat in front of her, but there wasn't enough room. Mama always said I was built for the field, and it had never rung truer as I tried to fit myself in that auditorium seat.

"Can't believe you're here." Gabby tucked her hair behind her ear. "Thought for sure you weren't going to make it."

"I told you I would." I shifted to face her, wincing as my knees banged against the chair in front of me. But it was worth it to see her blush and look away. I nodded toward the standing crowd behind me. "Wow, this place is packed."

"She's worth it. Trust me." Gabby smirked at me. When the lights dimmed, Gabby held her breath and grabbed the armrest between us. Our fingers grazed for a brief moment.

"Y'all give it up for Charlotte Martin!" the MC said loudly into the mic. The auditorium cheered and clapped, conjuring Charlotte to the stage. She gripped her temples with the tips of her fingers as she paced in front of the mic stand. She reminded me of how Mama looked after a long and frustrating day. She looked dog-tired—something I could also relate to.

"I gotta tell y'all—I'm *tired*." She took the microphone off the stand and paced the stage with it. "I'm sick and tired of seeing images like this. Can I get someone to hit the lights for me, please?"

When the lights went off, a projector went on.

"You guys may have heard about some of these cases. I'd like to share them with you anyway, because it's important to say their names. It's important to bear witness. So, here we go." She pointed her remote at the projector. "Harold Boyd was a Black man arrested under suspicion of selling loose cigarettes outside of a convenience store. A police office pinned him to the ground and put his knee on his neck, killing him dead—right there on the street. Say his name with me."

She held her mic to the crowd, who shouted the victim's name. "Harold Boyd!"

"Marcus Smith was jogging early on a Saturday morning and was shot with a shotgun in the back by a retired police officer. The excuse was that he *looked* suspicious. Say his name with me."

"Marcus Smith!" the crowd yelled.

"I know y'all know about this young man."

I caught my breath as I stared into the haunting eyes of Dante Maynard. It was the same photo the Shadow had used on the first round of flyers at the beginning of school. His eyes were innocent, cast in the partial shade of his hoodie. He wore a soft smile.

"This young man was a promising young basketball player in Shreveport. Just two months ago, he was gunned down at a gas station under suspicion of robbery. His crime was being Black in America. What is his name?"

"Dante Maynard!" the crowd said together.

The room went black as the projector shut off. Then the lights came back on.

"These murders happened within two hundred miles of where we're standing, all in the last two years. I repeat, these young men were *killed* in our backyard." She replaced the microphone on its stand. With a sigh, she said, "So, you see why I'm tired. I'm tired of hearing these stories. I'm tired of knowing there will be another police-involved murder of an innocent Black man in a few months. I'm tired of feeling helpless to stop it. And I'm tired of the officers not being jailed.

Dante Maynard was shot over two months ago, and the officer responsible for his death is still not in custody."

I squirmed in my seat, unable to get Dante's killer out of my head. Officer Reynaud was walking the streets, strolling around town with his thumbs tucked in his belt loops. He'd even been brazen enough to arrest Marion and accuse him of resisting arrest, even though he knew that was a lie. A crooked cop was terrorizing our community. And no one in power seemed to care.

She leaned into the microphone so that her voice boomed louder. "This is not a drill, folks. We need all hands on deck and for y'all to speak out. Using your voice to hold them accountable could save a life."

Someone in the crowd shouted, "We should fight back! Hit the streets right now."

"Yes, brother. I admire your enthusiasm. Gathering and implementing collective voices can be a powerful tool. But I hear the anger in your voice. I wanna caution you against violence."

"Why? Let's go Malcom X in these streets!"

"White people treat us like animals. I'm not going to give them what they want—the out-of-control Black man or woman fueled by rage. Let us use our minds. Let us build a bridge to a new world."

I wanted to agree with her—the bridge to a new world didn't have to be violent. It's what I'd tried to build by kneeling during the national anthem. I'd wanted to cut through the noise and make a statement for all to see, but it had backfired on me. I was still feeling the reverberations from that decision. And no one seemed to *understand* the message enough to seriously examine Officer Reynaud and his negative impact on our community.

So…did peaceful protests really work? Or did protests need to make more noise and shake things up? As Charlotte continued her talk about building bridges, my mind spun.

What am I thinking?

I shook my head, trying to remember my commitment to stay away from protesting. I was just here to support Gabby and keep her company.

Charlotte gestured to the side of the stage, wiggling her fingers for someone to join her on the stage. "And who better to teach us how to build that bridge than one of our local teachers. Maya, would you join me up here?"

Gabby's breath hitched at the same time mine did. She gripped my hand, her eyebrows upturned in surprise, her lips tucked underneath her teeth. We watched wide-eyed as Ms. Jabbar strode across the stage and grabbed the mic. My heart raced from the shock of seeing our English teacher and from the shock of Gabby's fingers gripping mine. I squeezed back, the warmth of her hand flooding my senses.

"Thank you, Ms. Martin." Ms. J adjusted the microphone so that it would reach her tall height. "Next weekend, you'll have an opportunity to use your voice in numbers. Join us for a peaceful demonstration outside of Monroe Town Hall. Bring your posters, bring your friends, and speak out against injustice."

The date was set: next Saturday. The rally ended in a call for action. It left me feeling less confused and prouder of the small act of protest I'd done on the field. I'd taken a knee, and because of the immediate backlash, I hadn't allowed myself to celebrate my exercise of free speech. I had a voice and had used it. What if we *all* used our voices?

We could shake the very foundations of this country.

"I guess we shouldn't be surprised." Gabby covered her mouth before she busted out a laugh. "Ms. J *and* Charlotte Martin. Wow."

Her enthusiasm was infectious. I couldn't help but return her smile.

"Wasn't she great?" Gabby beamed. "Ready to go?"

I nodded and gulped. Where we were headed, I had no idea. But I'd follow Gabby almost anywhere. She'd gotten Marion a better attorney for free, kept me accountable on our school project, and trusted me enough to share her favorite speaker with me. Wherever she led, I would follow. And I would work up the nerve to tell her what she meant to me—*tonight.*

"Oh, there's someone I want you to meet." She tugged my arm in the direction of a knot of students near the front of the room. She cupped her hands over her mouth and yelled, "Dave. Dave!"

It took me a minute to recognize the name, but I finally did. Dave was the guy Gabby texted with—the guy she'd leave a room to speak to. And I suspected he was the one who'd been making her smile as she drifted through the lunchroom, her fingers rapidly typing as she floated through the halls. This was *that* Dave.

I *hated* Dave.

Dave turned around, his light-skinned cheeks flushed as he ran his hand through his Creole curls. His hazel eyes twinkled as he caught Gabby's glance. His long arms stretched over the masses as he waved back. He weaved through the crowd with purpose and scooped Gabby into a hug that lifted her to her tiptoes.

"This is Dave," she said after she found her footing. Her eyes shone brightly as she looked from me to Dave, clearly enamored with him. I staggered as I seemed to lose my footing. "Dave, this is Rus."

"So, you're the football guy who took a knee?" He waved his hand with a flourish. "Hats off to you."

"Thanks, man."

"You ready for a party? Let's head to Raven Hall." He held his arm out for me to lead the way. I turned toward the door, but not before seeing his other arm wrap around Gabby's waist.

23

Raven Hall sat on the south end of the small community college campus. An eclectic mix of students lounged on the lawn, soaking up the moonlight. A girl in a cowboy hat strummed her guitar in the hallway. I stepped over her legs in order to get to the residents' common room, which opened up to a sizable backyard.

I silently seethed as Dave put his arm around Gabby and led her through the dorm.

This was not the date I'd envisioned.

I grabbed a bag of chips off one of the tables, not even bothering to ask whose it was. I shoved a handful of them into my mouth just as Dave wiped a bundle of curls off Gabby's forehead.

Worst. Date. Ever.

I didn't stand a chance against this light-skinned brother. They walked close together—the way people did when they were familiar. I wondered if texting had turned to touching. I mean, how could it not? He was tall and educated and had a bougie accent, and they both spoke with a sense of urgency and mutual understanding. In a lot of ways, they seemed better suited for each other than Gabby and me. They were more of a natural, obvious fit. But Gabby kept looking behind her, making sure I was keeping up. I was still in her thoughts. I just hoped I wasn't an afterthought.

"I've gotta talk to Spencer really quickly. Wanna ask if we can squeeze something about Saturday's march into this week's paper." Dave smiled broadly, revealing large white teeth. "We go to print tonight."

"Go, go!" Gabby waved her hands, shooing him toward the corner of the room where, I assumed, Spencer stood. "We'll be fine."

"I'll grab you a drink on the way back?" Dave raised his eyebrows, nodding as if he'd already received our responses. "Beer?"

I looked at my phone a dozen times, watching the time edge later and later. It was nearly eleven, and even though I wasn't grounded anymore, staying out all night wasn't exactly the way to earn my parents' trust back. I needed to be home by midnight, but this college party seemed to be just getting started.

I'd promised Gabby I'd come for *one* drink. But where were those drinks? That smooth-talking Dave had gone to get us some, but he was busy chatting with people on the patio. He leaned against the counter railing, looking like he had all the time in the world. College students didn't have curfews, but I did.

"I'll probably have to bounce soon." I leaned across the table. "How late were you planning on staying?"

"I don't know. Maybe a couple of hours."

I frowned, wondering what that kind of freedom must be like. Gabby's dad must be very trusting.

Gabby leaned over her chair, petting the tall grass with her fingertips. She drew her hand to her nose and laughed.

"Interesting choice." She smelled the tips of her fingers again. "That's not grass. It's oregano. I thought I recognized it. Here. Smell."

She snapped off a piece, then leaned over to me. She hovered over my lap, so close I could feel her breath grazing my neck. She waved her hand, begging me to take a whiff. I breathed deeply.

"Wow. That's definitely an herb." I had no idea what it looked like fresh—I'd only ever seen it dried and crushed in a spice bottle. I grabbed the bushy sprig from her fingers and sniffed it again. "Smells like pizza."

"I know, right? It grows like weeds. Whoever planted it probably didn't mean for it to take up the whole backyard." Gabby laughed. "You learn a thing or two when your dad's in the produce business."

"Someone say pizza?" Dave said from over my shoulder. His hands were full with three red Solo cups. He handed one to each of us, then looked at the twig in my hand.

"Smell." Gabby nodded.

There was no way that I was holding it up to his nose like Gabby had done for me, so I quickly off-loaded it into his unsuspecting hand. He made eye contact with Gabby as he inhaled, looking melodramatic as he flared his nostrils in wonder. She blushed and turned away with a small laugh. I was instantly annoyed.

"You're too much," Gabby said.

"I spoke with Ms. Jabbar after the lecture about Saturday's demonstration," Dave said. "She says she needs help gathering signatures for the petition."

"What petition?" I asked.

"The one to get Officer Reynaud fired." Dave raised an eyebrow, looking from Gabby to me like I should have already known about the petition.

"And hopefully jailed," Gabby mumbled into her cup. "Lord knows he deserves worse."

I nodded. Every Black and brown person within Reynaud's jurisdiction was in danger. There was no telling what he might do during another tense situation, but it wouldn't be just or fair. Something had to be done about him.

"I was thinking we could set up a table next to the Walmart entrance." Dave turned to Gabby, clearly intending to expand on his plan, but I had to interrupt.

"Wait. The Walmart in *Westmond*?" I sputtered a laugh, causing them to look at me.

Dave cleared his throat, clearly waiting for an explanation.

"You're kidding, right?" I raised my arms incredulously. Dave seemed like a smart guy, but his idea was making me reevaluate. Surely he was aware he was putting Gabby in a dangerous situation. My eyes narrowed. "You want Gabby to take a Black Lives Matter petition to a *white* neighborhood?"

Dave raised his eyebrows and crossed his arms, looking to Gabby for support. She blanched as she caught the heat of his gaze. She put her hands on her hips.

"Why shouldn't white people be as concerned as we are?" She tilted her head. "Rus, we need the whole community to condemn Officer Reynaud and police brutality. There have to be some white people who believe in this cause too."

I shook my head, becoming lost in thought. I could imagine Officer Reynaud answering a call of disturbance. Showing up to the Walmart parking lot, his eyes wild with hunger to catch the agitator who was trying to galvanize his own town against him. He'd gleefully cart Gabby to the station. It was the worst situation for her safety. But Dave thought differently.

"It's the perfect place." He turned to Gabby. "We need to build a coalition, don't you think? Target the neighborhood that protects Officer Reynaud."

"Yeah, Rus. We need to bring our voices to the scene of the crime." She popped her head up from her cup, an idea working behind her bright eyes as she stared at me. "Like you did on Shreveport's field. Or, you know what would be cool? You could speak at Saturday's demonstration."

"Gabby, come on…" I shrank away from her outstretched arm. "You want me to cause more trouble for myself?"

"We have the permits to assemble. No one's going to get in trouble, Rus." Gabby chuckled, nudging my elbow. "I know you have plenty to say."

Without waiting for me to agree, she looked to Dave. He rubbed his chin, nodding slowly as he worked out the details in his head. "That's actually a really good idea." Dave looked at his phone, checking the time. "If I hurry, I can squeeze your name into the school paper before it goes to print."

My muscles tensed. I'd barely survived my last protest, and now they wanted to throw me on the stage of the biggest protest this town had seen in decades? As Dave nodded

more fervently, I shook my head. Gabby swung her head to
each of us, looking for consensus.

"You in?" Dave raised his eyebrows, growing more impatient as the seconds ticked closer to the school paper's deadline.

"Nah." I held my lips between my teeth, avoiding eye contact with everyone—especially Gabby.

"Don't tell me you're one of those one-and-done brothers." Dave scrunched up his mouth. "You have a platform.
You have people's attention. *Use* it."

I pushed my chair away from the table and stood up. I was
exhausted—from the game I'd played tonight and from a lack
of sleep. But most of all, I was tired of people telling me what
to do. *Don't speak up. Use your voice* more.

I was being pulled from both ends, and I felt overextended.
I grabbed my jacket and made a beeline for the door, unwill-
ing to lose myself in any more causes.

My mood got increasingly sour as I stalked through the
dorm, tiptoeing around empty bottles and crushed Solo cups.
By the time I made it to the sidewalk, I was salty as hell.

One and done?

Dave was *killing* me. I didn't want to think about Gabby—
how disappointed she'd looked as he skewered me for being
a fair-weather activist. My activism had lost the game against
Shreveport and mangled my teammates' and my parents' respect. How was that fair-weather?

"Rus!" Footsteps padded down the sidewalk, closing in on
me. "Rus, stop!"

Gabby's small fingers nipped at my sleeve but I tore away,

redoubling my speed toward the parking lot. The auditorium stood in the distance. The parking lot was just behind it.

"Russell Boudreaux!" Gabby paused on the sidewalk, gasping to catch her breath. "Don't you dare leave me stranded at another party."

My knees locked into place. I had promised her I would never abandon her at a party like I had freshman year. And now I was breaking that promise. I ran my fingers over my scalp, cussing under my breath.

"He didn't mean anything by it." Gabby nodded in the direction of Raven Hall, where Dave was probably scratching his head at our abrupt departure.

"I can't win." I threw my hands up. My eyes started to sting, but I coughed the tears away. "Everybody back home says I did *too* much—that my kneeling might have gone too far. And then you and Dave think I'm not doing *enough*?"

"You can't hide from what you did. You took a knee in front of a whole stadium full of people." She gathered her hair off her face and gripped it at the roots. "Rus, you're braver than you think."

"I'm not brave." I shook my head. I was just a football player, a guy who wanted a shot on the field. I wanted to make opportunity for myself. And as much as these protests spoke of a bigger picture—of more equality in the near or distant future—what good would that do me now? "I blew up my whole *life* when I took a knee. You don't get it."

"You think I don't understand what it is to voice an unpopular opinion?" She raised her eyebrows, her nostrils flaring.

Before I could respond, she swung her backpack around her shoulder and unzipped the back compartment, packed to the brim like it always was. I leaned forward, wondering why she was going to show me her books.

There must have been two reams of printer paper stuffed in there. She pried her fingers between the stack and slid a page up so that I could see. It was an image of Officer Reynaud pointing his gun at a boy in a hoodie, his hands in the air. I recognized it from the security footage I'd just seen in the auditorium. The bold text on the bottom of the page said: No Justice, No Peace.

"Now do you see?" she asked expectantly.

"Wait a minute." It was obvious what this was. These were more Dante Maynard flyers. My eyes grew wider as I looked from the flyer to Gabby's face. "*You're* Dante's Shadow?"

24

My fingers twisted into knots as I fidgeted in the front seat of Gabby's fancy Ford F-150. It was much roomier than my small car, but my head almost grazed the roof. She pressed a button on the center console, and the sunroof began to retract.

I leaned back, watching the clouds drift across the sky. They were backlit by a bright moon, just as they had been the night I'd wandered from the party and seen Dante's Shadow running behind town hall. I'd replayed that night over and over again, wondering who would be so brave and reckless.

That was *Gabby* that night.

I almost couldn't believe it, but something about her revelation made perfect sense. I remembered the slight frame of the masked person, her agile and graceful movements as she ran through the alley. Her way with words was written all over the flyers, which dripped with the passion of activism. Of *course* the Shadow was Gabby.

"Paperwork," I said under my breath, remembering the excuse she'd given me the night she didn't show up to the team party. The taut leather squeaked as I turned to her, finally able to look her in the eyes. "This is why you ghosted me that night?"

"Yeah. I can't exactly have my phone on when I'm in the middle of civil disobedience." She laughed awkwardly as she shifted in her seat. She hitched her knee on the center console and faced me. "You're not alone in this fight. Do you see that now?"

"How did you get mixed up in this?"

"I take a college level course here on Tuesdays and Thursdays—biochem. Our school doesn't offer it, and I want to stand out in my college applications..."

I cleared my throat, urging her to get back on track.

"After class, I overheard one of Charlotte Martin's lectures. I stood outside the door to her classroom while she spoke about the history of policing in America, the dog whistles of law and order." She rested her head on her headrest, a heavy sigh escaping her lips. "That's where I met Dave."

I rolled my eyes at the mention of his name. As if she could read the anger in my thoughts, she spoke.

"He's a good guy, Rus. He really is. And he has an admin key to the school's newspaper room." She grinned mischievously. "That's a whole lot of paper. I couldn't resist."

"But why take the risk?" The way I saw it, the reward didn't outweigh the risks. Why was she going to such lengths to plaster her voice all over town? I didn't understand it. I slumped against my window. "Papering the town with those flyers—Gabby, you're bound to get caught."

"Not necessarily." She slouched behind the steering wheel, folding her arms. "Besides, even if I was arrested, I'd probably get a gold medal from Berkeley. They *live* for this kinda stuff over there."

"That's where you're going?" I blinked, trying to think about how far Louisiana was from Berkeley, California.

"I applied early decision, so I'm waiting to hear back, but I think I have a shot." She sighed, her eyes hooded as she looked into her lap. "I don't want to live close to home. Anywhere in the South, for that matter. We live in a city where a Black boy was murdered, and his killer is still walking free. It's too creepy."

"Beyond creepy." I shuddered as I thought of Officer Reynaud's smug face as he put handcuffs around Marion's wrists.

"About the protest on Saturday—speaking publicly won't get you into any more trouble than you're already in. If anything, it should have the opposite effect. Dave has invited other local papers. The media will gather public pressure against the Westmond police."

"It shouldn't be me up there." I shook my head. I wasn't the story here. I hadn't been shot or kicked off the field. I had yet to run afoul of Reynaud. But I knew someone who had. "It should be Marion."

I slid my phone out of my back pocket and scrolled through my contacts, searching for the one person who had more to say than I did. Marion had suffered greatly at the hands of the police and the football league. He knew how to speak to a crowd—I'd seen him do it countless times in the locker room. He could dig deep when he wanted to pull our team out of a rut. Now it was his turn to help himself.

With one eye on my keyboard and one eye on Gabby, I texted Marion.

"That's up to you. I won't push you. I know now what happens when I push you too hard." She shook her head, laughing under her breath. "I can't believe I told you. You're not going to tell anyone, right?"

"I'm no snitch." I folded my arms.

"Good." She nodded, then tapped the clock on the dashboard. "It's getting late."

"Yeah, I better get home." It was after midnight. But I was worried about Gabby, concerned that when I left her truck, she'd put on her black bandana and paper Westmond. There was a lot of unfairness going on between law enforcement and Black bodies. I knew that firsthand. Officers like Reynaud wouldn't think twice about cuffing her—even with her fancy truck and her house on the hill.

"Please don't put the flyers up by yourself." I grabbed her hand and squeezed it, just as she'd done during Charlotte Martin's speech. She blushed and squeezed back. "I would be your lookout, but I literally can't stay out any later."

"Relax, Rus. This isn't my first rodeo. I outran those cops last time."

"Yeah, because *I* pulled you out of the way." I glared at her, remembering the waifish figure running down the alleyway. She'd been doing this for a while, and by the determined set of her jaw, she was going out tonight—with or without my blessing. I ran my fingers over my scalp. "Text me when you get home? Seriously."

"I will."

My foot eased off the brake pedal, and the Civic shuddered to a halt beneath the live oak down the street from my house. The glow from my phone broke up the darkness as I scrolled through my texts, searching for a message from Gabby. Maybe she'd decided not to go out after I begged her not to.

Nothing.

I tried not to think about what she was doing, but I couldn't help it. It had been only fifteen minutes since I'd seen her at the community college, but that was long enough for Gabby to get into trouble. If she needed help, I hoped she would call me.

The clock in the corner of the screen bored into my eye sockets. It was just after 1:00 a.m., which meant I was well past any wiggle room on my curfew. I gently pushed the car door shut, careful not to make too much noise, and devised a plan to sneak in the back door, praying the footboards wouldn't squeak too much.

I gently pushed the door closed so that the latch wouldn't make a sound. I didn't want to wake anybody up, especially Pops. I wanted more than one night of being ungrounded, and coming in after curfew was not a good start.

The light and the TV were on in the living room, casting Marion's face in shifting shadows. He looked over when my keys gently clanked against the kitchen island.

"What up?" He gave a lazy wave over his stomach, his voice a little too loud.

"Shh, you'll wake them up." I sank into the rocking chair and waited a few seconds to make sure my parents were still asleep.

"Don't worry, I covered for you." Marion yawned. "Told Pops you were blowing off steam."

I wasn't sure if blowing off steam was supposed to mean that I was off banging Gabby or that I was off partying with the team. Either way, Marion had missed the mark. He had no idea what I was really up to.

"I didn't think you'd be awake." I tugged on his comforter, waking him up before he dozed back to sleep. "Why didn't you text me back?"

He drew his blankets around his shoulders. "'Cause I think you're talking crazy."

"It's really not *that* crazy. The local news will be there, so you can tell your side of the story." I said, parroting Gabby, suddenly more comfortable with the idea. If Gabby was fearless in the face of Officer Reynaud, then we could be too. And Gabby said it was permitted and lawful.

"You saw the video. The lawyer says there's no way the prosecutor will want to move forward with the case." Marion propped himself on his elbows, his eyes heavy with sleep. "I've got a meeting with him next week. And by that time... all this will be in the past."

"For real?"

Marion nodded, lowering his head back to the couch.

"But what about Officer Reynaud? He's still on the streets." My whisper came out in a hiss, but I didn't care. I was happy that Marion was on his way to clearing his record. But this was bigger than just Marion.

"I gotta steer clear of any more controversy. And getting a mug shot in front of town hall sure as hell would be a controversy."

"It's permitted, so you know we're not breaking the law. This is important, Marion." I tapped the couch with the tip of my sneaker. "And Ms. J will even be there to support us."

"I worry about you, Rus." He paused. Then, in little more

than a whisper, he said, "You're my boy for life, you know that. I got your back. But I need your help here. I need you to not make no more waves, you hear me?"

"You mean keep my mouth shut? Let you watch your football scholarships pass you by?"

"I'll be back on the field in no time. You can come to the lawyer's office if it'll calm your ass down." He shook his head, looking at the ceiling. "It's the most justice we can hope for. We're not going to solve racism. Not in this town. But I am gonna get back on that field."

25

Marion wiped the front of his dress shirt, practically vibrating with excitement as we sat in Mr. Samuels's office. Mama wrapped her arm around his shoulder and gave a playful tug on his ear.

"Ain't nothing but a conversation. Quit fussing," she teased, even though she was anxious herself. I could tell by the way her ankle kept twitching. Mama wouldn't believe Marion's exoneration until she heard it from the lawyer's mouth.

I was edgy, too, but I hid it better than they did. I hoped we hadn't come all the way to New Orleans to meet with a lawyer who would tell us the same thing as the court-appointed lawyer: *There's no hope for Marion, so take a plea.*

Mr. Samuels opened the door to his office and stepped into the small waiting room. He rubbed his hand over his short, salt-and-pepper-colored hair before straightening his tie.

"You must be Marion LaSalle," he said with an outstretched hand, brown and wrinkly like my father's. "Good to finally meet you."

"You too." Marion released his breath in a rush, like he'd been holding it in all the way from Monroe.

"Let's go to the conference room." He tilted his head, appraising Marion's size. "You'll have more room there."

"Yes, sir." He nodded, then looked back at me and Mama.

"Will they be joining us?" Mr. Samuels asked, opening his arms to include the two of us.

"Can they?" Relief painted Marion's words.

"It's up to you. This is your meeting."

With his nod, Mama and I fell in line after Mr. Samuels and Marion. The conference room was spacious, with large tan leather chairs. I'd read online that Samuels specialized in white collar crime, and it showed in his fancy office.

"Mr. LaSalle, it's so good to finally meet you. As you know, as soon as Gabby and her dad told me about you, I took your case pro bono."

"Yes, sir."

"I've been speaking with the DA. And if ever there was a good-old-boys network alive and well, it's in Monroe." He rolled up the cuffs of his sleeves, then rested his elbows on the table. "The prosecutor's office offered a plea bargain. As your lawyer, I am obligated to present you the offer, even though in my opinion, it is preposterous."

Marion nodded slowly.

"They are willing to drop the assault and battery charges if you plead guilty to the resisting arrest charge."

"But I didn't resist." Marion's chest rose and fell quickly as he panted. "Rus, you were standing right next to me."

"He didn't struggle." I nodded in confirmation. Mama

wrapped her arm around the top of Marion's chair, squeezing his shoulder. "It's on the video. Did they watch it?"

"They watched it." Mr. Samuels reached for his laptop on the corner of the table, which sat next to Marion's file. He turned it so that the screen faced Marion. Mama and I scooted toward him. Mr. Samuels pressed Play. "See that wiggle as the arresting officer grabs your arm?"

No. This couldn't be right. I'd watched that video over and over again. I'd seen every exonerating minute of it. It cleared Marion of all charges. Right?

Mr. Samuels paused the video at the moment that Marion squirmed under the force of Officer Reynaud's grasp.

"*That's* all they have?" I squinted at the screen.

"I've got to tell you. I've been a lawyer for over twenty-five years, and I've never seen a weaker case." He knit his fingers together, pursing his lips. He gave Marion a moment to compose himself, but he was slowly becoming unraveled.

"So, what do I do now? I thought you said the video evidence was going to work." Marion gripped Mama's hand tighter. His eyes flitted from his file on the table to Mr. Samuels's patient eyes. "I can't plea to something I didn't do."

"Nor would I advise you to. Most criminal cases don't go to trial, and many people agree to plea agreements, pleading guilty for crimes they didn't commit. That's the way the system works, especially for us Black men."

"Sorry, sir. We weren't expecting this." I wiped my forehead with a clammy hand. My dress shirt stuck to my skin, I was sweating so hard. "We thought Marion would have a shot of returning to the team."

"The team…" Marion's voice trailed off, his lip quivering.

"If I plead guilty to resisting arrest, and the other charges are dropped, then I'd be allowed to play, right?"

I saw the wheels turning in Marion's eyes. The reason he couldn't play ball was because of the league rule barring players charged with violent crimes. If those disappeared, then the league might let Marion suit up. But at a *significant* cost.

"You can't plead guilty." I leaned against the conference table, my palms sweating as I looked at Mr. Samuels. "It would go on his record, right?"

"That's correct. So, again, as your lawyer, I advise you not to take the deal." He shook his head. "You'd have a misdemeanor on your record. They'd put you on probation for years. It's not a fair deal at all. I suggest we go to trial."

"How long will that take?" Marion blinked past his unshed tears, his lips in a tight line. He was trying to hold himself together, but a tear escaped down his cheek. "Will it take longer than football season?"

"Unfortunately, that's likely. But we *will win.*" Mr. Samuels knocked his fist on the table. "I have two associates researching precedent just for you. We may have to wait a while for our day in court, but we'll stick with you on this. I'm concerned with fairness. It's what you deserve."

Marion cried openly in the car—big sopping wet tears that beaded on his thick lashes and soaked his cheeks. It was as if his body was purging all the hope of the past month, slowly closing the door on his dream of going to college on a football scholarship.

By the end of the car ride, his heavy breathing slowed to shorter pants. His sobs petered out to occasional sputters.

And slowly, the creases on his brow softened. His stomach growled, and he looked at me through the rearview mirror.

"Anyone else hungry?" he asked in a meek whisper.

"I know just what you need." Mama got in the right lane, and exited the freeway.

Marion didn't make a sound the rest of the car ride. By the time Mama rolled into the parking lot of Rudy's Diner, the tear streaks on his cheeks had dried. His face was blank, his hard facade slipping back into place.

"I gotta go pick up some lesson plans from the middle school." Mama's eyes tightened with worry as she looked from me to Marion. "You two gonna be okay for a while?"

We nodded as we discarded our collared shirts in the back seat. I'd wanted to take mine off since we left the lawyer's office. We walked across the lot to the picnic table behind the diner, where the employees took their lunch breaks. I fanned my undershirt, letting the cool breeze dry the sweat off my skin.

Before the meeting with Mr. Samuels, I'd thought Marion at least had a *chance* of coming back to the team, however remote it was. I hadn't allowed myself to fully envision a whole new world—a world in which Marion and I would never play together again—until I heard him heaving between teary gasps. The realness of it sank in, making me slump against the lip of the table.

"Is Karim's brother gonna hook us up?" I asked. Karim's brother was a line cook and slipped us free stuff from out of the back door.

"Yeah, I'm texting him right now." He buried his face instead of looking me in the eyes—probably embarrassed about crying in the car. "What you want?"

Marion's fingers flew over his screen as he typed in enough food to feed a village. I only asked for a burger, but he ordered three sandwiches for himself. Maybe he wanted to fill the void with food.

"I still can't believe it." Marion dropped his forehead to his knees, groaning to the ground.

"Me neither." I scratched my head, still trying to process the information Mr. Samuels told us. "Is everyone in the criminal justice system fucked?"

It was an honest question. The officers were responsible for unchecked aggression against the people they were tasked to protect. And the prosecutor was pursuing unwinnable claims in the hopes of getting a plea bargain. The world was backward.

"They ain't never gonna let up until I take that plea." Marion lifted his head and turned to face me. "Mr. Samuels thinks he can win, but he don't know Monroe."

The back door to the diner opened, and Karim's brother poked his head out. He tugged his hairnet over a chunk of hair that had slipped out.

"What's up, blood?" He stepped away from the door and the clatter of the busy kitchen behind him. He held his hand up for a high five.

"Hey, Hakeem," Marion mumbled under his breath, barely lifting his head in greeting.

I didn't want to leave Hakeem's hand hanging, so I hopped off the table and slapped it. Better late than never.

"What's good? You gonna hook us up?" I lowered my

voice, hoping Marion couldn't hear. "It's been a rough afternoon. We're in need of a pick-me-up."

"What happened to him?" Hakeem raised an eyebrow, chuckling under his breath. His smile faltered when he saw me shake my head. Then he looked at Marion, who had begun to tear up again. Hakeem got the seriousness of the situation and nodded, the smile wiped off his face. "I feel you. I don't know if I can slip *that* much food off the line, but I'll see what I can do. I'll be back."

"Everybody's gonna know." Marion shrugged, biting his lip. "Hakeem's going to tell Karim he saw me crying in the parking lot. And you know Karim's going to tell everybody on the team. That nigga can't keep a secret no kinda way."

I didn't do Marion the disservice of contradicting him. Our chatty team would definitely know Marion LaSalle had been moping in the parking lot by tomorrow morning.

"So, get in front of it." I shifted in my seat, gripping the unvarnished wood for support. "Send them the video and tell them the prosecutor is still going forward."

"Dang. My boy getting bolder and bolder by the day."

"This is exactly why we should be at the protest on Saturday. Aren't you tired of working with the system and getting nowhere?"

"I didn't send the video to anybody because I thought the charges would go away." Marion sniffled into his sleeve. "I didn't want to provoke the prosecutor. But you know what? That's bullshit."

"You ain't taking that plea." I gripped his shoulders, shaking him until he looked me in the eyes. He nodded and gripped my shoulders too.

"I ain't guilty of *nothing*. And I ain't going down without a fight." He howled, making room in his chest for a little kernel of hope. The flicker of his football dream was still alive, no matter how dim it was. "Guess I'll talk at your rally after all."

I wiggled my phone in front of his face. If we were going to Saturday's event, we were going to need all the help we could get. "Let's text the guys, see if they'll come too."

26

Marion paced in Terrance's living room, occasionally stopping to look out the window at the gathering protesters. From that corner of the house, he had an almost unobstructed view of the lawn in front of town hall. He rubbed his hands down the front of his crisp dress shirt, the same shirt he'd worn to his meeting with Mr. Samuels. It was his nicest shirt, and if he was going to beg the public to listen to his story, he was going to do it in style, looking like a man. He started pacing again, and Terrance nudged me with his elbow.

"Is he okay?" He leaned forward, speaking barely more than a whisper. "I don't know if this is a good idea."

"We already went over this." I gripped Terrance's shoulder. "We need the whole town to know what went down. Is everything ready?"

"Almost!" Gabby yelled from the foyer, where she sat in a pool of wires. She untangled the last wire from the pile and assessed the spread. Looking up, she pushed her glasses up the bridge of her nose. "Ms. J said they needed another AV cable."

"I got one upstairs." Terrance ran up the stairs two at a time.

"Marion." I stepped farther into the living room, intruding on his corner of solitude. He frowned as he peeked through the blinds. "You got this. We've played in front of audiences ten times the size of this."

"It's not the same." He shook his head, looking at me. "I don't know nothing about this kind of crowd."

"You'll be fine," I said, and I wanted to believe it. Last time I'd protested publicly, I'd received a largely negative response. But I didn't want Marion to compare today to *that*.

"Found an extra cord," Terrance said from the foot of the stairs.

"Any word from the team?" Marion asked. Terrance looked to the floor as he shook his head, causing Marion's lip to quiver. He sighed and straightened his collared shirt. "Let's do this."

Gabby handed me the box of wires, then threw her megaphone strap over her shoulder. Marion walked with only a crumpled-up piece of paper. The weight of his words was heavy enough. I wished I knew what he'd written, but he wouldn't let me see it. I would find out soon enough.

It was a short walk to the town hall lawn. We crossed the street slowly, deliberately. We reached the organizer table, which sat under a square canopy tent that blocked out most of the sun. Ms. J opened her arms to us.

"There are my fearless students!" She grabbed the box of HDMI and AV cables and gestured to the seating area to the right of the stage. "Some of your teammates are already here."

Bobby poked his head out from behind Ms. J, his sly smile growing as Marion walked nearer. It was impossible not to melt under his toothy grin. Marion was no exception.

"Y'all came!" A laugh escaped his lips as he clasped Bobby's hand, pulling him forward for a pat on the back. Karim stepped forward, slapping his shoulder.

"We not going to let you do this alone," he said, giving Marion's shoulder a squeeze, then brushing the wrinkles off his shirt.

"And Darrell?" Marion looked behind them, as if he might pop out from behind Ms. J too. Darrell had alerts set up on his phone so that any news of the Jackson Jackals would hit his inbox first. I knew he was aware of Marion's speech.

"Sorry, man." Karim shrugged, looking toward the grass. "I saw his cousin Gary roll up with a few of his homies, but Darrell wasn't with him."

"Dave! You made it." Gabby shouted over my shoulder. She grabbed my hand and pulled me through the small tent, but not before I caught Marion's reaction to our hand-holding. I'd have to fill him in later.

I liked the hand-holding. I'd like to do other things too, but I was willing to move at Gabby's pace.

Gabby's grasp on my hand was also not lost on Dave. His smile faltered a fraction as he digested the scene, then he pulled Gabby in for a half hug. He had a tendency to linger too long in his hugs with her, so I tugged gently on her arm, breaking their connection. It earned me an annoyed look from Gabby.

She rolled her eyes and whispered under her breath, "No pissing contests."

Right. Dave was *just a friend*. I knew that, and I'd happily remind him of that fact.

Someone cleared their throat behind me. I turned around

in the small space to find a short man in a navy blazer looking up at me.

"Afternoon, boys. I'm Chuck Wallace from the *New Orleans
Herald*." The reporter gave a small, awkward wave. "Would
you have time for a few questions?"

"Hi, Mr. Wallace." Dave perked up, tearing his gaze away
from Gabby to shake the reporter's hand. I was glad he stepped
in. I didn't want to mingle with any more reporters, not after
I'd fielded the unfair questions in front of the Shreveport stadium. Dave's enthusiasm compensated for my lack thereof.
"I'm a *huge* fan of your work. I'm studying Journalism and
Justice over at Central."

"Good to meet you. May I?" The reporter gestured to me,
and my chest tightened. He wanted to speak with us instead
of an overexcited Dave. "You must be Russell Boudreaux
and Marion LaSalle. I'd love to sit down with you both. Ask
you a couple questions."

"Everything we gotta say will be on that stage." I clenched
my teeth. I'd had enough experience with the press lately to
know that I wouldn't be heard.

"Here's my card. With my email and phone number on it.
Just in case you want to say more." He handed one to me and
Marion. "Our readers are interested in hearing your story.
Both of you." He nodded, then turned his attention to one
of the organizers.

"Wow, you got the attention of Chuck Wallace." Dave ran
his fingers through his light brown hair, a mixture of disbelief and wonder on his face. "I'm impressed."

"And all it took was one of us getting unjustly arrested and
thrown in jail." I rolled my eyes, annoyed that he was glori-

fying the media who'd spent the last few weeks demonizing me and Marion.

As far as I was concerned, if Chuck wanted to correct the record on the Westmond-Jackson fight, he could start with quoting Marion's upcoming speech.

"All right, y'all, let's get started." Ms. J clapped her hands toward the organizers, snapping everyone's attention to the stage.

I poked my head out of the canopy, surprised to see that the crowd had swelled to well over two hundred people. Marion shuddered next to me as he looked over my shoulder.

"That's a shit ton of people," he hissed as he ducked back under the tent.

Ms. J patted Marion on the back. "You're the first one up. You ready?"

"Yes, ma'am." Marion nodded, although his hands started to shake.

"You got this." I playfully punched his shoulder.

"And we got you." Bobby gave him a thumbs-up.

The stage was a wooden platform, set about three feet high. Even for her long legs, it was too high for Ms. J to handle without support. She hitched up one leg and looked to one of us for help. I stepped forward, lending her a hand so that she wouldn't have to crawl onto the stage. The chatter in the crowd dwindled to a murmur. All eyes were on her.

"Thank you for coming out on this fine Saturday afternoon! We want to kick this off with a special voice, one of my students and someone many of y'all know as the quarterback for Jackson. Black Lives Matter isn't just about our fallen

brothers and sisters. It's about standing against the devalua-
tion of Black bodies in all their shapes and forms. Marion's
plight *matters*."

Ms. J paused, letting the importance sink in. Marion's eyebrows twitched like Ms. J's words pierced his soul. He didn't
hear enough that his life mattered. He certainly didn't hear
it from his stepdad, and the league had let him down. But he
squared his shoulders, seeming empowered by the growing
applause from the crowd.

"Please welcome Marion LaSalle!"

"Hello. Hi." He paused to adjust the microphone. He
pulled it up about a foot and twisted the knob to tighten it
into place. "My name is Marion. And…and I'm here because
I'm poor and Black. I'm not like Bradley Simmons. I don't
live in a big house or drive a nice car. I don't even have a car.
Sometimes, I don't have food on the table. The only thing I
had was football and dreams. And now I don't even have that."

He took the microphone from the stand and stepped forward, so close to the edge of the stage, the tips of his sneakers hung off.

"I'm here because a Westmond player called me a nigga
and punched me in the face. I'm here because we live in a
community where that's acceptable. I'm here because I was
arrested for assaulting that player, even though it was clearly
the other way around. Y'all seen the video of the fight. Hell,
the prosecutor has seen the video. And every single referee
and cop saw Brad swing first. Officer Reynaud saw what happened. He's not just a murderer, he's a liar too. So—"

A screech of tires interrupted Marion's speech. Protesters
on the periphery of the square huddled closer, getting as far

away from the street as they could. Bradley hopped out of the tailgate of the truck, as if the mention of his wrongdoing had conjured him from thin air. He was followed by six other Westmond players. I recognized the long blond hair of one of them—Lawrence.

The guy who'd stood by silently while Marion was dragged off the field in zip ties.

Another truck pulled up, this time with half a dozen older men. Their faces were shadowed by camo baseball caps, their eyes shielded by sunglasses. I struggled to steady my breath—this was *bad*. I hoped they weren't packing, because men like this didn't ask questions before pulling the trigger.

They exited the truck slowly, their shoulders broad as they joined the Westmond players in the middle of the road. They weren't in any rush, and judging by their relaxed stance, they weren't afraid of repercussions. They didn't need to be afraid. They were protected simply because of the color of their skin and the size of their wallets.

"Don't mind us," Brad shouted over the murmur of the crowd. He elbowed one of his teammates, who handed him a crumpled piece of paper. He flattened the sheet on his torso, then held it at eye level—it was a flyer about the protest. "This is a public demonstration, right? After all, you invited us."

Marion's grip on the microphone faltered. Slowly, he lowered it to his side. He bowed his head, and even from my vantage point on the ground, I could see the courage seeping out of his body. His shoulders slumped. Ms. J tapped Gabby on the shoulder and motioned for her to hand over the megaphone. She held it up to her lips.

"All are welcome here. We're happy to see more people from Westmond in attendance."

"So we can see homeboy over there disrespect the flag again?" Brad pointed to me, his eyes glinting with a challenge. They dared me to react. They dared me to push through the crowd and slam him into the car.

I couldn't take the bait.

"This is a peaceful demonstration," Gabby said. I felt like I should have been the one to speak up, but I was afraid I'd lose my temper. Gabby was cool and collected, holding her megaphone high with a firm grip. "We have a right to be here."

"We just came to return something that belongs to y'all." Brad reached into the back of the pickup and grabbed two large trash bags. They were filled to bursting, the sun glinting off the black plastic. He threw one into the crowd, hitting a few protesters in the head. "Keep your garbage away from Westmond."

Gabby clasped her mouth, watching her flyers scatter on the lawn. She'd worked hard on those with the hope it would broaden her neighbors' consciousness. Instead, it was being used as a vehicle for vengeance.

"The way I see it, this is a Monroe issue—not Westmond." One of the older men stepped forward. He had the same nose and mouth as Brad, and I wondered if he was his dad. "So you need to keep your posters and your accusations on *your* side of the interstate. Don't be bringing this to *our* side."

Brad opened another trash bag, and his teammates reached in, each pulling out a wad of flyers. They tossed them into the crowd, pelting protesters indiscriminately.

Fuck this.

I lunged onto the stage and took the microphone hanging limply in Marion's hand. I gestured to the group of angry white men standing in the street.

"A boy was shot and killed by our shared police department. And you think this *isn't* a Westmond problem too?"

But I didn't need to hear their answer. I knew Westmond felt no accountability for Dante's murder or Marion's arrest.

"What happened to that poor boy was a tragic accident. And there's an investigation pending." Brad's dad held his hands up. He cocked his head. "That's justice enough for now."

"So, I guess you wouldn't mind if a tragic accident happened to one of your boys, would you?" Homegrown Gary rounded the side of the crowd, his hand hovering around his waistband. A collective gasp rippled through the crowd. We all knew where Gary carried his pistol.

I studied the Westmond folks, waiting for their hands to reach for their waistbands too. I wouldn't be surprised if several of them had concealed weapons.

I searched the crowd until I found Karim. I gave him a panicked look and flicked my head to the side.

Get him out of here, I mouthed wordlessly, flicking my thumb to the alleyway behind me. I didn't want this to turn into a gunfight. There was still time to deescalate things.

Karim quietly moved through the crowd until he reached Gary. He grabbed his arm and pulled him closer, whispering furiously into his ear. I pulled the microphone back to my mouth, waving to the crowd to encourage them to look to me instead of the Westmond agitators.

"These people are a distraction. I will not allow them to

derail this protest. We're here to talk about the injustices our community has endured at the hands of *their* police department. And deep down, they know we're right."

Marion stood straighter, spurred on by the truth. Raising his hands above his head, he pumped his arms, encouraging the crowd to rebound. It *worked*—one by one, people clapped and cheered as they turned their backs to the agitators and gave the stage their attention.

I held a finger up, a laser beam pointing squarely at Lawrence. "He saw the fight break out on Westmond's field, and he knows damn well his team co-captain, Bradley Simmons, punched Marion *multiple* times. Lawrence, you saw his face afterward. It was swollen and beaten. Speak up, dude! Say something to the police."

Lawrence blushed and looked away, bared raw for all to see his cowardice. Marion clenched his jaw and paced at the front of the stage. He cupped his hands around his mouth and yelled, "Speak up!"

Brad stepped in front of Lawrence, as if shielding him from the glares of the crowd.

"Your silence protects violence." I dropped the mic to my side just as Gabby brought her megaphone to her lips. I hopped off the stage to stand next to her.

"Silence is violence!" Her voice boomed through the speaker as she walked to Marion and stood next to him, spurring him to join her. She raised her right arm, her hand balled into a fist, and repeated the words. "Silence is violence! Say it with us."

The chant began in a trickle. Worried gazes darted from the stage to the white men, and back to the stage again. But as the chants grew louder, the crowd continued turning their backs on the Westmond agitators.

Silence is violence!

The words reverberated off the walls of the surrounding buildings, breathing life into the tattered Dante Maynard flyers that still hung limply on the side of town hall. The Westmond men seemed all but neutralized. They leaned against their trucks, arms folded, as our chants invaded their ears.

"Don't let them silence you!" Gabby beamed, her eyes bright as she caught my gaze. "Because silence is what?"

"Violence!" The crowd cheered, and I joined them—keeping eye contact with Gabby. Then they started chanting again, louder and more forceful than before.

My ears perked up as the sounds of sirens mingled with the protesters' chants. A line of police cruisers sped down Main Street and surrounded the town hall lawn. There must have been six cars, maybe more. I couldn't think through the thudding in my ears as I saw the one cop I feared the most.

27

Officer Reynaud slammed his car door shut. Cupping his hands around his mouth, he yelled, "Everybody go on home."

A murmur rippled through the crowd as they surveyed the escalation. We were surrounded by Westmond cops at a lawful demonstration in Monroe. We had more of a right to be here than they did.

"Where did I put that permit?" Ms. J's voice shook as she fumbled through her folder in search of the document.

Growing impatient, I grabbed the megaphone from Gabby's hand.

"We have a right to be here." I stood my ground with Gabby at my side. I brought her megaphone back to my lips, but Ms. J clasped my arm firmly. She gestured for me to give her the megaphone. Her eyes tight and her nostrils flaring, she was serious. I immediately released it into her hands.

"Officer, we have a permit," Ms. J said in her most dulcet tone. "I have the paperwork with me, if you'd like to come take a look."

"That won't be necessary." He jutted his lip out and shook

his head. Reynaud wasn't interested in the truth. He never was. "We got a call saying this was no longer a peaceful protest. That someone was making threats against Mr. Simmons's boy."

"Sir, as you can see here, this is a peaceful gathering." Ms. J opened her arms, inviting the police officers' closer inspection. People were armed with posters and chants—nothing more.

"We're just here to affirm that Black lives matter," Gabby said through cupped hands. It earned her another worried look from Ms. J.

Someone else in the crowd shouted, "Black lives matter!"

Then another and another, until the whole crowd was chanting at full force again. I climbed back onto the stage to see the chant spread like fire, lighting up the scared faces. Even Marion beside me was screaming at the top of his lungs that Black lives mattered—that *his* life mattered. I joined in, smiling widely. Maybe we could drown out their hate.

Or…maybe not.

Reynaud reached for his waistband, and I staggered backward, knocking into Marion. Reynaud's fingers were dangerous around his gun, and if he reached for his holster, we all needed to run.

But he didn't grab his gun. Instead, he unhooked his handcuffs from his belt and advanced on the protesters. With a flick of his wrist, his fellow officers did the same. I didn't know who they intended to arrest, but I didn't want to stick around. As part of the organizers, Gabby, Marion, and I were easy targets. I crouched near the edge of the stage and tugged on Gabby's sleeve.

"Let's bounce," I said through the side of my mouth.

"We can't just *run*." Gabby pushed away from the platform and made a beeline for Ms. J. I wasn't sure what our teacher would be able to do—she'd tried and failed to convince the police to recognize our permit to assemble. The farther Gabby moved away from me, the more anxious I got.

"This is now an unlawful assembly," a loudspeaker on top of one of the cruisers blared. "Anyone demonstrating in this area is doing so unlawfully. I repeat, this is now an unlawful assembly."

Grabbing a woman by the armpit, Reynaud snatched her forward, directing her to put her hands behind her back. He held her arms tight and cuffed her. Handing her off to another officer for processing, he unlatched a bundle of zip ties from the back of his belt.

Realization spread like wildfire through the crowd. They were going to arrest *all* of us.

Panicked people started hopping up, backing away from the advancing officers. A wall of people mashed toward the stage, separating me from Gabby even more.

Homegrown Gary scampered behind the stage and looked in both directions before fleeing down the alleyway. A hard tug on my sleeve snapped my attention back to the chaos.

"I can't get arrested again." Marion gripped my arm harder. "Let's get out of here!"

"Then *go*!" I ripped my arm away from his grasp. I couldn't just *leave* Gabby.

I searched the devolving demonstration and found her face down on the sidewalk, her hands held behind her back by

Officer Reynaud. She screamed against the pavement and my breath caught.

Gabby!

Her shoulder was at such an odd angle. It didn't seem natural for her arm to bend that far back. Reynaud was three times her size. He didn't need to pin her to the ground like that. I lurched forward, my hands balled into fists.

GET YOUR HANDS OFF HER!

I'd seen a friend brutally pinned to the ground like that. Less than a year ago, Marion was buried under the weight of two Westmond linemen. He'd screamed in agony as his shoulder popped out of place. I'll never forget the image of him writhing on the ground as tears escaped down his cheeks. Now the same thing was happening to Gabby.

I'll kill him. When I reached Reynaud, I'd kill him for sure.

I was yanked backward by two strong hands gripping my arms. I whipped around to find Marion tugging me in the other direction.

"Get off! Marion, stop!" I shoved against his grasp, but he didn't let go. I craned my head around to keep Gabby in sight. Her arm was stretched taut under Officer Reynaud's viselike grip. He ripped a zip tie from his other hand and pulled her arm farther back. With a final shudder of tension, the shoulder went limp, and I knew it was dislocated. "Let go of me."

Ms. J stumbled forward, looking alarmed as I thrashed in Marion's arms.

"Stop fighting and get out of here. *Now.*" She pushed me in the direction Marion was pulling.

"I'm not leaving Gabby!"

Gabby shrieked so loudly, it pierced through the crowd, right to my heart.

Everything inside me told me to run toward Reynaud and rip his hands off her body, even if it meant getting arrested. Even if I got hurt. Even if it meant I couldn't play. I lunged toward her, but Marion kept hold of my arms.

"Do as I say, Russell. You know what he's capable of!"

Ms. J's voice jarred me back to reality. If I charged a police officer—especially a trigger-happy officer like Reynaud—I could be killed. That was the reality of being Black in America. If I stepped out of line, I could lose my life. And nobody would give a damn.

Fuck.

Marion tugged on my sleeve before jumping off the back of the stage. I hesitated on the ledge, torn between what I wanted to do and what I should do—between rescuing Gabby or getting out of the town square, which was quickly devolving into a mass raid.

"I've got Gabby. Go!" Ms. J bounced on her heels, then ran toward Gabby and Officer Reynaud.

I stumbled off the platform, my heartbeat thumping through my ears. A tear burned across my cheek. I wiped it hastily away as I headed down the alleyway after Marion and Terrance, in the direction that Homegrown Gary had taken—the sound of Gabby's scream still ringing in my ears.

The screaming in the background disoriented me as I fled down the street. I wondered if one of those cries for help was Gabby's, and my mind flooded with the image of her lying facedown on the cement with Officer Reynaud pushing her into the pavement. Then watching the unmistakable pop of her shoulder as it gave way to his forceful grasp…

I shuddered.

My foot landed in a dip in the road, and my ankle landed at a weird angle. I hopped on one foot, then hobbled down the alleyway after the guys.

I'd seen Marion run under pressure on the field, seen him flushed out of the pocket and have to make a quick escape. He'd tuck the ball close to his chest and book it across the field with tight, measured strides.

This was not *that*.

He ran full tilt, his arms flailing like windmills as if he could use the wind to propel him forward—using any advantage to keep him from falling prey to the bevy of cops storming the crowd of protesters. Labored breathing and heavy footsteps sounded behind me. I looked over my shoulder and found Terrance struggling to keep our hurried pace. As a bulky defensive lineman, he wasn't used to the rigors of sprinting.

Gary darted to the right down another side street, and Marion, running in jagged lines to avoid potholes, turned to follow. My footsteps were equally as erratic—the frantic pats of our feet against the pavement echoed off the side of town hall.

For a split second, I forgot where we were going. But I was on autopilot, instinctively following the path away from the mayhem.

"This way!" Terrance shouted from behind me. He wheezed, pointing toward his house at the end of the block.

Turning quickly, Marion changed direction so fast that I almost careened into him. We caught up to Terrance, who huffed as he jogged and fished in his pockets for his keys.

There were more footsteps behind us—some hurried and frantic like ours, some more sure of themselves, steady as they stomped in pursuit. In either case, I wasn't taking the time to look. I'd made my decision to *run*.

Another voice called, "Stop right there!"

"Who's that?" I hissed, afraid to look. It was an unfamiliar voice that spoke with authority.

Please don't be a cop.

"I think one's following us!" Marion craned his neck, looking past me toward the alley. He cussed under his breath, confirming my biggest fear.

"Run faster," I said between huffs. "Terrance, where are them keys?"

"I had 'em a second ago." He pawed at his pockets. "Hold on!"

"Terrance!" I yelled. I hoped to God he'd picked them up off the registration table where I'd seen him drop them.

"Got 'em!" Terrance held the keys up. They dangled from his fingers, clinking in the wind.

He jammed them into the side gate, his fingers shaking as he turned the lock. The wooden door flung open, and we toppled forward. I landed on the stone pathway with a thud, catching myself with my hands before my face hit the ground.

Terrance shut the gate, then ducked below the top, out of sight of the watchful eyes of cops.

My breaths were ragged and loud, and I had to cover my mouth to keep from being noisy. Breathing through my nose pinched my nostrils, making it hard to catch my breath. I scrambled to a shaded corner of the side lawn and crouched against the fence across from Marion.

Large beads of sweat dripped down his forehead and caught on his eyelashes. For a moment, it looked like he was crying, like he had in the car ride back from New Orleans after that fancy lawyer had delivered the bad news about his case. I wouldn't blame him for crying. Shoot, I was fighting back tears myself. We had every right to be terrified.

Still on his haunches, Marion crab-walked to the latched gate, mashing his face flush against the wood so that he could look through the slats.

"It's still popping off out there," he said in a low whisper, hoarse and shaky with fear.

I scooted forward and squinted through the small opening, watching people scatter and hide. One of the college students I recognized ran through the alley followed closely by a cop with his club raised. A cop was going after a *white* student like that? What would he do to someone like *me*?

An influx of squad cars flooded the streets with sirens, some of them with Westmond PD emblazoned on their sides. I shoved away from the view, unable to look, but Marion kept watching at the other side of the gate. He held his phone up, recording video as the officer tackled the guy to the ground.

"I know the importance of a video. Maybe this'll help

him out later. You know, when they try to say he resisted."
He kept filming, no doubt thinking about the person who'd
filmed the Westmond fight. Even though the video hadn't
freed him from all the charges, it was still helpful. Maybe this
video would help the guy getting arrested.

"Where's Karim?" Terrance croaked. His eyes grew wider
as he looked from me to Marion.

I shook my head slowly, trying to remember the last time
I'd seen him. The last fifteen minutes was a blur of scattered
crowds and alleyways, a mash of panting breaths and hiding.
There was no telling where Karim was.

"Shit." Terrance ran his hand over his short, coily hair.
"Where was the last place you saw him?"

"He was getting cuffed near..." Marion's low voice trailed
off. He blinked away from me, turning his gaze to the grass.

"Gabby," I whispered. My jumbled memory began to settle into something I could hold on to. "You're right. He was
standing near Gabby."

"Rus." Marion shifted in his crouch, lowering his voice so
that the approaching footsteps couldn't hear us. "I'm sorry."

"My fault," I mumbled, barely loud enough for anyone to
hear. Regret seeped into my pores. We should have never
gone to a BLM protest.

"We had a right to—"

I held my hands up, cutting Marion off. I didn't want to
hear about the permits, about how everything was cleared
with the city, about the fact that we had a right to be in the
town square.

I didn't want to hear any of that.

Those were the justifications I'd used before all this happened. I used to believe in the power of protest, in the power of words to affect social change, but now...

Right now, I was sure of only one thing: I was squatting on the ground because I was being hunted like an animal.

This is it, Rus. This is what being Black in America is. And you can't change it.

Remaining crouched, we scampered around Terrance's house to the back porch, which was safely out of sight. We slipped into the house through the back door, resigning ourselves to a long wait until the dust settled.

28

It was almost normal, being in Terrance's house. I'd sat in this room with him and Marion countless times—sneaking booze out of his mama's liquor cabinet and staying up too late. I never thought I'd be prying his blinds apart to nervously watch the streets. These were strange times.

The red emergency light on the side of the fire station was blinking, flooding the street with a creepy glow.

"Where did everyone go?" I turned in the window seat and looked at Marion on the couch. He ran his fingers through his dreads, frown lines drilling into his forehead.

"I don't know," Marion mumbled.

"I'll try Gabby again." I tapped her number again, and the phone rang and rang. Each time I dialed, I hoped she might answer—as if the police would miraculously realize they'd been idiots and set her free. But the call emptied into a full mailbox. I couldn't even leave her a fuckin' message. I shook my head. Pretty soon, if I still couldn't get Gabby on the phone, I'd have to call Dupre Produce and speak to her dad—and I was *seriously* dreading that conversation. "Still nothing. What about you, T?"

"No one's answering. It just keeps ringing. Three-one-one is such a fake service." Terrance tossed his phone onto the coffee table. "But my mom texted me. She's trying to find another doctor to cover her shift, so she can come home. Anyone get in touch with Karim?"

"He isn't answering either," Marion said, bringing his phone from his ear. "He must be in jail. I mean, where else would he be?"

With a grunt, Terrance hopped up from where he was sitting on the floor and shuffled down the hallway in the direction of his bedroom. He called over his shoulder, "I need a break."

We sat quietly for a while, me and Marion, occasionally looking out of the window to keep an eye out for the cops. But the streets were pretty dead. There was only one sound that pierced the eerie quiet of the moment, that sliced through the silent darkness of Terrance's living room, and it was the buzzing coming from my phone.

Mama.

I stared at the screen, wondering if I should answer it. She could have been calling about anything, like asking me to pick up something from the grocery store on my way home. But I doubted that. Mama *lived* for the evening news, so by now she knew about the protest and the raid. That's why she was calling.

I let it roll to voice mail.

"That's *bold*." Marion raised his eyebrows. "You remember what happened last time you ignored her phone calls?"

How could I forget? After I'd spent the night in the tree house, Mama had put me to work for weeks. And that was just for kneeling and sleeping in the backyard. I could only imagine the punishment that would follow *this*. I'd be grounded through graduation—college graduation.

Marion jolted upright. Now *his* phone was ringing. He gave me a knowing look, reaching for his back pocket.

"Don't answer that." I held my hand up. "Come on, man. Please don't pick up her call until we figure out what we're going to do."

"What is there to figure out?" He scowled. "We can't do *shit*."

"Gabby's in Westmond, right? Look at the TV." I shoved off the window seat and edged closer to the flat screen above the mantel. A small crowd was beginning to form outside the Westmond precinct, demanding they release everyone who'd been rounded up tonight. "That's where Gabby and Karim are. We gotta be there."

"Jesus." Marion threw his hands up. He shoved off the couch and started pacing near the window. "You ain't thinking this through."

Ignoring Marion, I dialed Gabby again. It went straight to voice mail, meaning her phone must have died. In fact, it seemed that the only phone in town that was working was Mama's. She buzzed angrily in my palm, insisting that I pick up the call. But I pressed Decline.

Marion's jaw went limp. He could stay here if he wanted—and maybe he should stay put to avoid getting into more legal trouble—but I couldn't just sit here and do *nothing*. I tilted my head toward my car keys on the coffee table, eyeing them hungrily as a plan brewed in my mind.

"Don't be stupid." His eyes tightened.

I leaned forward, prepared to snatch the keys, but he was one step ahead of me. He lunged for the coffee table, knocking a decorative vase off-kilter in the process. It teetered on the table, wobbling close to the edge.

"Stop!" I swooped down to catch it before it shattered on the floor. It was enough time for Marion to secret the car keys in one of his pockets.

"What the hell, guys?" Terrance skidded into the living room, his mouth growing wide when he saw me on the floor with his mama's vase.

"It's nothing," I said, scrambling to my feet. I turned to Marion, who skirted the room to put the table between us. "Gimme back my keys."

"Can't do it. No." He shook his head. "You'll thank me later."

"Can someone tell me what's going on?" Terrance slapped his sides.

"*He* wants to go to Westmond. He wants to be a fuckin' hero." Marion rolled his eyes and paced in front of the TV. "Not sure if you remember all those angry white dudes from earlier, but they all live over there. I know *exactly* what's going to happen when we see them again, and we might not be as lucky as we were this time around. So the answer is *no*."

He pointed a shaky finger toward the parish line.

"That's enemy territory. I ain't marching into the belly of the beast. And neither are you." He waved his hands, effectively ending our conversation. As if on cue, his phone started buzzing again.

On some level, I knew Marion was speaking the truth. I had no plan to save Gabby. I had no power. But Marion didn't trust me not to act impulsively. He slid his phone out of his back pocket and tapped the screen, accepting the call. "Hi, Mama." He frowned across the room at me. "Yes, yes. He's right here."

My eardrums were still ringing well after I handed the phone back to Marion. Mama had given me an earful, and now she was laying into Marion. I'm sure he was getting the same dose of discipline she'd already dished out to me.

I'm so disappointed in you.

Y'all shouldn't have been down there in the first place!

You coulda been hurt.

The streets aren't safe.

Y'all should be home!

Marion held the phone away from his ear, holding his head back as Mama barked another order. This time I could hear her exact phrasing.

"Put Rus back on the phone!" she boomed from Marion's outstretched hand.

"She wants to talk to you again," he said apologetically.

"I know." I snatched the phone from his outstretched hand, more than a little annoyed that he'd answered Mama's call.

She breathed into the line, the kind of long breaths she used after arguing with Pops. She was trying to calm herself down, lower her blood pressure, which was probably dangerously high.

"If I had my druthers, I'd have you in the car and headed home now." She let out a deep sigh, and I could almost see her lips pursing as she said, "But you're going to have to stay there. I already called Terrance's mom, and she's going to leave the hospital as soon as she can. She said she'll be there within the hour. But you need to stay put. The streets are not safe right now. The area is crawling with cruisers. I swear your dad and I hear sirens zipping down Calumet every fifteen minutes. Stay at Terrance's, you understand?"

I nodded vigorously, partly distracted by the news on the TV, at the growing demonstration brewing in Westmond's town square. The thickest knot of people stood in front of the police station, where countless protestors had been locked up. Where Gabby was.

Mama obviously couldn't see me nodding, so she cleared her throat and asked me again. "Russell, do you *understand*?"

"Yes, ma'am."

"I'm dead serious this time. There's a lot of energy and guns out there—a whole lotta 'shoot first, ask later.' And I don't want you to get caught in the crosshairs."

"I know. It's pretty..." My voice trailed off. I stepped farther into the hallway so that the guys couldn't hear the panic in my voice. "It's pretty scary outside."

"Honey, you *should* be scared. We all should be."

When I hung up the phone, I didn't have the energy to speak to the guys. I stormed down the hall and dropped to the stairs, finding a moment's peace in the silent darkness.

After a while, the quiet darkness began to cave in on me, so I joined the guys in the living room. But even then, the space felt cramped, tight. And as the night crept onward, I felt trapped, bound to the spot as the world burned around me. It took all the willpower I had to obey Mama's instructions.

Sometimes my mind would drift to my keys, and I'd think about where Marion might have hidden them. But I couldn't help but think of Mama's warning. Her voice swarmed my thoughts.

You should *be scared. We all should be.*

Is that what the cops wanted? To scare people into submission? To back us into a corner so that our only option was silence?

Maybe Darrell *was* right. Maybe silence *was* safety.

Because right now I didn't feel safe—not by a long shot.

My knees buckled and I plopped onto the carpet in front of Terrance's massive flat-screen TV. Images of this afternoon's protest flashed across the screen. Pictures of Ms. Jabbar at a previous rally speaking passionately alongside Charlotte Martin and the other speakers, of Gabby with her bullhorn today. The fiery passion of earlier was now chilled—chilled by the arrests and police violence, chilled by the banner scrolling across the bottom of every local news channel.

Monroe and Westmond protests now deemed riots. Anyone in the vicinity will be arrested for disturbing the peace.

29

Marion and I laid low at Terrance's house until midday, just to make sure the dust had settled. Even though it was a Sunday afternoon, the streets were empty. My hands were still shaking as I slid behind the wheel of the Civic. We were scared, and we had every reason to be. It would be just like Officer Reynaud and his fellow officers to patrol the streets, arresting anyone who was driving while Black.

I didn't take Calumet—it was too much of a main thoroughfare. Instead, I weaved through side streets and back roads, keeping my head down just like my parents taught me and driving under the speed limit all the way home. As we inched closer to home, we got closer to the parish line that separated Monroe and Westmond. A police cruiser turned on its lights behind me, and my heart almost stopped.

Oh, no.

My face went cold as I watched it speed up, swerve around the Civic and cut in front of me before it turned onto the main road. I panted, trying to slow my heart rate.

I felt like a dog escaping the dogcatcher.

The rapid blades of helicopters chomped at the wind as they circled above the freeway—right near the parish line. My heart raced every time they drew closer, and my jaw unclenched every time the sound faded. I tried not to let my face betray my worries. Marion was clearly becoming more unraveled by the minute as his good dress shirt became more wrinkled and untucked and his eyes grew wider with every helicopter pass.

I was a mess by the time I swerved into the driveway, and Marion looked equally frayed. We scrambled out of the Honda, looking over our shoulders as we made our way to the porch. Mama stood there in her robe, hands on her hips with a dish towel flung over one shoulder.

"I ought to skin you alive." She shook her head slowly, her nostrils flaring. She snapped her fingers, then pointed straight through the door. "Get in here now."

"Mama." My voice cracked as I fell into her arms. I cried into her shoulder, the adrenaline and fear becoming unraveled with every tear I shed. I couldn't keep myself together anymore.

"Baby, you're okay." Mama patted the back of my head, rocking me back and forth in the doorway, her slippers shushing against the floorboards. She whispered over my shoulder, "What happened?"

"Gabby got arrested. It was…really, *really* bad…" Marion cleared his throat after a while. "We think Karim might be in a cell too. But we can't get through to him."

"Come on inside," Mama said a little softer than before. "Your daddy and I got the news on."

Crammed in the living room, we watched the live feed

from the Channel 5 news chopper as it zoomed in on a growing crowd of protesters. A newscaster on the ground held her microphone out to Charlotte Martin, who stood on the steps of the Westmond Police Department.

"We're outside Westmond PD, where the police are holding more than a dozen protesters from yesterday afternoon's demonstration in front of Monroe Town Hall. The protesters said they were peaceful. The police say otherwise. Ms. Martin, what do you think of the situation?"

"We will not leave this police precinct until they release the protesters. Their First Amendment rights have been violated." She unfolded a sheet of paper and leaned over the microphone, her lips moving rapidly as she read out the names.

"They *do* have Karim." Marion bobbed his head from side to side, like he'd already known for sure.

"And Ms. Jabbar," I mumbled under my breath, waiting to hear Gabby's name read off Charlotte's page. Finally she said Gabby's name. I released my breath in a rush of air.

"At least she's with Ms. J." Marion shrugged, twisting his lips like even he didn't find solace in that fact.

"Does her dad know?" Mama rubbed my hand with both of hers.

"I don't know. I don't have his number."

"I'll go give him a call." She got up from the couch, headed down the hallway to her bedroom.

I turned my attention back to the TV, unable to look away from the gathering crowds outside the precinct in Westmond.

Charlotte Martin finished her list of names then, grabbed the microphone from the reporter. She stepped so close to the camera, I could see her pulse thumping through her neck.

"We have a right to demonstrate against police brutality, and the police proved the point of our protest once again. And as long as these charges stand and a murderer walks the streets, there will be no peace."

My muscles relaxed at the sound of Charlotte's promise. If I couldn't be at the police station to get Gabby out, I was glad that she was there commanding the media's attention, forcing people to hear about what the police had done to Gabby and all those protestors yesterday.

Fury and indignation swirled in Charlotte's eyes. Even through the screen, you could feel the heat. There was no chilling her speech. She held the microphone so close to her mouth that the felt head brushed her lips. "No justice, no peace!"

No Justice, No Peace.

I winced when I heard the phrase that was on the posters Gabby had pasted all over town last week. My heart sank, knowing there was never going to be justice in Westmond. Not for people like us.

Judging by the fire in Charlotte Martin's eyes, she knew it was going to be a fight and she was ready. She turned her back to the camera and shouted it again to the crowd, "No justice, no peace!"

And by the look of the police in riot gear—batons drawn as they made an impenetrable wall in front of the station— there would be no peace tonight. I was certain of it.

Mama sprang from her rocking chair during the commercial break, keeping busy by opening mail from the stack on the counter. Keeping her hands occupied was her way of processing, but Pops was the opposite—he wanted to dig in.

"Change it to Fox, will ya?" Pops waved his hand at Marion to grab the remote during the commercial break. He fumbled through the clutter on the coffee table and grabbed it, changing the channel.

Another reporter stood in front of the Westmond shopping mall on the other side of town. There was a group of white protesters standing outside with tiki torches. Some had rifles slung over their shoulders.

"We just want to protect our businesses in case these people lose control and come over from Monroe," a man said into the microphone. A woman behind him waved her poster across the screen.

White lives matter.

Unbelievable.

White people weren't being killed in the streets without consequences. No one had to tell them their lives mattered, because their worth was baked into the very foundations of this country. I wanted to throw the remote across the room at the TV. Swirling in rage, I buried my face in my hands and screamed, louder than the protesters on the TV. When I looked up, the creases on Pops's forehead were severe.

"I can't..." It was too much to handle. My head spun, and I backed away from the TV and went straight to my room, where I pulled the covers over my body.

My thoughts clouded with images of Brad pelting the crowd with Dante Maynard posters, with the screams of Gabby lying pinned to the ground, my helplessness in the face of it all. Every passing minute replayed the same images, and I could feel the hope seeping from my body.

What was the point of protest if it blew up in our faces *every single time?*

There was never any hope of changing the system. And the sooner I accepted that, the better.

The sunset was starting to blink through my blinds by the time I heard the sounds of pans clanking against the stove. Mama was making dinner, but I wasn't hungry. I curled up in bed, tucking my knees close to my chest. A soft knock at my door stirred me, but I didn't answer. I didn't have any words to offer anyone. The door hinges creaked, and a few short footsteps later, my bed dipped to the side as Pops sat on the edge of the mattress. I buried my face in my pillow.

"Just got off the phone with Mr. Dupre." He cleared his throat.

My body stiffened at the mention of Gabby's dad, and a spike of adrenaline surged through my veins. My face felt cold. I couldn't take any more bad news—especially where Gabby was concerned.

"Please tell me she's okay." I turned over and propped my head on my pillow so I could see his face. The circles under his eyes were darker, more severe than they looked after he pulled a long day on the job.

"He's got her home safe." My dad's voice wobbled. "Looks like her shoulder was dislocated, but the ER doc was able to… pop it back into place."

I cringed into the pillow, imagining *exactly* how much pain Gabby was in. When Marion had dislocated his shoulder last year, he said the pain was excruciating—like it was on fire until the medic popped it back into place. And even then, it was still painful.

Pops's lip twitched as he watched me. He opened his mouth like he was about to say something, but he turned away. His Adam's apple bobbed as he gulped down a tear, but one escaped down his cheek. Seeing Pops cry was a rare sight—I couldn't remember the last time I'd seen it. He was always so buttoned-up about his emotions. I drew my legs to my chest, trying to hold myself together. But I was gutted.

I'd brought this on. I was the cause of the pain behind his eyes. So many people laid their hopes and dreams at my feet, and in the course of a few weeks, I'd trampled them. I was glad Pops couldn't look me in the eyes. I wouldn't have been able to meet his gaze.

"I thought things would be different for you kids. I really did." He continued looking at the wall instead of at me. "Thought things would be different for me too. The nineties were—that was another time. I helped bring my team to the state championships my junior year. The Black, left-handed quarterback from Nowhere, Louisiana. And then senior year, when I'd earned my starting spot on the team, people started showing up to games with bananas. Every time I walked across the field, they threw them from the stands. I remember when my coach told me to warm the bench, I needed to do it for the other players. I was a distraction."

I thought about how demeaning it must have been to have bananas thrown on the field, to have white people hollering like monkeys, dehumanizing Pops. Then I thought about Brad splattering our truck with eggs and toilet paper, scrawling the word *garbage* across the window. Both were public forms of humiliation and racist as hell. How much had really changed?

Pops turned his head slowly, the shame pooling in his eyes as a few more tears scurried down his cheek. "Can you believe that? *I* was the distraction. Not them people throwing bananas in the stands." He pursed his lips with a sigh.

I could believe it because it had just happened to me and Marion. I bet the league thought Marion was a distraction too. Maybe that's why they swiftly pushed him off the field instead of dealing with the troubling inequities happening on their watch: kids slinging racial slurs and referees pretending not to see violence.

"I tell you, I wanted to mouth off to my coach. I wanted to tell him *he* should try playing under the same conditions, see how distracted he was. I wanted to call those people racists, but I—" he brought a fist to his mouth and coughed a cry away "—I didn't say anything. And I warmed the bench for the rest of my final season. Maybe if I hadn't sat quietly on the bench—if I'd pushed back on my coach, I might have played more, might have caught the attention of a college scout. Maybe I'd have gone to school and spent my time bending over books instead of toilets—although ain't nothing wrong with it. It's a good livin.' But I think about what coulda been sometimes."

I'd never heard this version of events before. Pops always blamed his fall from grace on an old weight-lifting injury he couldn't shake. But to hear that his football career was taken away from him because of racism—it changed the way I viewed him.

"You're a good kid, Rus. Real good." He rested his hands

on my leg. "And you did something I couldn't do. You spoke up for yourself and for Marion."

I opened my mouth to say something, but he held his hand up.

"I wasn't brave enough to do that in my day." His lip trembled. He leaned forward and gripped my leg tighter. "You did the right thing, okay? And I couldn't be prouder."

I'd been waiting all season to hear those words come out of his mouth, to get my dad's approval. He'd withheld it for so long, I'd forgotten what unconditional love and support felt like. When he stood up and opened his arms, I scrambled off my bed and hugged him—tight, leaving no room for any lingering bitterness.

After a while I pulled away, feeling that familiar pit of doubt in my stomach.

"But protesting didn't do anything." The weight of guilt felt heavy on my shoulders, and I dropped my head, sniffling into my knees. "Nothing good came from it."

Right now, Gabby was probably in a sling—in *pain*. I'd felt a degree of responsibility to keep her safe, and I'd failed.

"The police response—that ain't got nothing to do with you, understand? Nothing. But here…" He brought his fist to his chest, right over his heart. "A person's gotta be able to live with their choices. I guess what I'm saying is, you've got a good head on your shoulders, and you made the right choice."

My breath hitched. I'd *made the right choice*? It was the validation I'd been craving for weeks. My chest loosened as I exhaled with satisfaction.

Kneeling was a risk, but staying silent would have been just as risky. If I was screwed either way, at least with kneeling, I'd *tried*.

Unable to hold back the tears, I wept into my hands. Pops wrapped his arm around my shoulder and whispered, "Everything's going to be okay."

"But everything's still such a mess. How can I fix things?" I asked.

"You'll think of something. And I will support you."

Bared raw, I lay in bed another hour. By nine o'clock Mama worried that I hadn't eaten, but I really wasn't hungry—for food or for company. When I finally got up, I texted Marion, telling him that I needed to be alone, then sank to my desk.

Chuck Wallace's business card stared up at me, daring me to call the number embossed across the middle. I thought about taking him up on his offer to do another interview, but I quickly dismissed that option. Every attempt at speaking up for myself had landed me in a dead end. Or worse—almost in jail. I had no reason to believe Chuck Wallace would be any different from the other reporters who had distorted our story.

I peeked through a crack in my door, rubbernecking to see the TV in the living room, where Mama and Marion were still watching the news. The crowd numbers had swelled until thousands of people flooded the parking lot of the Westmond Mall. There were more White Lives Matter signs, more racist chants. My pulse quickened, and I closed the door. I promised myself I wouldn't look at the news anymore. It only served to enrage me—the reporters always seemed to miss the point.

I turned off the internet, then sat at my desk, crammed in the corner of my room. Chuck's business card taunted me. I slid open the top drawer and tossed it in there so that I could forget about it. I had *so* much homework to do.

I struggled through precalculus, then moved to English, where I had to complete the presentation essay for the *Beale Street* project I'd been working on with Gabby. Of course, in true Ms. J fashion, the story and the assignment were probing reflections of real life.

Just when I thought I was finished with activism, it sucked me back in.

I stared at the page a long time, unsure what to say. My fingers grazed the keyboard over and over again until I wrote my first words.

This is an indictment.

What began as a trickle soon became a deluge. I poured myself onto the page, filling it with details of Dante Maynard's shooting, Marion's unfair arrest, Gabby's dislocated shoulder, Ms. Jabbar's curriculum. And the white silence that surrounded it all.

From all angles, I'd been boxed in by violence and injustice, and *still* every fiber of my being bucked at the notion that I should accept it. My protest had been mangled into something that it wasn't. My spoken words had been distorted beyond recognition. But there could be no interference from words on paper. No noise. No biased reporter twisting my words. No angry fans spewing hate. There was just me and the certainty of the page.

Writing became the balm that soothed my hopelessness. There was nowhere to hide from words in my notebook.

I was tired of people telling me to stay in my lane, calling me to focus on the game instead of the injustice closing in around me. I was suffocating from the confines of racism, trapped. I couldn't focus on anything else.

Get them back on the field.

That's what Marion and I always said to each other. That was why I had to spit truth where it would really hit home. I had to go *big*. I had to *turn the heat up*, as Gabby would say.

A plan brewed in my belly as I poured myself onto the page, my eyes stinging from angry tears and frustration.

I thought of Gabby screaming at the top of her voice in the Shreveport stadium, calling their fans hypocrites when I'd knelt. Her face flushed as she emptied her lungs in her shouts—the picture of unabashed defiance.

A person's gotta be able to live with their choices.

That's what Pops had reminded me to do. I needed to stop second-guessing myself, stop internalizing all this guilt I had for using my own voice. That was my *right*. I chiseled away the self-doubt I'd allowed to calcify around my decision to kneel.

I funneled my convictions onto the page—my call to arms against apathy. I was well beyond six pages by the time I wrote the final sentence, well beyond the scope of the assignment. But Ms. J wouldn't mind. I emailed her the submission just after midnight. But I was still restless.

I needed to send it to one other person.

Feeling bold, I pulled open my desk drawer and retrieved Chuck Wallace's business card. I hastily typed his email address into the top of a message and pasted my indictment onto the blank page. Then I attached the video of the whole Westmond-Jackson fight—the one that the prosecutor was sitting on. For a moment, I hesitated with my finger hovering over the button, unsure whether this was a good idea...

Click.

It was in Wallace's inbox now, and that sent an unexpected surge of relief through me.

As the churning in my stomach subsided, I fell into a fitful doze, still unsure if justice would be served and if my voice would truly be heard.

#

My eyelids fluttered open at the sound of firm knocks at the front door. After a poor night's sleep, my eyesight took a while to adjust to the thin light poking through my curtains. It was still early—*really* early.

Who's knocking this early in the morning?

I heard my parents' bedroom door open and the tired shuffling of my mom's slippers on the way to the front door. Blinking rapidly, I tried to wash the sleep out of my eyes. I grabbed my phone off my nightstand, squinting to see the time. It was just before 6:00 a.m.

I slipped on fresh clothes and followed the sounds of low chatter coming from the front of the house, wincing as my feet padded against the cold linoleum. When I passed the kitchen island, Marion set two plastic cups in front of him. He opened a two-liter bottle of cola, sending a hiss through the house.

He poured a full glass, then slid it across the counter. "Drink up."

"What's going on?" I asked, rubbing my forehead groggily.

"You're gonna need caffeine."

His hair was dewy like he'd just taken a shower, and he was already fully dressed in a tracksuit. I frowned down at the soda, which was not exactly the ideal breakfast beverage, but a familiar voice snapped my attention to the door.

"Thank you, Mrs. Boudreaux," Darrell said from the other side of the screen door. "We appreciate you being so cool."

"It's all right, boys." Mama nodded at him. She gripped her beige robe tighter and stepped to the side so that Marion could squeeze beside her. More footsteps pounded up the porch—solid, heavy ones that could only belong to more football players. I scooted closer, curious to see what was going on.

"Morning, ma'am," Bobby said from over Darrell's shoulder.

"Ma'am." Terrance yawned sleepily from the top step.

"Sorry to disturb you like this," Ricky said shyly. "We're ready when you guys are."

"What are you guys doing here?" I poked my head out of the door to find the team standing on my front lawn. And not just the offensive line—the *entire* Jackson Jackals looking back at me expectantly.

"Marion called a team meeting," Darrell said over his shoulder as he hopped down the stairs.

"When?" I turned to Marion, a sleepy eyebrow raised.

"Last night, when you shut out the world and wouldn't get out of bed." His eyes tightened, and I could tell he was worried. "I'm still co-captain of this team. Am I right?"

I nodded. Of course he was still part of the team. Hell, Marion pretty much *was* the team. We'd been suffering from his absence. I'd been trying to drill that into his head since he got suspended from league play. My gaze swept across the lawn, taking in every loyal team member, then back to Marion, who had a familiar mischief in his eyes.

I grabbed my phone out of my pocket and turned it off airplane mode. A flurry of message notifications popped up from our team text thread, buzzing my phone excitedly. I had missed a lot since I'd locked myself in my room. But one thing I still didn't have was a text or call from Gabby.

I gulped, uncomfortable with her silence and worried that she was in pain. What if her shoulder had popped out of place again? Would she need surgery?

I thought about calling her, but it was ridiculously early. She needed all the rest she could get. I shot off a quick text, letting her know I was thinking about her and that I was sorry. I ended it with a plea.

Call me back when you wake up? Please??

Coach Fontenot's old Chevy pulled up. He opened his car door, nodding to the nearest players before loudly clearing his throat. He wrung his hands while he crunched across our gravel driveway, looking at the ground instead of at the crammed doorway. He seemed nervous.

"Hello, Cheryl," he said, wringing his hat in his hands. "We need to talk to your boy."

Mama tilted her head and pursed her lips. "Which one?"

"Sorry, Cheryl. I need to talk to *both* of your boys." He flicked his head toward me to come outside, then nodded toward Marion, stepping aside to give him room to lead the way. "We have some team business to discuss."

★ ★ ★

Behind my backyard, just beyond the tree line, the team settled in for our emergency team meeting. Bobby's feet dangled from the tree house above, while Darrell leaned against the rope ladder. Terrance sat nearby on a protruding rock, biding his time for his turn to go up to the tree house. It was a meeting I'd never imagined would happen *here*.

The whole team was assembled, and it was all because of Marion. I scratched my head, looking at his squared shoulders and his raised chin. He looked strong and confident, unlike his frazzled appearance the other day. I didn't know what had caused this shift in him, but I wanted whatever he'd had.

Coach walked up the gentle hill to where Marion stood. He took off his hat and smoothed his thinning hair, a solemn gesture.

"I know it's unusual for me to be at one of your meetings. But I thought that, under the circumstances, it was the right thing to do. First off, I wanted to apologize to y'all for not providing leadership *off* the field, especially when y'all needed it the most. And I guarantee you, I'm not gonna make that mistake again." He bent his head in an awkward bow, then gestured to Marion. He was, after all, the reason we were here, and Coach was ceding the floor to him. "Marion… your meeting."

"I think I can speak for everyone when I say this season has *sucked*," Marion said, stepping forward. Strained laughter rippled through the team. *Sucked* didn't even begin to describe our senior season. Marion grinned as he continued. "Okay, it's been *terrible*. And not just because we lost a couple games—

although that never feels great. But because of all the other shit we've had thrown at us."

He held his arms out, as if he was allowing all the horrors of the semester to commune with us. I gritted my teeth as I remembered the ridicule and the humiliation, the arrests and the violence. Such *violence*—from Marion's bloodied face to Gabby's dislocated shoulder. We were just students, not soldiers in a war zone. We deserved better. This season had marked a cosmic shift in all of our realities. We'd normalized the events as they happened, but that was impossible to do as we took stock of it as a whole.

"But I am not hiding anymore!" Marion boomed, pounding his fist in his hands in a show of mettle. "We can't let them tear us apart. So are we gonna come together or what?"

"Yeah!" Terrance mumbled from beneath the tree house. Only a few lackluster voices joined him.

Marion stepped forward, inching farther down the slope, his eyes fiery. "I said, are we gonna come together?"

"Come on, guys," I said, clapping my hands. I joined Marion's side, shouting one of our chants, "Jackals on three, Jackals on me. One, two, three—"

"Jackals!" the team shouted in unison, with more energy this time.

The vacuum of leadership, the frayed disputes, the mounting failures—all of that felt like a wound on the mend. When we gathered and supported each other, I felt whole again. Well...almost whole.

I wished Gabby would call me back.

"We've got another brother who was locked up this weekend." Marion's voice traveled above the energized chatter coming from the team. "That's the *second* time in a month that one of us has been jailed for *no reason*. Karim didn't deserve that. He doesn't deserve being home right now, fighting trumped-up charges. I didn't deserve it either. And we cannot let that go unanswered."

"Sho' can't," Darrell shouted from the rope ladder. He licked his teeth underneath his closed lips, looking like he was ready to throw down.

"Luckily, we've got *this*." He slid his phone out of his back pocket. "'I am determined to live an unencumbered life. But I am experiencing an uptick in blatant, unabashed racism, and it sickens me. It should sicken you too.'"

Blood drained from my face as I recognized the words from my open letter—my angry, rambling letter I'd sent to Chuck Wallace last night.

"Where did you get that?" A searing heat crept up my cheeks.

"The internet, son. It's *everywhere*. I see you took it all the way to the top this time." Darrell held his phone up for all to see the letterhead of the *New Orleans Herald*. I leaned forward, barely able to believe it myself. "Get out all your phones and read this, if you haven't already. The article is called 'An Indictment Against Racist Police.'"

I wasn't surprised Darrell had already seen it, with his Jackson Jackals news alerts. Of course he'd found my article.

Diving my hand into my pocket, I got my phone. I hadn't received any confirmation email from Mr. Wallace, no follow-up. I scrolled through the articles on the landing page and there is was: my indictment, with my name underneath.

"Holy shit," I said, half laughing, half coughing.

"'Marion LaSalle's only crime is being Black and poor,'" Marion read aloud, popping his head up when he read the sentence. I was afraid he would be angry—I put his whole case in the letter. But his mouth widened into a smile. "You got that line from my protest speech."

"It was a really good speech, bro."

"I'm just glad people are actually gonna listen this time." He held out his hand, which I took, and tugged me into a hug. I slapped him on the back, relieved to finally have my best friend back in the thick of the team.

Darrell snaked his arm around our necks and bounced up and down, a welcome change from the tense locker room atmosphere that had plagued the Jackals for the past month. He raised his hand, signaling he had something more to say.

"Negros be getting indicted left and right for crimes they didn't even commit. Pleading guilty for shit they ain't even guilty of. Man, look what Russell did. He turned the tables on 'em. He indicts every single white person in this country who looks the other way." Darrell held his phone closer to his face and scrolled through my words. "Listen to this.

'If you believe that killing a boy in broad daylight is a tragedy but don't have the guts to hold his killer accountable, this message is for you. I am pointing my trembling finger at you, an indictment. Your continued silence is the fuel that keeps the fires of police brutality burning, and for that, I hold you personally responsible for Dante Maynard's death, and for any victims of a corrupt system that denies liberty and justice for all.'"

The words sounded more powerful when the guys read them out loud—not at all like the whiny words that were bouncing around in my head. This was what I'd wanted, my unfiltered words rising above the noisy newscasters.

"I can't believe you wrote that." Terrance stood up. "Especially after what happened Saturday."

"Maybe that was exactly the right time to write this," Ricky said into his lap, still scrolling through my letter. "I'm glad someone brought attention to what's going on down here."

"Rus, what happened to Gabby..." Terrance's voice trailed off as the memory of Saturday's mayhem flashed across his eyes. "I'm sorry, man."

"I really didn't think that shit was possible. And I've seen some crazy shit go down. But the way they stormed the crowd..." Darrell shuddered, his lip quivering as he gripped my shoulder. "How Gabby doin'?"

"She got out last night." I buried my head in my hands. "Her shoulder got dislocated. She has to see a specialist and might need surgery. I haven't heard much else."

"She deserved better," Darrell said.

"We *all* deserve better." I raised my voice so that my brothers could hear me. "Last month, I acted without telling you guys why. So I'm telling you now. I could not stand for an anthem for a country that sees me as a criminal simply because I'm Black. I knelt for Dante and Marion and all the other innocent Black people who have been victims of unchecked police aggression. And at this week's game, I'm going to do it again."

This time, I'm kneeling for Gabby.

"You ain't gonna be alone this time." Darrell shook his head, looking at the teammates on either side of him to make sure everyone was on the same page.

"From now on, we stand together." I turned to Marion. "Which means you're coming out there too."

"Nah, Rus. You know I can't suit—"

"Coach." I turned to him, my hands on my hips. "We've got the media's attention. All eyes are on Monroe, so it's time for you to blow up the league's spot. Put pressure on the league to lift Marion's suspension—*publicly*, so they can't hide behind their stupid rule book."

"I—" Coach shifted nervously on the lawn, almost like he didn't have the nerve to challenge them. But after a moment he straightened his stance, setting his jaw tightly. "I'll give 'em hell."

"Thanks, Coach," Marion said, clasping his shoulder. He watched Coach walk across the yard, then turned to me. "So what now?"

"I don't know." I bit on the inside of my cheek as I weighed my options. "We could call the governor, now that we've got all this attention."

"You got his direct number?" Marion chuckled as he wrapped an arm around my shoulders. "I'm just playing. His old racist ass ain't gonna come help us."

"You never know. I just published an article in the *New Orleans Herald*. So, stranger things have happened."

"Slay the baller way." Marion tilted his chin up and cackled toward the morning sky.

31

We rounded the corner to the front of the house, my phone dinging in my pocket. I was about to flip through my notifications, when I saw another visitor at my front door. A figure stood on the porch, dressed head to toe in black. Even down to the black-on-black Converse, this person could blend in with the shadiest shade. I'd seen them before, papering flyers all over town, risking life and limb to speak truth to power. It was Dante's Shadow in the flesh, cradling a sling against her chest.

Gabby!

How could I ever have mistaken Dante's Shadow for a boy? Her baggy black sweatshirt concealed her chest, but those skinny jeans gripped her hips—hips that couldn't belong to any dude. I'd been a fool for not seeing what was in front of my face, and I was determined not to let that happen again.

"Guys, I'll see you later?" I said over my shoulder. Darrell's chuckling made me whip around. If he started talking shit about Gabby again, I'd for real shut him up.

"Oh, okay I see how it is." Darrell clutched his chest, pre-

tending to be offended. "You get a girl, and you kick us out
your house."

"I missed your sorry ass." I tousled his short hair, glad to
be mending fences with him. I didn't even bother correct-
ing him. Gabby wasn't really my girl—not *yet*. But I'd be her
guy if she let me.

"Yo, D, can I catch a ride to school with you?" Marion
shouted from the porch steps, his mischievous gaze darting
from me to Gabby as he waited for Darrell to respond.

"Fine, but hurry it up. You got a lotta schoolwork to catch
up on." He smiled at me. "Don't worry, Rus. I'll crack the
whip."

Marion darted into the house and was back in a flash, before the screen door could slap the doorframe more than a
few times.

The guys trickled off the front yard, headed toward their
cars along Calumet Street. I turned my focus to Gabby, who
was sliding her hood down. Her natural coils caught the
morning light, and I thought she was possibly more beautiful than she'd been a few days ago. Sling or no sling, Gabby
was fire.

"What are you doing here?" I gripped my temples.
"Shouldn't you be at home in bed or something?"

"It looks worse than it feels." Gabby swiveled to show me
her sling, which she'd already decorated with a Black Lives
Matter sticker.

"I'm sorry." I hung my head low, too ashamed to look her
in the eyes. "I shouldn't have left your side during the rally.
And when Reynaud grabbed you, I should have stopped him."

"Ms. J told me you were fighting Marion to get to me. I

knew I had to see you as soon as I could. To put your mind at ease."

"It's working." I inhaled deeply, catching hints of Gabby's honeysuckle scent. Yes, my mind was at ease now that I knew she was safe.

"Um...but are we gonna talk about you blowing up the internet? I'm out of commission for two days, and you grab the national spotlight?" Gabby leaned against the faded white railing. Her smile widened, and she threw her head back in a cackle. "You're an absolute mad genius! Look at all these copycat articles popping up."

She hiked her leg on the ledge of the railing and scrolled through her phone. I leaned in closer, but not to look at the articles catching the coattails of the *New Orleans Herald*.

"Come here." I scooped her into my arms, careful not to jostle her bad shoulder. Feeling her warmth for the first time in a long time. I held her secure on the railing, her feet grazing the wood floorboards, our faces hovering close to each other. She leaned forward, rubbing the tip of her nose to mine.

"You gonna kiss me or what, Boudreaux?"

And that was all it took.

My lips pressed into hers. A blend of emotions collided as we kissed—the months of longing, the layers of protest and anger and frustration. The recent nights of separation, when I didn't know if she was okay. All of it went into that rush of release.

I opened my eyes for a brief moment, long enough to see the blinds scramble back into place. Mama and Pops had clearly been snooping. My lips stiffened, making Gabby turn to see what I was looking at.

"Were they watching?" She pointed over her shoulder.

"Yup." I nodded, tucking my lips between my lips. I was embarrassed but determined to return my attention to Gabby. I gripped her arms, but recoiled once I saw her flinch. "Shit, I'm sorry! I didn't mean to move it. How does it feel? Are you in pain?"

"I'm fine." She waved her hand dismissively when I tried to inspect her arm and shoulder more closely. "Can't be worse than the injuries you guys get, right?"

I scrunched my mouth up, thinking about the time Marion dislocated his shoulder—the look on his face when it had popped out of place was just as bad as the agony plastered across it when the trainer held him down and popped it back into place. I shuddered, shaking the image out of my mind. It made me picture Gabby in the same agony, and I seriously did not want to imagine that right now.

As if she could see the discomfort in my face, she interrupted my waking nightmare.

"Women have a higher pain threshold than men. So don't worry about me." She held her good arm up and posed like Rosie the Riveter. She flexed the puny muscle and smiled smugly. "'I am woman, hear me roar,' and all that."

"We'll see about that." I eyed her skeptically, realizing she might be a tough patient—just like Marion. He could hide pain well. By the way Gabby was trying to minimize her injury, she was exactly the same.

"Want a ride to school? We might make it to first period if we hurry."

"Sure," I said, even though I could drive myself. Ever since

Pops had fixed the Honda, it had been running without incident. But that didn't matter. I'd go anywhere with Gabby.

The screen door hinges moaned as I swung it open. My
parents were standing in the kitchen, suspiciously out of
breath, like they had run to their places moments ago. They
were shameless snoopers. Pops hid his smirk behind a cup of
coffee at his lips. I grabbed my backpack and skidded out the
door, waving goodbye over my shoulder.

"So when do you get to take the sling off?" I asked as I
opened the passenger side of Gabby's truck.

"About a week, just in time for Halloween." She grinned
devilishly.

"Don't tell me you still dress up…" I rolled my eyes, even
though I loved her childish excitement over the holiday. I
buried my unease about couples costumes deep down, hoping that she didn't see worry lines on my face.

"You *don't celebrate Halloween*?" She almost squealed as she
clasped her hand over her mouth. "Oh, Rus. That might be
a deal breaker."

"What'd you have in mind?" I raised a skeptical eyebrow
at her.

"I have a couple ideas." She put the truck in gear and eased
around our circle drive. "I was thinking about being Ruth
Bader Ginsburg. You know, the Notorious RBG. I could run
around in a graduation robe with a lace collar and talk about
equal protection and feminism and stuff like that."

"Including intersectional feminism?" I tilted my head, a
smile tugging at my lips. When her mouth fell open, I said
with a chuckle, "See? I listen."

"Yes, you do." She smiled up at me, slowing the truck to a

halt. Reaching out with her good arm, she grabbed my hand, then leaned across the center console for another kiss, and I gladly met her halfway.

Our parking lot was packed to capacity for the October 25 rematch between Jackson and Westmond. We saw the reporters before they saw us, and we did our best to avoid them. Don't get me wrong—we were grateful for their attention on the racial inequities happening in Monroe. They'd hammered on every angle of our story *every day* this week, putting so much pressure on the prosecutor to answer for his disparate treatment of Marion and Brad, he had no choice but to drop the charges.

And that meant the league had no choice either—Marion was *back*. His suspension was finally lifted.

We slipped through a maintenance door on the far side of our stadium, giving a group of reporters the slip. It was one of the perks of having the rematch on our turf—we knew the layout better than anyone. Our footsteps echoed down the corridor as we ran undetected to the locker room.

Marion stopped on the threshold, looking to his cubby—the one next to mine. It was dusty from not being used most of the season. The corners of his eyes pinched, betraying his emotions.

"You got this." I slid my duffel bag down the locker room aisle, making plenty of room for him to take his rightful place. I looked down the bench and saw Karim was suited up. Nothing, not even arrests and bogus charges, would tear our team apart again. We were all going to play this game.

We put our gear on quickly, more quietly than usual. This

was a solemn game, filled with weighty importance. To me, it symbolized reclaiming our space. And there was no better place to do that than on our home field.

Westmond had home field advantage last time, and they'd squandered it. Now it was our turn, and we would not be making the same mistake.

"We ready?" Darrell yelled when we were packed closely together in the football tunnel.

"'Course we are." I smiled confidently.

"I've been waiting almost two months for this." Marion hopped on the balls of his feet, eagerly awaiting the announcer's call to the field.

"I give you, the Jackson Jackals!" the announcer boomed through the loud speakers.

We bolted onto the field, feeling the warmth from our fans, who greatly outnumbered the Westmond side of the stadium. The whole town must have shown up to fill our stands. Maybe even some of the neighboring towns too.

The Westmond stands were still packed—this was the highly anticipated rematch. And they were plenty vocal about their continued disdain for us. They booed and jeered, even louder and fiercer than they had during our last match. But our fans drowned them out.

The band behind us started to play a familiar song. It wasn't the anthem, but something else I knew.

"Is that 'This Is America' by Childish Gambino?" I asked Marion, who was equally as wide-eyed as I was.

He nodded, mesmerized by the white-gloved bandleader doing Donald Glover's weird dance from the music video. Then the color guard stood up. Instead of their batons, they held up poster boards. Each one was a blown-up image of one of Gabby's flyers.

The dancers shimmied down the aisles, weaving through the crowd as they did their own protest. And the band blared the notes of Gambino's protest anthem. They must have been working on this all week, just so they could show Westmond what Monroe was really made of.

My chest tightened, and I turned away for a moment to gather myself. My open letter had set so many things in motion and inspired other people to be activists in their own way. I wasn't the only person with something to say. I felt less alone now that others were stepping forward.

When I turned around, one of the Westmond football players was crossing the field. He took off his helmet and ran his fingers through his blond hair. Lawrence approached Marion, the tips of his cleats grazing the line between the field and our sidelines.

"What are you doing over here?" I stepped forward, my hands raised. "Come on, dude. Don't start nothing."

"I just wanted to…" He looked down at the turf, his checks turning bright red. He looked up at Marion, his eyebrows upturned. "I'm sorry, Marion. I should have spoken up sooner. And I definitely shouldn't have said the N-word. I'm really sorry."

"Yeah, like *before* you saw Officer Reynaud take me to *jail*."

Lawrence's cheeks turned a deeper shade of scarlet. He was ashamed for his inaction.

"You had so many chances, man." I shook my head slowly, thinking about how much *easier* this season would have been if this one guy would have opened his mouth and *told the truth about what he saw during the fight.*

"I read your article." He bit his lower lip, still avoiding eye contact. "About how white people being silent is part of the problem. I called the prosecutor's office Monday afternoon, and gave a full witness statement. I don't know if it helped but... I'm sorry."

He turned to walk back across the field, his eyes downcast. But I stepped off the sidelines and onto the field, calling after him, "Wait."

Lawrence turned around, and I held my hand out between us. When he grabbed it, I pulled him in for a pat on the back.

"Better late than never." I held his gaze.

"Thanks," he said, breathlessly.

A voice keened above the rest—Bradley Simmons's. He ripped his helmet off and pointed in our direction.

"TRAITOR!"

"Get your boy in check." I tilted my head, raising an eyebrow.

"Yeah that dude's a fucking asshole, right? Don't tell him this, but we're going to vote him out as co-captain later tonight. I'll make *sure* of it."

"That's a start." I waved at Lawrence before heading back to our sidelines. The music from our band faded into silence, and I knew what was coming next.

"Please rise for the national anthem." The announcer's voice echoed through the stadium.

The opening notes of the anthem filled the stadium. I looked to Marion, nodding for him to lead us in kneeling.

This was for him. For Gabby. For Karim. For me. He sank
to his knee, and I quickly followed.

O say can you see by the dawn's early light.

Bowing my head, I prayed that my silent protest shook the
stands. I was using my right to speak truth to power. The
Westmond cheers grew more feverish, but they were drowned
out by Ms. J's voice ringing in my ears.

Challenge your notion of patriotism.

For the first line of the song, we were the only ones kneeling. But then Terrance's knee dipped to the ground. Then
Karim. Bobby. Ricky. Darrell leaned on my shoulder, and
in stark contrast to the last time I knelt—when he tried to
snatch me up off the ground—he took a knee, resting his arm
around my shoulder in solidarity.

Whose broad stripes and bright stars through the perilous fight.

The stands behind us creaked, causing us to turn and look.
The Jackal fans were no longer in their seats but on their
knees. I caught a glimpse of Gabby in the front row. Flanked
by her dad and brother, she waved at me before wiping her
teary face on the sleeve of her sling.

And the rocket's red glare, the bombs bursting in air.

Coach Fontenot dropped to his knees at the end of the
line. His face placid, his angry vein safely stowed. He looked
down the line and met my eyes with a nod. Then he shook
his head, and I knew what he was thinking. The Clemson
recruiter was somewhere in the stands eyeing this with disappointment. I jutted my chin out.

If Jim Regan didn't want me to use my voice, then Clemson wasn't the school for me. I held my chin high, uncertain where my future would land. I knew only that, wherever I ended up, I'd never be silenced.

EPILOGUE

The December College Fair in nearby Baton Rouge was held in Louisiana State University's gym, which was ten times the size of Jackson High School's facilities. Booths were crammed closely together, lined in a zigzag pattern to funnel people through. There were so many choices, so many paths to follow. College application deadlines were coming up at the beginning of January, and I still didn't have any scholarship offers.

I was a free agent—for better or worse.

LSU was another one of those dream schools—it was Division 1, a formidable program, and close to home. I looked around their state-of-the-art gymnasium, thirsty for a chance to attend this school. But I'd already checked with them twice. They weren't looking for any more tight ends this year, not even for walk-on spots.

But there was something out there for me. Somewhere.

Gabby texted me a wonky-faced emoji, followed by a thumbs-up. Her text said: **Break a leg**, followed by a very saucy invitation to meet her in her greenhouse when I got back. I stuffed my phone back into my pocket, hoping she hadn't made me blush.

My heart flipped, then flopped as I remembered our inevitable fate. This was our last semester together, then she was off to school on the opposite side of the country. I'd miss her next year.

"Excuse me?" An excited guy in a loose denim shirt waved from across the aisle.

Me? I mouthed, pointing at my chest. I looked to my right and then my left but didn't see anyone else responding to him.

"I knew it was you." He squeezed out of the side of his booth and weaved his way through the crowd toward me. He was taller than I'd expected—almost as tall as my six feet three inches.

"Uh, hi." I waved awkwardly.

"Russell Boudreaux." He thrust his hand out to me, then ruffled his hair with a laugh. "Sorry, *you're* Russell Boudreaux. Of course you already know that. I'm Skyler Prewitt, a receiver at Stanford."

"Oh, hey, nice to meet you. You guys have been playing awesome this year." I shook his hand, eyeing the recruiting pamphlets on his tabletop. None of them looked football specific.

"We could use a player like you. Have you ever thought about going to school out west?"

"Do you have any scholarships available?" I asked, hoping the answer was yes. I'd heard Stanford had a great journalism department. I wasn't *just* interested in football. I wanted to cultivate other passions too.

"Hold on, let me get someone from the athletic department on the phone." Skyler raised his index finger in the air as he dug in his pocket for his phone. "I have a feeling Coach Shaw is gonna want to talk to you. Especially with the application deadline coming up."

I'd never considered going to Stanford—literally *never*. All I knew about Stanford was that their football program was pretty decent and the school was super expensive. I couldn't afford Stanford unless I got a scholarship. Skyler nodded, his smile widening as he spoke into his phone. It looked promising. Maybe Coach Shaw needed a tight end like me.

And then a thought bubbled up in my head—something that brought the promise of a future with Gabby. My interest was piqued.

"How far is Stanford from Berkeley?"

★ ★ ★ ★ ★

ACKNOWLEDGMENTS

I owe such a debt of gratitude to my agent, my north star who helped me edit my pages and navigate the world of publishing. To my agent, Carrie Pestritto, and the whole team at Laura Dail Literary Agency, thank you for pulling me out of the slush pile and taking a chance on me. Your guidance and expertise are invaluable. Know that you are heartily appreciated.

To Tashya Wilson: your enthusiasm for this project was infectious from the very first moment we met and I am so grateful for your insight and passion. And a huge thank-you to Bess Braswell for taking the torch and helping me see this book to the finish line. It has truly been a pleasure working with you both.

I also can't forget Connolly Bottum, whose editorial support on this project was invaluable, or Viana Siniscalchi, who shepherded *Kneel* through its early stages.

Big shout-outs to Boris Anje and art director Gigi Lau for creating the beautiful cover art—you truly brought Rus to life!

Brittany Mitchell, you did so much to publicize this book during these unprecedented times. I appreciate your hard work, as well as Linette Kim's, who did such a phenomenal job with library outreach. I also want to thank my publicists, Laura Gianino and Justine Sha…and give a round of applause to the entire HarperCollins sales team. Y'all are rock stars!

Tracy C. Gold, you read this manuscript in its infancy, when it was truly a rough draft, and you helped me sculpt sturdy bones for this book. And to Michele Bacon, thank you for being an early reader and then being one of the last people to read these pages just to make sure everything was in tip-top shape. You two are my beta reading editing gurus!

Thank you to Michael Noll and S. Kirk Walsh for teaching and inspiring me in our writing workshops in Austin, and to the Writers' League of Texas, the South Bay Creative Writers Group in Redondo Beach, and the Southern California Writers' Conference for teaching me about the publishing space and for hosting workshops that helped me hone my craft. Also big thanks to Fatemeh Razipour, who let me camp out in her Persian restaurant in Torrance in the same booth every day (like the neurotic writer that I am) so that I could eat good food while writing this book. I am so full of gratitude (and koobideh!).

To my parents, Dr. Deena Buford and Dr. Reginald Buford, thank you for supporting me through this journey. From grad school to finance to writing children's fiction—you've been by my side. To Glen and Susan Metts, thanks for regularly calling me to tell me you're proud. It means so much to me.

And to my partner, Jonathan Metts: thank you for reading all of my pages, for being my biggest cheerleader, and for finding the sun with me.